BOMBSHELLS

BOMBSHELLS

SARINA BOWEN

Tuxbury Publishing LLC

For Claudia, without whom there would be no Anton Bayer.

ONE

Anyone Get it on Video?

September

ANTON

IT'S a Wednesday afternoon during the preseason, and I should really be in the locker room. But I'm standing in an office in the Bruisers' headquarters, waiting to find out if I still have a NHL career.

Practice starts in thirty minutes. If they wanted me down there, I'd already know, wouldn't I?

My hands are clammy and my heart rate is erratic. So this is what it feels like when fate brings the hammer down. If only I could go back in time and make better choices. I wouldn't be standing here sweating.

Couldn't they just fire me already? I'm dying here.

Prayer probably won't work, even if this is one of those moments when I'm tempted to bargain with God. What would I even say?

Dear Lord—I'm sorry for all the cockiness I displayed last year. You know my stats were great during my rookie season. But then I kinda self-destructed.

I'm sorry I didn't leave the bar earlier all those times when I should have.

I'm sorry about missing the team jet that time in Arizona when I had no business being so hungover in the middle of a road trip.

On the matter of a certain compromising photo, I think we can both agree that the incident with those women was not really my fault. But I do apologize for putting myself in that situation and allowing for that tacky result.

But I am most sorry for the worst sin of all—squandering all those opportunities. You gave me a shot at greatness. But I started my second season on the struggle bus. And after that disastrous game against Chicago, you (in your infinite wisdom) sent me down to purgatory—aka the minor league team in Hartford. I had to watch on TV while the Bruisers went to the playoffs.

This summer I repented. I ran seven miles every day, even on the ones when New York City was as humid and gross as a used practice jersey.

I didn't skip a workout in the gym, either. In the evenings, I've drunk only a single light beer. Did you ever hear the joke about how light beer is just like sex in the bottom of a canoe? Because it's fucking close to water.

Oh hell! I can't even pray like a grownup. I just told a dirty joke to God.

Just then, the door swings open, and my heart plummets as Hugh Major walks into the small room, chest out. He's followed by Eric, my father's cousin, who is also my agent.

And Eric looks *grim*.

Oh shit. This is really happening.

Up until this very moment—when I saw that look on Eric's face —I still held out some hope that, after my strong showing at training camp, they'd give me one more chance.

Fuck my life. I deserve this. But it's still going to bite the big one.

"Well, son," Hugh says as Eric shuts the door. "You sure had some trouble last season."

"I know, sir," I say evenly, because a man doesn't cower from his fate. "My production was not up to my own standards."

"Nor mine," he agrees, even as a cold drop of sweat makes its way down my back. "You're capable of so much more."

"And I'm going to prove it, even if I have to do that in Hartford."

"Huh." He frowns at me. "How about you do it downstairs on the practice rink instead? We're going to roster you. But you'd better give us something to show for it."

"*Yessir*," I say, my ears ringing with confusion. Did I just hear that right? I'm *staying*?

I glance at Eric's stern glower for clarification. Why does he look so dark when…

His lip twitches. Then it twitches again.

That Bastard! He knew how this was going to go. He was just fucking with me.

"Keep your head down, kid. You know you've got to," says Hugh.

"I can," I insist, dragging my gaze back to his. "I got this."

"Then get down there and show us all." He gives me a nod and —done with me now—lets himself out of the room to deal with someone else's drama.

I don't breathe until he's gone. I'm drenched in cold sweat. And Eric, that fucker, is chuckling silently. "You jackass!" I hiss. "I about sharted myself just from the look on your ugly face when you walked in here."

"I *know*," he says with a snort. "It was priceless. And no less than you deserve. Honestly, Hugh should have yelled a little more and thrown some furniture around. Maybe that would put you into the headspace you need this season. "

"But I *am* in the right headspace," I insist. "I've been there since I got sent down to Hartford in March. Now I'm fitter than I've ever been. Even since high school, when I was in lust with a distance runner."

Eric shakes his head as he opens the door to shoo me into the hallway. "Let me guess—you ran half-marathons every day just to get into her spandex?"

"Yes."

"Did it work?" he asks as we head for the stairs leading down to the historic lobby of the renovated warehouse where the Brooklyn Bruisers make their home.

"Oh, sure," I recall. "Totally worth it. She was skinny, but man did she have stamina." But I'm getting off topic. "This time I ran

3

for *me*, though. Nobody will be able to outskate me. I'm fit and ready. They won't be sorry they took this chance."

Eric stops in the middle of the grand lobby, beneath the video screen showing highlights from last season. "That's the problem. It's your third season. They shouldn't have to feel like they're taking a chance. You're not a rookie anymore."

Well, ouch. "Yeah, no kidding. But things are already different." I swipe open the door that leads to the practice facility.

"Tell me how," he says as we enter the tunnel.

"I already told you my new rules."

"Say it again," he says. "Loudly. So the gods of hockey can hear you."

Man, I love Eric, but I hate being treated like a kid brother. There's no getting around it, though. He was this team's first Bayer. It's not his fault that he had to retire at the top of his game, after too many knee surgeries.

They picked me up that same season, so my nickname became *Baby Bayer*, and I can't seem to shake it. I don't enjoy the constant reminder that I was the second-choice Bayer.

Then again, my behavior last season helped the name stick.

This year will be different, though, because of these rules I made for myself. "No boozing," I grumble. "No whoring." Eric smirks. "And no scandals."

"Good," he says. "It's a start. Although rules are what you make of them. And none of those three things is the real problem. It's *focus*, Anton. And we both know it."

"Yeah." He's right. But so am I, because the rules are meant to give some structure to my life. They'll make me into a different man. A *better* man.

A man who can focus.

At the bottom of the tunnel, I swipe myself into the last secure door at the edge of the training complex. "I gotta suit up now."

"Good thing," he says cheerfully. "Have a great practice."

"I will." Seriously. I'll never take this for granted again. Every time my ID card lets me through this door, I'll say another hallelujah. "You're still a shit cousin for making me sweat it, by the way."

"Maybe." He walks away laughing.

4

IN THE DRESSING ROOM, I head for my locker. It's right where it used to be, between Drake and Campeau. I'm so ready to buckle down and skate. And I won't stop until we win the cup in June.

"You're late, Baby Bayer!" O'Doul calls. "Change, already."

"Sorry," I say, preferring not to explain where I've been. "Let's do this, boys!" I slap Drake on the back. "Who's ready to skate until we puke?"

"You talk a good game," my friend replies, pulling up his socks. "But I bet you're really just planning the first big prank of the season."

"Nah," I say, tossing my T-shirt into my gym bag. "I've retired the whoopie cushion and the rubber chicken." This will be the year that the hockey blogs know me for my stats, not my reputation as a party boy.

It's time to settle down. Hell—it's past time. "Where's my jersey?" I ask, glancing around the room. It's not at my station. And I feel an honest-to-God shiver, like the hockey gods are reminding me one more time that nobody owes me a seat in this room.

"Oh, uh," Drake says, frowning. "Jimbo only made it half way around before something came up." He points at a rolling laundry cart in the center of the room. "I found mine in there."

"Thanks, dude." I slap my upper body pads on and then cross to the cart. Sure enough, there's my practice jersey right on top. *BAYER* it reads, number *70*. "One better than 69," I used to tell the ladies in the bars after games.

I reach for the jersey. But just as my fingers close around the fabric, a hand comes shooting up from beneath the other laundry in the cart and *grabs me by the wrist*.

I shriek like a teenage girl at a Taylor Swift concert.

The room erupts with howls of laughter.

"MOTHERFUCKER!" I yell as Castro stands up in the cart, shedding a pile of jerseys. Then I clutch my chest, where my heart is beating wildly. "You will PAY, asshole!"

He doubles over laughing. "Anyone get it on video?"

"Oh ya," says the rookie Wilson in his big Wisconsin accent. He's clutching his phone and laughing. "That'll be a classic. You jumped a *yard*, Baby Bayer. Shoulda gone out for basketball."

"Assholes," I grumble, lifting the damn jersey over my head. "You all think you're so funny." The whole room is still laughing, even Ivo, the Finnish kid who barely understands anything we say.

I stomp back to my gear and put on my hockey shorts.

"Oh, man," Drake says, wiping his eyes. "What a way to start the season. How you gonna pay Castro back?"

As soon as I hear the question, my subconscious is making plans. I could steal that lucky peanut-butter sandwich he eats before every game. He might open it up and find a damp sponge in there instead. Or—since we live in the same building and share a laundry room—I could put a new purple T-shirt in his whites laundry and turn all his underwear lavender.

But wait. No.

Slowly I turn to Drake. "I'm not."

"What?"

"I'm not going to get him back. I'm done with jokes and pranks," I tell him. Even if revenge does sound nice, because my heart rate is still elevated from Castro's jump scare, my focus needs to be elsewhere.

"*Sure* you're done." Drake rolls his eyes. "You can tell me all about it tonight when we go out."

"Where?"

"Some warehouse party in Long Island City. Doors open at midnight but the real fun doesn't start until one, prolly."

But I'm here to skate. I didn't bust my ass all summer to get drunk at a warehouse party. "Maybe next time," I tell Drake. And then I pat him on the shoulder and grab my skates.

THE FIRST THING I see when I walk out to the main practice rink is a whole lot of journalists and photographers. They're here to preview the new team roster and check out the new, expanded practice facility.

"Bayer! Over here!" a photographer calls. I give him a wave and a smile. I'm so juiced for the new season and a new chance to prove myself. The circus-like atmosphere only feeds me.

The second thing I see is our head coach.

"Anton!" Coach Worthington lands his piercing gaze on me. "Good showing yesterday at the track. I had no idea you could sprint like that."

My chest practically expands from this compliment. "Thank you, sir. I worked hard this summer."

"It shows. I was impressed. This is the year you settle down and put up the stats you're capable of."

"Yes, sir. That's going to happen."

"I have some ideas." There's a glint in the older man's eyes. "We're going to practice a couple different defensive pairings this year. You'll skate with O'Doul in some preseason games and Tankiewicz in others. Gotta keep 'em guessing. We have so much strength on the blue line. Let's make it all count."

"Yes, Coach. I can't wait." His optimism is contagious. Everyone is buzzing about how this will be a big season for us. It was only a few years ago when the Bruisers were moved to the city and rebranded as a Brooklyn team. The GM got fired, and then the coach, too.

Everybody said Nate Kattenberger was a fool, that an internet billionaire couldn't make a world-class hockey team out of his pricey investment.

They were wrong.

Nate is only part of our story now. Now there's Rebecca Rowley Kattenberger—his wife—who owns the team. We've got a terrific GM, a great staff, and twenty-three players who are determined to get back to the finals this season.

Thank you, Jesus, for making me one of them. And I'm sorry about that dirty joke earlier.

I know I'm lucky to be standing here in this state-of-the-art practice rink in the Brooklyn Navy Yard. It's a bit of a zoo today because the team is holding an open practice. There are little kids in the stands wearing purple Bruisers jerseys. And photographers angling their giant cameras toward the ice.

Practice hasn't started, and most of the guys aren't out here yet. But out of the corner of my eye, I see an unfamiliar skater in full goalie padding. My attention is snagged by the fluid, strong strides of his skating. Goalies have to be phenomenal skaters, but there's something really stylish about this one. I wonder who he is. Some college kid getting a tryout? A draft pick I haven't seen before?

"We're going to run a lot of back-checking drills," Coach says. "Our whole season could hinge on how many fractional seconds it takes us to recover a lost puck."

"That makes a lot of sense," I agree.

The goalie has reached my end of the rink now, where there is a little girl smiling and waving at him. He comes to a fluid stop in front of the plexi. He scoops a puck up off the ice and then shows it to the little girl, sending her into paroxysms of joy. He tosses it over, and the little girl lets out a whoop and leaps for it.

I smile as a reflex, because I was once that kid, desperate for a moment's contact with one of my idols at the rink.

But then? The goalie unclips his helmet and hauls it over his head, revealing a head of long, thick hair. Hold the phone—this goalie is a *girl*. No—a woman. With rich brown hair and lush olive skin. She shakes out her hair, which seems to be in the process of escaping whatever braid or ponytail that had confined it. Then she smiles, giving the little girl a wave.

And I can't fucking breathe. Her smile lights up her eyes, which are a warm brown. She is like the living, breathing picture of female perfection.

In a goalie's pads. Fuck me.

"*Anton Bayer*," Coach snaps. "We were having a conversation. And now you're staring at a girl."

Dazed, I look back in his direction. "Sorry, sir. I just didn't realize..." The sentence has no rational conclusion. I just didn't realize that a ten-second look at a woman from ten yards away was enough to make me feel so much. Curiosity. Intrigue. Hunger, even. Who knew I had a thing for goalies?

"Yeah, the Bombshells' season is starting up at the same time as yours," Coach says. "It's going to be an adjustment sharing this facility."

"Exactly," I agree, as if I'd been thinking the same thing. And in truth, I had forgotten all about Rebecca's investment in women's hockey. "The, uh, new renovation looks great, though."

Coach grunts his agreement. Over the summer, they'd done a lot of work on the practice facility. The full-sized practice rink—where I'm currently making an ass of myself in front of Coach—got five hundred additional seats and a new, high-tech roof. There's a new stadium-worthy scoreboard hanging from the ceiling.

And—this is the wildest thing—an entire new story was constructed on top of our state-of-the-art locker room facility. So our dressing rooms are still there, but there's a new suite for the women's team above us.

I'd known all that. It's just that it hadn't really sunk in that there'd be actual women here in the building with us. And I really hadn't anticipated that my brain could be stolen by the goalie on day one.

Lordy, I'm going to have to watch myself. Coach was absolutely right when he said this is my year to settle down and contribute. It isn't just my sprints that I've been training. It's my mind. I need to be tougher than I've been.

Focus, man. Come on.

Coach checks his expensive watch. "Let's do this, Bayer. We're starting. Get out there."

I vault over the wall to get in a couple of warmup laps as my teammates troop down the chute to join me. I lean into my glide, lengthening my stride and stretching my legs. But as I round the ice, something silver glints at me from the surface. I stop, lean down, and remove my glove to pluck some kind of hairpin off the ice. It must have escaped when the world's most sensuous goalie shook out her hair.

So much for avoiding her. I straighten up and skate hastily toward the end of the rink where I'd seen her disappear. And there she is, helmet under her arm, watching my teammates warm up. She's wearing a frown now, which puts a crease in her forehead. I have the urge to smooth it out with my fingers.

But that would be creepy and weird, so I speak to her instead. "Excuse me, miss? I think you might have dropped this when you were giving that little girl the puck. Nice move, by the way. You made her whole year."

The beauty turns, and her eyes widen slightly. "Sorry. Are you speaking to me?"

"Yeah. I don't know your name. But I found this on the ice." I hold it out, and her eyes widen again.

"O-oh," she stammers. "I didn't…" She catches herself. "Never mind. thank you. I hope you didn't trip on it."

"Nah. No worries."

She reaches out and takes the pin from me, brushing my palm with her fingertips. And just that small contact ripples through me like an electrical current. "Welcome to Brooklyn," I hear myself say in a husky voice. "Was today your first practice?" That would explain the number of journalists.

"Yes," she says with a quick smile that I feel right in the center of my chest. "Was it that obvious?"

"What? No." I laugh. "I didn't see any of it."

Behind me, an assistant coach blows the whistle, calling for the first drills.

"But I'm about to have my own practice now," I add.

"Well, good luck to you, then. I hope it goes better than mine."

"Thank you." Still, I linger a moment longer, staring into those soft brown eyes. "You have a nice day," I say stupidly. Then I force myself to turn and skate away.

I didn't even get her name.

TWO

Like the Caribbean Sea

SYLVIE

IT ISN'T until he skates away that I remember to breathe. Everything about my encounter with the big, blond hockey player was strange.

In the first place, I didn't know a man's eyes could be that brilliant shade of turquoise-blue. I missed the first thing he said to me, because I was wondering how that color was possible.

And then there's the hairpin. I don't wear them, but my mother did. We had the same thick hair, which she wore in pretty up-dos, while I'm more of a ponytail girl.

My mother died a year ago, but since then, I've been finding hairpins everywhere. She leaves them for me to discover.

Yes, that sounds crazy, but that doesn't mean it isn't true. Reality worked a little differently for my mother than it does for other people. She was a deeply spiritual, mystical person. She was dedicated to prayer, joy, and inner knowledge. And her intuition went well past the normal range and right into, well, *freaky*.

I'm convinced that her spirit was just stronger than everyone else's. She was a cosmic force. And even though she's left this earth, she's still sending me frequent signs. Like a silver hairpin on the bathroom sink at home, where nobody has been but me. And a copper one in the pocket of the dress I wore to her funeral. There was even a hairpin with a tiny jewel on it that appeared on the windowsill one night when I was washing the dishes. I set down the sponge, and it was just *there*.

So the appearance of a hairpin just now at this rink, where I never expected to be, is just more proof of her divine powers. And her nosiness, too. Maman is trying to tell me that she's still beside me, even though I've suddenly relocated five hundred miles from our home in Ontario.

Brooklyn was never part of my travel plans. Fifteen months ago I graduated from college. I had hoped to make the Canadian women's team, but they already had a full bench of excellent goalies, and none of the women's pro teams had knocked on my door.

There were only five teams in the league—that made for ten professional women goalies on a continent of millions.

Then, three months after graduation, my mother died, and I stopped thinking about hockey. Or anything, really. Mourning will do that to a girl.

So I was floored earlier this month when the phone had rung and someone had said, "Hi, Sylvie Hansen? This is Bess Beringer. I'm a sports agent, but I'm also in charge of recruitment for the Brooklyn Bombshells. I know this is last minute. But how do you feel about guarding the net for Brooklyn?"

For a moment, I'd honestly thought I was being pranked.

But Bess had been dead serious. "The season begins in ten days. I realize you probably weren't planning to change your life today. But if it's possible, we'd love to have you."

"Would I be trying out?" I'd asked, still a little unsure that the conversation was real.

"I have tape from your final playoff game. And I just got off the phone with Sasha Marshall. We hired her, too. And she wants you in front of the net."

"Sasha Marshall," I'd whispered. Hearing my college coach's name had made it real.

"That's right," Bess had said. "At the last minute we lost a goalie who decided to play in Sweden. And Sasha thought of you. Can I have her call you?"

And that had been that. Seven days later, I'd been on a plane to New York. I'd barely had time to pack and tell my closest friends that I was leaving Ontario.

There's one person in particular that I did not tell. Bryce Campeau, a center for the Brooklyn bruisers, and the man I once believed I would marry.

He's going to be astonished to see me standing here. If he ever looks up.

The Bruisers are clustered around their coach, listening intently. People expect big things from the Bruisers this year. It's too early to talk of the championship, but they are well-positioned for the season. Which means I basically have a front-row seat to watch Bryce fulfill his dreams.

He stands stock sill in his skates, his whole being focused on his coach's words. Bryce is the most serious man I've ever met. And when he finds out I've suddenly appeared in Brooklyn, he'll —

Okay, the truth is that I'm not exactly sure what he'll do. He and I have lots of history, but not the romantic kind. He'd lived in our family's house throughout my teen years, billeted as a junior hockey player on one of my father's teams.

We'd often had players living with us. They had been brash, silly boys, and I hadn't paid them much attention. But Bryce had been different from the start. At seventeen, he'd been a man already, with a serious expression and moody, dark blue eyes. Like me, he'd had a French-speaking mother. And like my mother, he was a devout Catholic.

But Bryce was alone in the world. He never met his father. His mother tried her best to give him a good life, he'd said, but by the time he came to live with us, she had died of complications from liver disease.

"She drank. A lot," he'd told us frankly. "She quit many times, but it got her in the end."

So there'd been this kid, only seventeen years old when he'd arrived, and motherless. He'd been playing for an Ontario team and could barely understand his coach, or my father, who ran the program.

My mother had taken one look at his solemn face and the gold crucifix around his neck and saw a kindred spirit. She'd basically adopted him on sight. She could tell he needed someone to fuss over him—someone to make foods that he liked and organize his life and sit beside him at Mass on Sunday.

And I'd loved him from the first moment I watched his broody gaze scan my home, taking in my mother's collection of prayer candles and the carefully set table. He'd walked over to the mantel, noticing that one of Maman's statuettes had tipped to the side. And he carefully righted it. "Thank you for to bring me here in your home," he'd said in very halting English.

I'd liked the soft, measured tone of his voice. And I'd really liked that he needed my help with the language. As a French speaker myself, I would often come to his rescue, translating whenever he required it.

My father had required him to speak English at the dinner table. He'd known that Bryce needed to learn. But Maman and I had been his port in the storm. We spoke French when my father was out of the house, and we helped him adjust to life in a new city.

I'd hid my crush on him as best I could. And he and my mother were *thick as thieves*, as we say in English.

Bryce had lived with us for four years. And when, at age twenty, he'd left to play for Montreal, we'd all been so incredibly proud of him.

I'd missed him terribly, but I'd been self-aware enough to know that he viewed me like a little sister. Besides—I was headed off to college at the University of Michigan.

And there had been holidays and summers to look forward to. We had become Bryce's family, so he spent his free time with us. I'd lived for those moments when he'd watch movies with me in the den, and my mother would spoil him rotten.

Then—a couple years later—my mother died very suddenly. One day she was home with my dad and baking cookies. And the next day she was just gone. She had a brain aneurism and drove her car into a ditch, dying behind the wheel of her car before the police even arrived.

We'd been devastated. Bryce—recently traded to the Bruisers

—was the first person I'd called after my father broke the news. "Sit down, I need to tell you something. Maman is gone."

The next few days had been a blur. Bryce told Coach Worthington that the mother of his heart had suddenly died, and Coach took the extraordinary step of sending him home to us for a week. He'd missed three games to come to Ontario and hold my hand at her funeral.

My father was beside himself. He'd loved her desperately. "My beautiful rose," he'd sobbed at the kitchen table the night after the funeral. "I don't know what I'm supposed to do without her."

Bryce had finally teared up, too. It had broken me to see them so sad, so I'd gone to bed, tucking myself in and wishing I could wake up and have my old life back—the one where my mother hummed to herself in the kitchen while she made tea.

Later, Bryce had come into my darkened room, climbed into bed with me, and held me in his arms. That had never happened before.

"Sylvie," he'd said quietly. "I want to love like that, Sylvie. The way your father and your mother were to one another. That could be us. Some day we will be together for real."

"*Oui*?" I'd asked, stunned. "*Vraiment*?"

"*Vraiment*," he'd repeated. "She wanted me to take care of you."

"She did?"

"*Oui*. And I promised her I would. You are so special to me. You are everything. Fate sent you to me. I know it." He'd said a lot of things that night that I'd never expected him to say.

Then he'd kissed me. I'd already been on emotional overload, but Bryce's kisses had been the only thing that made me feel better about the terrible, gut-wrenching loss I'd just suffered.

My achy heart had held Bryce's promises tightly. Thoughts of our future together had sustained me for weeks after he left.

I should have known, though. Words spoken in the dark after you bury someone you love are not weighed and measured like other words.

Our friendship returned to its usual ways: texts from the team jet and the occasional phone call where he would speak to my father and then to me.

I'd thought about him every day, though. Bryce's whispered word in the dark —*someday*— got me through a lot of difficult hours.

But he hadn't brought up our future again, and eventually I'd grown impatient. This spring—six months after my mother's death —I asked Bryce when we could be together for real. "I would come to Brooklyn," I'd offered. "To be with you."

It had not gone over well. His stammering reply was not at all what I'd hoped for. My heart sank as he'd uttered phrases like "too soon," "incredibly busy," and "focused on my game."

"When, then?" I'd asked, trying to hold my heart together.

"Sylvie, I don't know. If you come here just for me, you are all alone much of the time. That is not right. The time is not right."

Alors. I had fallen for Bryce when I'd been a naïve girl of fifteen. But now, at twenty-two, I am a much wiser woman. I know what words of true love sound like, and they don't sound like that.

After that dreadful conversation, I wised up. I made myself stop dreaming of a future with Bryce. I went to work in the front office of my father's hockey organization. I even looked around for nice men to date, trying to get my mind off of *him*.

I didn't find any, though. It was a lonely, quiet time in the house with my father, both of us straining to hear the echo of my mother's voice.

Things began to feel easier for me this summer. Less sadness. More ordinary joy. And just when I'd stopped pining all the time, the phone rang, summoning me to Brooklyn.

So here I stand, twenty yards from Bryce in this beautiful rink, wearing a Bombshells practice jersey. My maman would say that fate brought me to his doorstep once again.

She did, in fact, predict this.

If that sounds crazy, it's because you never met Maman. She believed in fate. So does Bryce, by the way. He is forever seeing signs in ordinary things. So I wonder how he'll feel when he sees me.

As for me, I really don't know what to think. Part of me is full of skin-tingling wonder that I've been sent by fate or God or luck to be with Bryce again. Maybe he'll look over at me and understand that our paths are meant to join forever.

The other part of me knows that it's a long shot. I want to be loved *desperately*. I want to be cherished. I want a man who needs me in his life even when it's inconvenient.

Bryce has already failed this test once. But since I'm here, I think I'll school him on a few things. I'll show him that I'm strong, and that I am full of life and ready to be loved, even if not by him. I could even have some fun with this. I will show him what he's missing. He won't know what's hit him.

If he ever turns his freaking head and looks in my direction.

Someone else turns, though. It's that other man—the one with the eyes like the Caribbean Sea. He glances at me and then gives me a quick smile.

And it's *quite* a smile. My heart might be broken, but my eyes are not. His eyes linger on me for a long beat, and then he slowly turns his face back toward the coach.

But I still feel his attention directed this way. I don't know why, but I sense his interest.

The back of his practice jersey says BAYER. I've heard that name before. He's a defenseman, and one of Bryce Campeau's friends.

No one else glances this way, though, and I've been waiting here a long time.

So I turn and leave for the brand-new women's locker room.

THREE

Big No No

ANTON

"MAN, I NEED CALORIES," I bellow in the locker room after practice. "Pizza at Grimaldi's? Who's with me?"

Bryce Campeau raises a hand and gives me a serious nod.

"Excellent. Leave in ten?" I twist my head around, looking for my buddy, Drake. "Anyone seen the Drakerator? Why did he leave the ice early?"

"Blood-sugar crash," O'Doul mutters.

"Oh, shit," I say. Drake is a type 1 diabetic. Managing his condition during peak athletic performance is tricky. Sometimes he gets things a little wrong and starts to crash. And it's often worse at the start of the season, when his metabolism has to readjust to the daily strain of professional sports.

Hoping to check on him, I head for the treatment rooms. But Drake comes skidding into the dressing room, his face red, looking harried.

"You okay, man?"

"No," he says shortly. "I just fucked up big time."

"Damn. You want me to find Doc Herberts?"

"Not necessary. And not what I meant. My blood sugar was a little wonky, so I headed off to find the juice and the test kits I keep in Doc's office, right?"

"Sure."

"Well, they moved it."

"The juice?"

"The whole office!" He throws his arms wide. "It's upstairs now, on the new floor. So I'm, like, dizzy as I climb those new stairs, and I'm in this hallway I've never seen before. I don't know which office is which, so I start poking my head into all of them."

"Whoa. Did you find it?"

He winces. "Eventually. But first I found this super-pretty girl in a treatment room, grabbing some tape. So I say, 'Hey doll, could you help me find Herberts's office?'" He scrubs a hand through his hair.

"Wait, you called a stranger *doll*?"

"I *know*, okay? But I was using one-syllable words for a reason. Everything started looking yellow around the edges, and I thought I might pass out." He heaves a sigh. "I didn't."

"Well, that's good."

"Sorta. Turns out that girl is a *player.* I think she said defense. There was yelling. I didn't get all the details."

"Question." Jimbo, our equipment guy, raises his hand, like a boy in school. "Do they still call her a defenseman even if she's a defense*woman*?"

"They could say D-man," someone suggests. "Oh, wait…"

"Does this story have a punchline?" I ask. A guy could go all day without finishing a thought in this room.

"She ripped me a new one," Drake grumbles. "She went *off*. And it didn't help my case that in the middle of her telling me what a turd I am for treating her like a waitress or a puck bunny—her words—I basically staggered away from her, found Doc's office, and grabbed my juice and chugged it."

"Oh, man." I just shake my head.

"So she thought I was an asshole twice—"

"Which you were," Castro points out. "Even if you were not totally in control of your faculties."

"Right. And I just kept on being an asshole, trying to stay conscious while she delivered a long lecture about making assumptions."

"Assumptions you made," Castro points out again. "And by the way, the women's team officially starts today."

"Wow, thank you for that timely information," Drake grumbles. "The girl was *pissed*. Now I gotta watch my back every time I walk into this place."

"Come to lunch with Campeau and me," I say. "Sounds like you could use the calories. And we'll guard your six."

"Thanks, man." Drake pushes himself off the doorframe. He still looks a little off. I'm thinking we'll need to take a taxi over to our favorite pizza place.

The three of us leave the dressing room and troop down the hallway together. It still has that new-paint smell from all the work they're hurrying to finish. We exit via a set of secure doors into a hallway that widens toward a glass brick tunnel. From there, the floor slopes upward from our practice facility to the Bruisers' corporate offices.

Drake stiffens as we reach the tunnel. "Uh-oh."

Glancing up, I see three women ahead of us. They're stopped, as if waiting for someone else to join them. And, whoa, it's like the Charlie's Angels of hockey—a blond, a redhead, and the brunette beauty I can't stop thinking about.

Her face lights up when she sees us, too. I'm just about to call out a happy greeting when my teammate Campeau says, in a shocked voice, "*Sylvie!* What are you *doing* here?"

This is a development I wasn't expecting.

And if I'm not mistaken, her beautiful smile grows a little uncertain. "Um, *surprise!*" she says as we approach. "A week ago Bess Beringer called me and asked me to be the second goalie for the Bombshells."

"You—" Campeau swallows. He looks stunned, and maybe a little pale. "Here?"

"Here," she says firmly. "In Brooklyn."

"In Brooklyn," he echoes like a dummy. He takes a long beat to digest this news. "Where are you staying?"

She puts a hand on her hip. "With you, of course. You have a double bed, right?"

Campeau blanches.

She laughs. "Oh, *monsieur crédule*! I'm just teasing you. This is my roommate, Fiona. We have an apartment together." She indicates the blonde.

Bryce finally breathes. "An apartment? Where? Is it safe? There are some places in Brooklyn where you do not want to live."

"Let me just stop you right there," the redhead says with fire in her eyes. And when she speaks up, I swear Drake ducks behind me, using me as his human shield. "Isn't Sylvie a grownup who can decide on her own where to live?"

"But—"

"Do you ask your male friends if their apartments are safe?" she presses.

Sylvie laughs. "Charli, stand down. Bryce met me when I was a silly, impulsive teen. He probably can't help asking these questions."

The redhead crosses her arms. "Fine, but on day one I've already witnessed two of these guys saying ridiculous things to grown women. And the day isn't even half over."

"Hey, Bryce," I say, squeezing my teammate's elbow. "Aren't you going to introduce us to your friend? We're sharing a workspace, right?"

He gives a stiff nod. "Sylvie, meet Anton Bayer, a defenseman, and Cornelius Drake, winger."

"Cornelius?" the blond woman asks, incredulous.

"Neil," he corrects.

"Ah." She smiles, and her eyes dance with humor. "I'm Fiona, also a forward, and the captain of the Bombshells. This is Charli, who plays defense."

"And Sylvie is the goalie," I say, because I can't help myself. And I can't stop looking at her. Even in her street clothes, with her hair smoothed after a shower, her cheeks bear the high color of an athlete after practice. She has wide-set brown eyes and the cheekbones of a Swedish supermodel.

But there are lots of pretty women in the world. I couldn't even tell you why this one makes me feel wild and loose inside. Like I've just had three drinks and gotten on a roller coaster.

"Yes," Fiona says, putting a hand on Sylvie's shoulder. "We

have two incredible goalies. It's going to be a great season, boys. I hope your stats can keep pace with ours."

"Oh, bring it on." I laugh. "How does five bucks a goal sound? You versus me."

"But we only have twenty games," says Charli, the woman who Drake is afraid of. "That's not a fair bet."

"I'm a D-man, though," I point out. My job isn't running up the score.

"How many goals did you have last season?" Fiona asks.

"Five."

"So you like losing money?" she asks, and the women laugh, which puts the sparkle back into Sylvie's eyes.

"New year, new opportunities," I say lightly. "Do we have a bet?"

"Ten bucks a goal. Might as well keep it interesting." Fiona shrugs.

"Done," I say, knowing full well that I'll most likely be paying Fiona some cash every week. If they picked her for captain, she should easily average a goal a game.

But that's okay with me. I'll just have to make frequent visits to their new apartment—wherever it is—and pay up.

FORTY MINUTES later we're sitting in Grimaldi's putting away the pizza at a rapid pace. Except for Campeau, who looks shellshocked.

"What's your deal with, uh, the new girl?" I ask as casually as I can. Campeau isn't the kind of guy who gives you a whole lot of info about his past. I've spent a lot of time with the guy, and I barely know a thing about him. And not because I didn't ask.

"Sylvie," he says quietly, like it's difficult to say her name. "I really fuck things up with her."

My blood stops circulating. I barely met the girl, but I don't want to hear that they were lovers. I don't know what's wrong with me. "She's your ex?"

"No." He shakes his head. "Remember when I miss some games last fall to go to Ontario?"

"Yeah, when your mom died?" Drake asks.

"Not my real mom, but the mother of my heart. I billeted in their home as a junior player after my own mother died. And Marie was wonderful. I was very close with the family. Sylvie is Marie's daughter."

"Ah. But something happened between you two?" I press.

"No, and yes. After the funeral we were both very sad. I said some big things to Sylvie, about what the future might hold. I love Sylvie. I would do anything for her."

Brooklyn's best pizza turns dry in my mouth.

"But I should not have said anything. I should not have made any promises. And I should not have kissed her."

The image of Sylvie lifting her head for a kiss wrecks my brain. But after I take a drink of water and get a goddamn grip, I realize that nothing Campeau just said makes any sense at all. "Wait. Why not? If you love someone, why not say so and then kiss the girl senseless?"

He puts his head in his hands. "I was not ready. You already know how hard it is. We have to focus on the game."

"For that girl I would multitask," Drake says, speaking my own thoughts aloud.

"This season will be everything," Campeau says. "This one is for all the..." He frowns, searching for a word.

"Marbles?" I guess.

"Yes. I cannot afford to fuck up. I literally cannot afford it. The team offers last month to renegotiate, but I turn it down."

My water glass stops halfway to my mouth. "Wait. They offered to extend you early?" If the team wants you badly enough, they'll remake your contract way before the June cutoff.

Campeau nods curtly. "Yes, for a three-year deal. But the number was not very generous. We said no."

Something goes wrong in my gut. Campeau was Mr. Serious last year, when I was busy fucking around. He got the job done, and the team offered to extend him for three—really four—more years.

23

And he said *no?* Because of a couple million dollars? "Nate and Hugh are very savvy," I say slowly. "Of course they'd lowball you a little bit. But you would have all that added security against an injury, or even a bad season." Even if my cousin wasn't an agent, I'd still understand this on a gut level. The team offered him a *career*.

Campeau shrugs. "I do not plan to have a bad season. But I also do not plan to propose marriage before it is finished. I need the wins, the cup, the contract, and the girl. In this order."

Drake and I exchange a brief glance that's full of *what the fuck?*

"You understand," Campeau continues. "I need the stats. If I am to give Sylvie a good life, I need a big, multiyear contract. I need to reach the next level."

That is a story I know all too well. We all need the stats. We all crave the next level. Maybe I'm just a punter, and Campeau is the real deal. But what if the "next level" is an illusion? What if every single day of my career will feel just as perilous as the last?

"Sylvie wanted me to invite her here. She wanted to come to Brooklyn. And I did not offer." The Canadian sighs. "She stopped talking to me. She makes new friends. She even posted a picture on Instagram with a guy on a date."

"Cold, man," Drake says, reaching for another slice.

"No, it isn't," Campeau defends her. "We were never a couple. She wanted it. I always knew that. But I was living in her parents' *home*. A man does not go there."

"True," Drake says. "No sticking it to the coach's daughter. Big no-no."

"Big no-no," Campeau repeats. "She was just a teenager when we met, too. I love her. But…" He heaves a sigh. "The time was not right. The time still is not right."

"But here she is in Brooklyn," I say, twisting the knife a little. Because I'm still stuck on the whole *I love her but I should never admit it* thing. "What are you going to do now?"

"I have no idea," he says. "First, I will make sure this place where she lives is safe. If it is not, she can come and stay with me. I have a pull-out sofa."

"Women love that." I chuckle. "When they're in love with you, and you offer them the pull-out sofa."

Drake snorts out a laugh.

"I am so fucked," Campeau says.

"Yup! Entirely fucked." I take another slice of pizza and eat it with gusto.

FOUR

An Ocean of Mercy

SYLVIE

I STRIKE A MATCH, and the flame leaps forth with a familiar hiss. I tip the glass candle holder and carefully light the wick. Then I shake out the match and lay it on a saucer, since I'm not keen to set my new apartment on fire.

Apart from the unfamiliar location, this ritual is as familiar to me as breathing. It's three o'clock, the magic hour. My mother always lit candles in the afternoon. Tradition holds that Christ died at this hour.

"Google says that three o'clock in Jerusalem is really eight in the morning here," I'd once pointed out during my contrary teen years.

"That is not the point, Sylvie," she'd replied. "A ritual is for remembrance. The meaning is here," she'd said, tapping her chest.

I watch the candle flicker in its cup, and now I understand. These days, I light a three o'clock candle whenever I'm able, and nothing could be a more potent reminder of Maman.

I kneel for her in front of the candle and close my eyes. I say the prayer in French, as she taught me. *"Vous avez expiré, Jésus, mais…"*

It's a comforting prayer. Who wouldn't want an afternoon reminder of an ocean of mercy? I'm basically a lapsed Catholic like my father. And I only say the prayer once instead of the three times the ritual calls for.

But then I address her. "*Maman*, please be careful about hairpins on the ice. Someone could trip." In the silence of my new apartment, I feel more self-conscious than usual, even though I know Fiona is out shopping for throw pillows. "Okay, a hairpin probably won't kill anyone, but it's not a good look. I'm sure you were just reminding me to be patient. Especially with Bryce. The look on his face, though…"

I fall silent, remembering his expression. It wasn't joyous. First, I saw shock, followed swiftly by confusion. And then discomfort, especially when I made that joke about sleeping in his bed. I swear all the color drained from his face.

"It wasn't the reunion I'd hoped for," I tell my mother. "I thought he'd laugh and maybe pick me up and twirl me around. But he just looked like I'd run him over with the Zamboni."

Sure, I'd expected some surprise. But a small part of me thought he might see it as a sign.

But, nope. He was definitely stuck on the shock phase.

"I could be patient," I whisper. "If I thought that patience was the issue. And we already knew he doesn't like surprises." He'd had too many of those in his life already, many of them bad. Bryce likes order and planning and preparation.

But I'd sprung myself on him, because I wanted a big romantic reunion. Laughter, followed by the kind of kiss that sailors gave their women after returning from war.

I didn't get it. And after that awkward greeting in the hallway with my teammates, I'd hurried away to regroup.

The candle flickers gently. It's not a sign. My mother only communicates in lost hairpins and memories. "You did tell me to be patient," I whisper. "A year ought to be enough, though. He doesn't love me, Maman. It wasn't real. I wish you were here. I wish you could tell me what to do."

My voice cracks a little bit. I miss my mother so much that it aches. She and I were nothing alike, just as Bryce and I are nothing alike. But that doesn't mean we didn't get along. She was so strong and beautiful, and I thought she'd be with me forever. Instead, she was cut down on a sunny autumn day.

Nobody plans to die young. Nobody except my mother, that is. She'd had a will, which I guess is something responsible people do. But she'd also left me a letter.

It began: *Dear Sylvie, if you are reading this, then I have left this Earth. But I will never leave you, my baby girl.*

Maybe I should have waited to read it, because that first line cut me in half. The tears in my eyes made it hard to keep reading. She said so many loving things. And she reminded me to work on my patience.

But she followed that by telling me that I will be loved deeply and completely. And that Bryce was my soulmate.

The letter is tucked away in a shoebox now. It hurts too much to read it. And it won't do me any good to read it again, anyway. Maman was amazing, and many of her words will doubtless prove true.

But as I sit here staring into the candle's flame, I can't help thinking that she got a few things wrong.

It hurts, too.

FIVE

The Right Kind of Screw

SYLVIE

"YOU HAVE TO ADMIT," Charli says from a corner of our sofa. "*Bombshells* is a terrible name for a team. What were they even thinking?"

"It's not terrible at all," Fiona argues from the other end. "I love it. A bombshell is a sudden revelation. An overwhelming surprise. That's what we're supposed to be, in this scenario—the thing that makes New York realize that women's hockey is great. Plus, you get the alliteration with Brooklyn."

"But it *also* means sexpot," Charli sputters. "It's evil marketing. They think they can only sell tickets by sexing us up. If they print posters with a naked woman riding on a missile, I will quit on the spot."

"Hey," I argue from the floor, where I'm stretching my quads on the new rug I bought yesterday. "The logo is a cartoon bomb. No boobs in sight. But if it meant we could be paid more, and that a women's team could be profitable, I'd almost be willing to play topless."

I'm joking, of course, for two reasons.

First, I don't need the money because my bookkeeping job followed me to Brooklyn. "You can work remotely," my dad had said. "And I'll cover your apartment," he'd added during the frenzied twenty-four hour period where I had to decide if I was going to change my whole life and move to Brooklyn. "Just go and give this thing a whirl. Don't worry about money."

And the second reason I'm joking about flashing my tatas for ticket sales is that I'm hoping to get a rise out of Bryce, who's in my bedroom right now. That's right, in my *bedroom,* where I always hoped he'd end up.

Be careful what you wish for, though. A couple hours ago he texted me, asking if he could come over. So I washed my hair and put on makeup, as well as a low-cut sleeveless top.

In my defense, it's a warm September afternoon.

But when he came through the door, Bryce didn't even give my outfit a glance. He was carrying a small toolbox and a brand new deadbolt lock, the kind you can install above the perfectly functional locks already in place on our door.

He'd given me a perfunctory kiss on each cheek and got straight to work installing the extra lock, while my teammates looked on in amusement.

To be fair, Bryce's helpfulness is one of the things I've always loved about him. All the players who ever lived with us did chores. "This *eez* not a hotel," my mother would say, pinning a schedule to the refrigerator. Everyone in our home was responsible for taking out the trash or washing dishes or vacuuming the floors, at least when they weren't on a tour bus in the hinterlands of Canada.

Bryce's contribution was on another level, though, right from the start. He'd call on his way home from the rink to ask if my mother or I needed anything from the store. He fixed doorknobs that had stopped turning, he hung shelves, and changed the oil in my mother's car.

"So resourceful," my mother used to say. "The finest young man I've ever met."

Forty minutes ago, when Bryce had installed the lock on our front door to his satisfaction, I'd brought him a soda and led him into my room for a moment away from the prying eyes of Fiona and Charli.

"Listen, I appreciate your concern," I'd said. "But I feel very safe here." I'd sat down on the bed and patted the spot next to me. "I'm only two blocks from the rink. It's a nice neighborhood."

He'd sat down, too, but at a respectful distance, his serious blue eyes nowhere near my cleavage. "Your father thought it would be a good idea."

"Hmm?" I'd asked, distracted by my own agenda. *Kiss me you fool. Why won't you just lay me out on this bed and make love to me? Finally?*

"The lock," he'd said, giving me a frown and putting the soda on the bedside table. "Your father worries about you, too. You know…" He'd turned and climbed onto the bed on his hands and knees, making my heart leap. But it turned out he'd only been looking out the window. "*Merde.* You are only on the third floor. And these burglar bars are loose. Someone might climb the fire escape. I will tighten them."

That had been forty minutes ago. He's already made a trip to the hardware store for just the right kind of screw.

Although the *right kind of screw*, in my opinion, is not something you can get at the hardware store.

It's no use, anyway. We have a big team meeting in a half hour —the Bruisers and the Bombshells together. So if I'm going to convince Bryce to ravish me, it's going to have to be another day.

Having given up, I left him to his screwdrivers and came out here to stretch my sore muscles on the rug and listen to my team-mates' chatter. We've known each other for four days, but they've been intense ones. I've moved to a new city, and I've had my first two grueling practices with my new team.

I'm tired, but happy. Playing hockey as a professional? There is no better job in the world. And I like these women. Fiona is just as bubbly and confident as a team captain should be.

And Charli is… not. She's angry, although she hasn't told us why. But she's also smart, with a biting wit that frequently makes me cackle.

The buzzer rings on the wall, and I startle because I'm not used to the sound of it yet.

Fiona pops off the couch. "I'll get it!" She spends a moment on the handset and then presses the button to admit someone.

"Who is it?" Charli demands.

"A couple of Bryce's friends," she says. "He asked them to stop by before we all go to the meeting."

"It better not be that one who called me a *doll*." Charli tosses her red hair. "I still can't believe that. Two hours—that's how long we'd been in the building before one of the self-important million-aires revealed his sexist attitude."

"They'll adjust," Fiona says with a shrug.

"Will they?" Charli points a finger toward my bedroom, where Bryce is still performing his unsolicited home repair.

There's a knock on our door, and this time I get up to answer it. The first thing I see when I open the door is a pair of bright, turquoise eyes. They're smiling at me.

And then they take a slow trip down to my cleavage, before rising back upward.

My cheeks flush, even though I wore this top for that exact reason. "Hello there," I say, just as I notice the object in his hands. It's a toilet seat. "Gosh, is that for me?"

"It is, and aren't you lucky?" I'd forgotten that his voice has a slightly husky texture. I feel it right in the center of my chest. "Some men bring flowers, but I brought a new seat for the throne."

"*Why?*" Charli demands from somewhere behind me.

"Well—" Anton clears his throat. "Mind if I come in?"

I realize that I'm blocking the door while I stare at his pretty eyes. "Of course!" I leap out of the way.

"Campeau asked us to pick up a few things that he thought you needed."

"A toilet seat?" Fiona asks, skeptical.

"Replacement!" Bryce yells from the bedroom. "You do not know who lived here before."

"Actually, we do," Drake says, entering the apartment behind Anton.

Charli growls.

Drake moves to stand in the corner, in a pose that positions his hands in front of his testicles. "This is the apartment where Becca and Georgia lived until Georgia moved out to live with Leo, and Becca moved in with Nate. After that, Becca's sister lived here."

Bryce emerges from my bedroom. "Thank you for stopping at the store."

"My pleasure." Anton tosses the toilet seat—frisbee style—toward Bryce, who catches it. Then he hands me a small bag that contains four nine-volt batteries. "For your smoke detectors," he says. "Safety first." He gives me a wink that manages to mock Bryce and look sexy at the same time.

"Thank you," I say. "You didn't have to come all the way over. I could have gotten the batteries."

"We live across the street in 220." Anton lifts his chin toward the windows, where a luxury condo building is always in view. "Are we going to this meeting, or what?"

"Absolutely." Fiona claps her hands like the team captain that she is. "We'll leave in five minutes." She gets up to gather her practice gear, since the Bombshells have practice after the meeting.

In the silence that follows, Charli and Drake eye each other warily. Anton ignores them both, taking a slow tour around our new living room, stopping in front of the prayer candles I've placed on the mantel. "Does this fireplace work?" he asks. "It's pretty."

"I doubt it," I say.

He touches one finger to the blue glass candle holder and then turns around to look at me with those beautiful eyes. "How are you liking Brooklyn so far?"

"It's gorgeous," I say a little stupidly. My goodness, he must get a lot of attention from women.

"You're from Toronto, right?"

"Montreal and then the Toronto suburbs. We left Quebec when I was a little girl. When my father retired. And you?"

"Pennsylvania. But then Colorado, where I played on a minor league team."

"You ski?" I ask him. Colorado skiing is pretty great.

"Of course!" His eyes dance. "You too? Mont Tremblant? Did I just butcher that pronunciation?"

"Yes." I try not to laugh.

"Tell me how to say it right."

"Mont Tremblant. Use your nose."

He braces his feet on the rug, spreads his arms, and tries again. "MONT... TREMBLANT."

It's better this time, but exaggerated, and I hear myself giggle. "We'll work on it."

"Awesome."

___

AT THE MEETING, I sit down between Fiona and Bryce. When our coach calls Fiona to the front of the room, Anton Bayer slides into her empty seat. I turn my chin to give him a polite smile of acknowledgement.

He gives me a smile so hot that I feel a little flushed as I return my attention to the meeting. Some men just radiate sex appeal, don't they? I can't even say why. Something about him just runs hotter than other men.

"Good afternoon!" Rebecca says from the front of the room. "This will be an unusual gathering. I'm well aware how busy you all are. The season will soon be in full swing, and you'll be off on busses and planes having the season of a lifetime."

"We all know who's getting the bus," Charli whispers from behind me. "And who's on the jet."

"So," Rebecca says, "I wanted to have the rare opportunity to gather here just one time, as two teams with a common goal—to move Brooklyn hockey forward into a new era."

We all clap. Even Charli, I think.

"Everyone here could be part of a history-making moment in sports. I mean that. I feel it, too." Rebecca puts a hand to her heart, and every player in the room is completely quiet. She's short, with a curvy build. She's one of those tiny dynamo types. My mother would have said, *she has unique energy.* And everyone present has given her their complete attention.

I'm told that Rebecca used to be the GM's assistant, before she was ever the girlfriend and then wife of the owner. And well before she owned the team herself. She used to pick up coffee and dry-cleaning for the men who ran this place.

"When I was a little girl," she says, "I learned that girls take dancing or art classes. I didn't have any friends who ran track or played hockey. Not one. And I need you all to hear that messaging matters. Everyone in this room heard a different message. Someone gave you the idea that you could be an athlete—maybe your parents or your siblings or a teacher. Even if you had this fire burning inside you from an early age, somewhere, some person showed you what was possible."

I feel a little teary all of a sudden, thinking of my dad tying my first pair of skates onto my three-year-old feet.

"Everyone in this room has risen to the top of his and her field. That is commendable. But I want to take a moment to illustrate that it means a different thing to be a Bruiser than to be a Bombshell. The salary cap this year for a men's team is fifty-two million dollars. The salary cap in the women's league is two hundred and seventy thousand."

Someone whistles under his breath. And I see Anton wake up his phone beside me. He opens the calculator app and divides two hundred seventy thousand by twenty-three.

I already know the answer, because I worked this equation myself. It's $11,739. That's the average salary on my team. It works out to a few hundred dollars a week for the duration of the season.

"Jesus Christ," he whispers under his breath.

"Now, gentlemen. I will never tell you that you don't deserve your fame and glory. You sweat for every new rung of this crazy ladder that you've climbed. Your achievement is not arbitrary. The *reward*, however, is. Some people in this room make six or seven million dollars a year. And some of them make eleven grand. Because that is how the screwy world we live in values your contributions."

Rebecca pulls no punches. The room is so silent that I can hear my own heartbeat.

"Who gets to decide, though?" she asks. "It's so arbitrary. Football, basketball, baseball, and hockey all do well on TV. Soccer is not a money sport in this country, but it is in most other parts of the world. I'm sure my husband could draw us up a multivariable equation that explains where the money comes from, and where it goes."

I think I just fell a little in love with Rebecca Rowley Kattenberger.

"As much as I'd like to change the bare facts of the pay equality in hockey, I can't. Not this year, anyway. But that doesn't mean I can't make a few changes and contributions."

She paces at the front. "I'm not allowed to pay my female players amounts exceeding the salary cap. But there are a few benefits we've granted to all employees of Brooklyn Hockey LLC. And these benefits accrue to everyone who works here, because that means that it's not a special stipend for the women. Number one: more amenities in the locker rooms. And healthy smoothies are now always available in the players' lounge."

Everyone cheers.

Huh. I guess millionaires like a free smoothie as much as the rest of us normal people.

"Number two: all employees will carry a Kattenberger 5000 phone, provided by our organization."

Now the women hoot, because we've heard about the Katt phone, and we want one.

"And this is my favorite new benefit—every hour you spend on charity work for the Brooklyn Sports Foundation will be compensated at twenty-five dollars per hour. And we're going to do some great things this year. Georgia and I have some big ideas, and we're going to share them with you."

The blond publicist stands up. "That's right, guys! We've done a lot for Brooklyn charities over the past few years. This year we've got a new one. Hang on. Let me just…" She points a clicker at the projector, but nothing happens.

"Let's guess what it is!" one of the men calls. "Save the whales!"

"Can we sponsor a dog rescue?" Anton calls out. "I love puppies."

"That's because you are one," Rebecca says, and his teammates hoot and laugh.

The screen finally lights up. It reads: *Hockey is for Everyone.* "Each year we participate in this promotion," Georgia says. "But now we're going to take it further." She clicks the remote, and the words fade out and back in again, until it reads: *Sports are for Every-one. Bring it, Brooklyn!*

"When we say 'Hockey is for everyone,' it's wishful thinking," Georgia continues. "Of course, we welcome all kinds of fans. That will never change. But think of all the boys and girls in Brooklyn who will never get a chance to skate. There are very few skating rinks in New York City. And we can't give up enough of our ice time to make a real dent. But there are more than fifteen swimming pools in Brooklyn, and yet most of New York's children never get swimming lessons. There are unused basketball courts and soccer fields, too."

Rebecca chimes in. "'Sports are for everyone' probably seems obvious to all the fitness freaks here today. Which is basically everyone but me."

"We love you anyway!" someone calls out.

"Oh, I know you do!" she says with a smile. "But seriously— the kids of New York don't have enough opportunities to move their bodies. And guess what? Their health will suffer as a result.

"The men and women of Brooklyn hockey have a special power as role models. You can show boys and girls in your community another way to be in the world. How it feels to be part of a team. How your body feels different after a hard practice. How your muscles learn to do things that seemed impossible just a few weeks before."

She clicks the presentation forward. "This year, I want everyone in this room to think of himself or herself as an ambassador for sport. Georgia and I have created several new programs to help us accomplish this goal. And I think every one of you can make a unique contribution. There are signup sheets on the wall."

At the side of the room, Georgia reveals a whiteboard with several categories on it. *Skating lessons, swim lessons, soccer clinics,* etcetera.

"Look, guys. I know that time constraints are real. You have a big job to do here in this building, and you're all dedicated to your own success. That's what I love about you. So the scheduling is going to be tricky. That's why I'm also hiring a dozen coaches to run these programs for us, so that you'll only have to drop in when you're in town…"

A hand shoots up. It's one of the Bruisers. "Are we really going to teach these kids to play soccer? What if we don't know the rules?"

"The YMCA coaches will help you out. And if you really can't mingle with kids, you can stick to the black-tie fundraisers. Your famous faces always bring in the cash."

"Even Baby Bayer's face?" some heckler teases.

"Oh, especially his," someone else chirps.

I just bet it does.

"Our first ticketed fundraiser is coming up in November. But our fitness classes for teens begin in two weeks."

Charli's hand waves in the air. "Will the time commitment be significant? Most of us work other jobs just so we can afford to be professional hockey players."

"It's only as significant as you make it," Georgia says. "The Bombshells' practice schedule is in the evenings, to match with the game schedule. We wanted you to have big blocks of time in the early part of the day for other commitments."

"And they wanted all that ice time for the men," Charli says under her breath.

"But no pressure. And if you do participate, you'll earn twenty-five dollars an hour."

There are a few more questions and comments, and then the meeting is dismissed. "Bombshells, come and get your welcome packets," Georgia says. "And don't forget to look at the signup sheets. You don't have to commit right this second, though. I'll move the sheets online after today."

I head right over to the signup sheets, so that I will have first pick. There are teen swimming instructor and lifesaving coach slots in the middle of the day. I'm a great swimmer, and that sounds like fun. So I write my name down immediately.

At twenty-five American dollars an hour, this is perfect for me. I can earn some extra cash and play with kids. What's not to like?

"Swimming coach," Bryce says from right behind me. "Do you know where the pools are located?"

I turn around and offer him the pen. "I'll find the place okay. Are you going to join me?" If he's *that* worried about my welfare, maybe he will.

"No." He shakes his head. "I do not speak enough English to teach people to swim. What if someone struggles, and I forget the word for..." He makes a frantic motion with his hands.

"Kick?" I try.

"*Oui.*" He puts the pen back on the ledge where it belongs.

Okay. Fine. There goes my opportunity to parade around in my bathing suit in front of him.

His loss, right? I leave him and head over to the table where Rebecca is handing out welcome packets to the Bombshells. The gym bag with our team logo on it—a cartoon bomb with the wick sizzling and ready to blow—is delightful.

Inside, I find a Bombshells T-shirt. On the back it reads: *Under-estimate us. That will be fun.* There's also a brand-new Katt phone with a sleek yellow case, which I know I'm going to be playing with all evening.

Beneath that, I find an invitation on thick, creamy paper for a black-tie benefit dinner to be held in November.

And, finally, a VIP card for the Colorbox Nail Salon, entitling the bearer to a free mani-pedi every week through April.

"Oh, sure," Charli grumbles. "The little ladies need pretty fingers and toes to play hockey."

"That's not it at all," Rebecca says from right behind her.

Charli, at least, has the good sense to flinch.

"I own that salon," Rebecca says. "And I always tell people that I think better with my feet in a tub of warm water. So I just thought some of you might enjoy the same."

"Thank you," I say quickly. "The perks are really fun. I can tell you're thinking hard about making this job sustainable."

"We're trying," Rebecca says. "Brooklyn is an expensive place to live. And we're not allowed to factor that into our salaries. So we've made sure that players have access to housing that's close by. And some meals on the road. We'll do what we can."

"Thank you," Charli says, her chin down, her expression chagrined. "I do appreciate it."

She is saved from further explanation by a whistle from Fiona at the front of the room. "Practice starts in twenty minutes, girls. Let's suit up."

On my way out the door, I glance once more at the signup sheets. Bryce put his name down for soccer coaching, so we definitely won't be working together. But right under my name on the swimming sheet, the name *Anton Bayer* has been freshly scrawled.

He seems like a fun guy. The kids will enjoy his company.

That's got to be why I feel a strange little prickle of anticipation, right? It's because of his attitude. And not because I'm suddenly picturing him shirtless.

Nope. It's not because of that. Not at all.

SIX

Polish and Brighten

ANTON

I AM the last man on Earth who should coach swimming lessons. I don't really like the water. But teenagers should know how to swim, so they'll like it better than I do.

This is a selfless act on my part. That's my story, and I'm sticking to it.

"Are we going to lift?" Drake asks me on our way out of the meeting. "It's chest day."

"Of course we're going to lift." This is the season where I will take nothing for granted. "Let's go."

The weight room is a little crowded today, because everybody has the same idea. But that's okay. Drake and I make good use of the bench, and I like the camaraderie of the weight room during the season.

Plus, there's gossip. Castro's wife wants to redecorate their apartment. O'Doul picked a date for his wedding. And Beacon got a dog.

"I got a teenager and a toddler," he jokes. "It's chaos already. Why not add a dog?"

"Bring on the chaos!" somebody else yells.

"I don't know," Drake says, adding a plate for my last set. "It's

41

going to be different around here. With the women and all. Now *that's* chaos."

"How do you figure?" I ask. "They have their own weight room. Their own locker room suite, too. They won't be in your way." I take a breath and then lift the bar overhead, grunting like a beast.

"But they're still here in the building," he points out. "We might have to change our behavior. Clean it up a little."

"Do you mean, like, fart less often?" someone asks.

"Exactly," he says gravely.

"Dude, what?" Castro yelps. "Nobody can just *decide* to fart less often. Your ass might explode."

"But you could do it quietly," Drake says, and he's completely serious. If I weren't pressing nearly three hundred pounds of iron over my body, I might laugh.

"Look," Trevi says. "You're overreacting. There have always been women in the building. My wife, for starters." She's Georgia, the co-head of publicity. "There's a female trainer, a female massage therapist. There are women in the front office, the travel department, the GM's office. A woman owns the whole damn team!"

"But that's not what he means," Jason Castro says as he wipes down the leg press. "He means there are women in the building doing his same *job*. They're not support staff. They're also the stars of the show. His fragile male ego has taken a hit."

"It has *not*," Drake argues. "You're putting words in my mouth. I simply meant that the tone around here is going to change some. I didn't say it was a bad thing."

"You're *afraid* of the Bombshells," someone teases.

"Yeah, especially that angry redhead."

"I'm not *afraid* of her," he grumbles. "Just, uh, a little wary."

"Huh. You do look a little pale, my friend," Leo says. "Have you tested your blood sugar lately?"

Drake gives him the finger and marches out of the room.

I've finished my last set when Drake comes tearing back into the room. "Guys! You're not going to believe this, but the locker room is different."

"Since yesterday?" I ask, skeptical.

"Yeah, there's some strange thing in the toilet stall. A device."

"A strange device," Trevi muses. "Like, a bidet? They were doing some renovations."

"No, it's not a bidet. Look."

A few of the players follow Drake into the locker room, including me. But I was headed there anyway. Soon, we're crowded in front of a toilet stall. "Look," Drake says, eyeing the metal unit on the wall. "What's that?"

Castro is the first to laugh. And then so do I. "It's…"

"Just…" Tankiewicz howls.

"Maxi…pads…" I can't breathe. "And tampons!"

"Don't you have a sister?" Castro snorts.

"But what's it doing in our locker room?" Drake demands. "Are we being evicted?"

"No, fool," Castro says. "Maybe they hung it in here by mistake. Calm down, man. There's nothing to worry about."

Drake crosses his arms, still looking unsettled. "But there are other changes, too. There are cotton balls and Q-tips by the sinks."

"Huh." I strip off my sweaty practice shirt and toss it into a laundry hamper. "That's good. We need clean ears so we can hear Coach yelling at us." I strip off the rest of my clothes and grab a shower stall. The water is the perfect temperature, proving that everything that really matters is still the same.

There's a new shampoo dispenser in here, though, so Drake will probably make a big deal out of that, too. Before, there was just one product in here—a three-in-one soap that was supposed to clean every single part of my tired body. And that was fine.

Now there are choices. The first dispenser contains a lemon-verbena body wash. The second is a shampoo for dry hair—with avocados and coconut. There's also one for volume, with bamboo extract.

I like both avocados and coconut, so I push the button for that one. Easy choice. My shower takes three minutes, because I'm quick like that.

When I step out to grab a towel, Drake is stepping out of the stall next to mine. "Holy hell. Will I smell like a woman now?"

"Nah," I say. "There's nothing feminine about coconuts. Big, hairy nuts? Come on, man." I grab a towel and toss him one.

"Where will it end, though?" He shakes like a wet dog. "Look, there are new products on the sinks. What is *that*?"

I walk over and pick up one of the bottles. "This one says *Daily Perfecting Cream*. It claims to polish and brighten."

"You could stand to be brighter," Leo cracks. "Try that one."

I give him the finger.

"Careful!" Drake barks. "We can't just spread any random thing on our bodies."

"Then why do you pick up jersey-chasers in bars?" Castro cracks from inside a shower stall.

"I'm serious. You don't know what's in here." He picks up the bottle and squirts a glossy white blob onto his palm. Then he lifts it cautiously to his nose, like it might be radioactive. "Whoa. What is that? Here—smell this."

Trevi emerges from the shower stall. "I have a great nose. I bet I can guess it in two sniffs."

"Wait." Castro steps out, too. "I'm married to a girl who loves her products. I can guess it in one sniff."

"Can not," I argue. That's why I love these guys. We can turn *anything* into a competition.

We all crowd around Drake, leaning in to get the first sniff.

"I'm getting…berries," Castro whispers.

"And flowers," Trevi says. "Gardenia?"

"Oh God. Flowers? It's worse than I thought," Drake complains. "Who's *doing* this to us?"

"Not gardenia," I argue, taking a deep sniff. "Lilac?"

"Nah." Trevi smells it again.

That's when O'Doul walks into the locker room, catching three bare-assed men, nose to nose, sniffing a gooey liquid out of Drake's palm. "What the fuck, boys? What is that?"

We all straighten up quickly, as if caught with something far more scandalous than bath products.

"Never mind. I don't even want to know." He gives us a grumpy look. "Video meeting in ten minutes."

"But what's with all the new stuff in the locker room?" Drake presses. He's like a dog with a bone. "We don't get it."

"Hey, just ignore that stuff. Rebecca wants to provide perks for her female players—like shakes and stuff. But the salary cap rules say that she can't give them anything unless it's for everyone who works here."

"Ah," Castro says. "That makes sense. Although maxi pads in our shitter is a bridge too far."

O'Doul shrugs. "Not my circus, not my monkeys. But you guys *are* my monkeys. And we need to keep our eyes on the prize, guys. There's a video meeting for all monkeys in ten minutes."

"Roger." I head for the dressing room and my clothes.

Bryce Campeau is sitting on the bench poking at his phone. "Hey, thank you."

"For what?" My mind is still on maxi pads and gardenias.

"For earlier. Going to the store for Sylvie's things."

"Oh. No big deal. How's that going, anyway?" I pull on my briefs.

"The smoke detectors work, but I do not love the burglar bars."

"No, man." I jump into my jeans. "I mean—how is it going with *her*. And you." I eye my friend, the broody Canadian. He looks uncomfortable.

"She is annoyed with me. But I can't change the circumstances. I can't make my life less hectic. It's not a good time to change our relationship. I can't give her the attention she deserves right now."

"So you're just going to make her wait for it?" That's cold.

"I only want the best for her. Right now, I can't be my best."

"You'll help keep her safe, but you won't sweep her off her feet."

"Yes."

And I've got nothing.

"Will you keep an eye on her?"

"What kind of eye?" I ask, grumpy now. Keeping my eyes on her is all too easy.

"She is very sheltered. New York will be a lot for her."

"Didn't she play for the University of Michigan? That's a huge school."

"I still worry. Just watch out for her. As a favor to me."

"Sure, man. Sure."

I'm a good teammate, and a good friend, even when I think my friends are crazy.

Besides—I plan to be around the neighborhood a lot this season. No more clubbing. No more late nights, and no more scandals. This will be the year when I make everything happen.

I guess it's just as well that the only woman I've been interested in since last spring is basically off limits.

Three rules, I remind myself. *Let's not break 'em.*

SEVEN

Sniper Speed

SYLVIE

IT'S MY FIFTH PRACTICE, and our preseason is flying by at top speed.

And so is the puck, unfortunately.

The Bruisers' goalie coach snaps a puck toward me. I'm forced into the butterfly position, protecting the five-hole. We've been practicing for forty-five minutes, and I'm dripping with sweat, my muscles shaking.

So I'm slow to recover in time for his next shot. I lunge to the left, deflecting sloppily with my stick. The puck drops to the ice. It's not a goal, but it creates a rebound opportunity that would cost me in a real game.

The coach blows a whistle, "Reset!"

I basically stagger out of the crease to help the other goalies gather up all our pucks.

This practice session is a huge opportunity for me. The Bombshells don't have their own goalie coach, but the Bruisers' guy invited us to work out with his netminders today.

That means I'm practicing alongside veteran star Mike Beacon and up-and-comer Silas Kelly, as well as the other Bombshells goalie, Scarlet McCaulley. She's twenty-five and an alternate for Team USA.

She's also kicking my ass. Our season opener is ten days away, and it's painfully obvious that I'm not ready yet. Scarlet has spent the last forty-five minutes stopping everything that moves. And the men are also crushing it.

I started out strong, but the pace of this session has been brutal. My instincts are still sharp. I stopped a lot of pucks that the coach slapped my way. But then I got tired awfully fast, and now half the time my body can't close the deal.

It's humiliating. At least Scarlet looks good. The goalie coach won't necessarily go back to his pals and say, *Tommy Hansen's kid is going to sink the new women's team before they even get started.*

"We've got ten minutes left. Let's do some harder shots," Coach says, skating backward. "I always get help for these, because..." He crosses his left hand to his right shoulder. "Already had one surgery to repair the repetitive-stress injury I gave myself shooting on goalies. Don't need to go under the knife again."

That's when two players skate onto the ice from the bench. The first one is Leo Trevi. But when I glance over to see who the other player is, I find myself looking into the sturdy gaze of Bryce Campeau.

It just figures, since Bryce is the other super-frustrating thing about my stint so far in Brooklyn. He's not avoiding me, exactly. We've had lunch together twice. And when I left a message for my father the other day, asking a simple question about the WiFi hookup in our apartment, it was Bryce who rang the doorbell two hours later to fix it for me.

That's exactly the type of attention I'm getting from Bryce. The polite, obligatory kind, followed by two cheek kisses and the occasional text to ask me how I'm doing.

So I'm frustrated—with Bryce, with my performance, and with so many other things. I've only been here for ten days, but so far Brooklyn is a tough nut to crack.

Leo and Bryce line up a series of pucks on the ice. They'll skate past the four goalies, firing on us each in turn. Longer shots provide more reaction time, but greater force and speed.

Then the drill begins. The coach and his assistant skate through the foreground, obscuring our clear view of the shooters and their setups, while the two players fire at us.

Leo shoots the first puck on Silas, who handily stops it. Then Bryce gets a missile off on Scarlet, who just barely swats it away with the tip of her glove.

Suddenly there's a puck hurtling toward me at high speed. I dive, but miss it as it whistles past my ear and into the net's upper corner.

Damn it. I pick my exhausted self up just in time to misjudge a shot from Bryce, sending that one through the five-hole.

Focus, Hansen, I coach myself. I know I can do this.

It works, too. I get the next one from Leo. No problem. And then I stop three more from Bryce. But as I'm batting away the third one, I realize that the speed of that puck wasn't much to deal with.

And neither is the next one. I watch as he fires a shot on Silas, and then on Beacon, both of them at jet speed.

I have to look away to dive for a shot from Leo. But then Bryce comes back to me and sends me a puck at the speed of a grand-mother riding on a donkey.

He's *soft-balling* me, I realize. Bryce can see that I'm struggling, so he's throwing me a series of easy shots. He's *coddling* me.

And I am livid.

It's funny what anger will do to a girl's game. I am ferocious as I stop the next two shots from Leo. And when Bryce sends me another yawner, I slap it back to him so hard and so accurately that he has to dodge out of the way to avoid taking a shot to the nuts, because he's not wearing any pads.

"*Merde*," he curses softly.

"Whoops," I say through gritted teeth. And I give him a look so bitter that his eyes widen in alarm.

But the boy does not learn his lesson. For the remaining few minutes of the exercise, he takes it easy on me. After ripping meteors at every other goalie, he sends me pucks that would embarrass a high school center.

I am incensed. I don't need Bryce to humiliate me like this, when I'd been doing a fine job of it without his help.

When the coach finally blows the whistle, calling our session to a close, I gather up the pucks with everyone else.

"Whoa, that was intense," Scarlet says, still breathing hard. "Great session, huh?"

"Yup. Great," I manage. At this rate, I'll spend the season sitting in the corner of the bench opening and closing the door for other players on shift changes, while Scarlet plays every last game.

I wait until the coaches depart. And then I skate up to Bryce, who's moving one of the extra nets out of the way. "What the *hell* was that?" I hiss. "Why would you treat me like a child, instead of an athlete?"

Bryce jerks his head back in shock. "I did not treat you like a child."

"You absolutely did! Don't try to make my life easier, Bryce. That is not why I came to Brooklyn. And that is not what you're supposed to be to me—my protector. You're supposed to—" I bite off the rest of the sentence. *Kiss me. Love me. Want me.*

I don't say these things out loud. I shouldn't have to. And furthermore, we're not alone. When I glance over my shoulder, I spy Anton Bayer crossing through the vestibule, in earshot of everything I'm saying. And his eyes look worried.

Luckily, I don't have to stop yelling at Bryce. I can just switch to French, and insist that he *doesn't ever* take it easy on me in practice again. On penalty of death. Or at least a good maiming.

"*Je suis désolé, Sylvie. Je ne veux pas.*"

He's trying to appease me. But I'm still so angry I could burst.

So I turn on my skates and walk away without another word.

EIGHT

Such a Grind

ANTON

OH MAN. The moment Sylvie busts me for eavesdropping on her argument with Campeau, I high-tail it out of the rink.

Not that anyone asked me, but she was absolutely justified in her anger. Anyone could see that he wasn't shooting at her the same way he did for everyone else. That's not what the coach asked of him, either. A player can't grow without practicing at the highest level.

Yet any fool could also see that he'd done it out of love. There's no way he intended to humiliate her. That's just not the kind of guy he is.

I'm still thinking about them when I slip into the back of the video room, where the defensive coordinator is showing us tape in preparation for our first preseason games.

"This rookie sniper was named the MVP of the Junior World Championships in 2018…" Coach drones.

Campeau's thing with Sylvie is none of my business. And signing up to teach swimming lessons with her was probably a stupid move.

My little crush is only going to get worse.

The coach drones on about New Jersey's scoring style, and I try to pay attention.

WHEN COACH IS DONE, I somehow manage to enter the lobby from the video room at the same moment that Sylvie bounds out of the tunnel, heading for the door.

"Hey," I say, startled by the reappearance of the girl I can't stop thinking about. Her cheeks are flushed. Stealing glances at her for a week has taught me that she always has high color in her cheeks, as if she burns a little brighter than other women.

"Hi," she says, slowing her pace as she approaches. "You're not waiting for Campeau, are you?" The name sounds extra French when she says it.

And maybe I'm a jackass for thinking this, but I'd really like to hear her mutter French into my ear in bed. "Uh, no. No. Don't know where he is."

"*Good.*"

She sounds so fierce, I have to laugh. "Walk out with me," I say with more nonchalance than I feel.

"Are you going to give me a lecture about patience, or gratitude?"

"Fuck no, I don't give lectures. I'm usually on the receiving end of those."

Her face breaks into a startled smile, and she follows me out onto the sidewalk. "Well, I probably deserve one. But I'm not in a forgiving mood yet."

"Are you in the mood for tequila, though? That's what I offer my friends after a shitty day." It's true, too. I'm not one to dole out advice. Who wants to turn into his father?

"I'm not much of a drinker," Sylvie says, tossing her lush hair over her shoulder. "But I could use some food."

"How do you feel about spicy Szechuan?"

"I feel *great* about it. You don't have to cheer me up, though. If you have things to do."

"Woman, it's chow time. And you're saving me from masturdating."

"Um, what?" she says, giving me a startled look.

"That's a Frankenword for taking yourself out to dinner alone. Masturdating."

"A Frankenword?" She gives a shout of laughter and claps a hand over her mouth. "You are ridiculous."

"True facts. Now follow me, newbie. It's time for your introduction to the best cheap Chinese food in Brooklyn."

She hitches her gym bag up on her shoulder and follows me down the street.

SOON WE'RE ENSCONCED at China Garden and splitting a first course of green dumplings in tangy plum sauce.

"These are *magnifique*," Sylvie gushes, plucking up another dumpling with her chopsticks. "How did you find this place?"

"Georgia Trevi. She has a thing for dumplings."

"Bless her. And thanks for bringing me here. I was clearly in need of an intervention."

"Hey, no problem." I sound casual enough. But that's not how I really feel. Sylvie has hovered at the edge of my consciousness these past ten days. Every time both teams are in the practice facility, I somehow manage to hear her laugh, or spot her down the corridor.

And now I have her alone. It's no crime to buy a girl some spicy noodles and chicken after a bad day, but I feel a little guilty nonetheless. And it occurs to me now that Bryce Campeau hates this restaurant and never comes here.

Thanks, subconscious. Good work.

"You know," I tell her. "You're not the only one who's struggling to prove herself."

Sylvie glances up at me. "No? You too?"

"I didn't have a great season last year. And now it's all riding on this one."

She sets down her chopsticks and puts her chin in her hand. "Do you believe in fate?"

"Um...?" Do I? "Not really." Although every time Sylvie smiles, I'm not sure of anything anymore.

"My mother did. She raised me in a very spiritual household. And now that she's gone, I think about it all the time. So when I got the call to come to Brooklyn, I thought it meant something big, you know? That my life was on a path to move forward." She makes an exasperated face. "Ten days in, and I'm not sure anymore."

"Ten days, huh?" I nudge her shoe under the table. "Well, I guess you gave it a thorough try."

She smiles at me suddenly, and I feel it warming me like a heat lamp. "No lectures from you."

"That's not a lecture. That's sarcasm."

She beams. "Fine. So I shouldn't throw in the towel yet. What is your story? What happened last year?"

I'm not looking forward to telling a pretty girl how I fucked up. But I suppose it's only fair. "This will be my third season in Brooklyn. My rookie year I worked hard, and I had some early luck, I guess. But then I let myself slide. I took the summer off. And when I came back in the fall, I partied too hard."

"Oh boy." She points at the last dumpling. "This one is yours."

I push the platter toward her instead. I would feed this girl a mountain of dumplings if she'll just smile at me again.

She nabs it, and—*bam*—big smile. I almost forget what I was talking about.

Oh right. Failure. "It didn't go well for me last season. My stats sucked, and we were all adjusting to Tank's style of play." Tankiewicz is a veteran defenseman we got in a trade a year ago. "He's a great player, but it caused some adjustment on the ice."

It was the kind of wrinkle that teams experience all the time. But I'd already been off my game. "I didn't catch on fast enough. None of my tricks were working. And at the end of January, Coach shipped my ass down to the minor-league team in Hartford."

Sylvie flinches, even though she's known hockey all her life, and has probably heard tales of woe like mine before. "You're back now, though."

"Yeah, Coach told me if I worked my ass off all summer, I might make it back."

"And that's what you did?"

"You bet. I found a trainer here in Brooklyn and basically lived at the damn gym. It was such a grind. But every morning I asked myself whether I wanted a real career, or whether I wanted to be one of those guys who has to frame his jersey and hang it on the wall, because everybody already forgot his name."

"And here you are," she says.

"For now," I add, because I've learned not to take a thing for granted.

"My fitness is a problem, too," she says, pouring more tea out of the pot for both of us. "It turns out that a year of mourning wasn't very good for my game."

"Your mother died," I say quietly. "Campeau told us about that."

"She did," Sylvie says, folding her hands. "She and Bryce were very close. It really upset him when she died. And things got kind of weird after that…" She shakes her head and doesn't say more.

But I'm curious, and kind of a bastard, so I have to ask, "What's the deal with you guys, anyway?"

She looks out the window, where there's steady foot traffic past the restaurant. "We've always been good friends. And for a while there I thought we'd be more. But I was wrong."

My stomach clenches for her. Is Campeau really that stupid? This woman loves him, and he's unmoved by that?

"Can I ask you a question?" She turns to me with those giant brown eyes. "You don't have to answer if it makes you uncomfortable."

"Anything."

"Does Bryce have a girlfriend? He should just tell me that. But…" She gulps. "It would help me understand."

"*No*," I say softly. "I really don't think so. I've never heard him talk about anyone special."

"Including me, I suppose." Her smile is wry.

"Well…" I have to tread carefully here. But, nope, he never talks about her. "He always said how close he is to your family. I know you all mean a lot to him. But he is also the most buttoned-up guy I've ever met. I mean—I'm an open book. An over-sharer. But Bryce doesn't talk about his feelings."

She fiddles with the chopsticks' wrapper. "It's true. You're right. He's a man of deeds more than words."

"Exactly," I say quickly.

"His deeds could use some work, though," she grumbles.

Our waitress appears, placing a heaping plate of spicy Szechwan chicken down on our table, along with a molded bowl of white rice.

"*Yessss*," Sylvie says with the gusto of a lover in the throes of passion. "Come to *mama*."

We dig in, and I have the dual pleasures of spicy chicken and watching Sylvie enjoy the food. We also ordered a noodle dish. And that food doesn't stand a chance. We both pile food onto our plates with enthusiasm.

"So we're going to teach some kids to swim next week?"

"That's the idea." Sylvie heaps some noodles beside her chicken. "Did you read the handbook? Some of these kids don't even own bathing suits. So we're bringing bathing suits with us. And it's not just a course on swimming. It's a lifesaving course. They can apply for lifeguard jobs if they pass."

Wait, what? "They never get in the water, and we're supposed to teach them to be lifeguards? Does that sound plausible?"

"If they're strong enough, a little fearless, and willing to listen, anything is possible." She dives in with her chopsticks.

"Are you, uh, a decent swimmer?" I ask. "I took a lot of swimming lessons as a kid." I leave out the fact that I hated every one of them. "But I've never been responsible for a bunch of wet teenagers who can't swim."

"I went to swimming camp every summer as a kid. I used to race. And I had my lifesaving certificate."

Seems like I should have seen that coming. "Guess I'll be following your lead, then. I'll admit I'm a little worried about teaching non-swimmers to save lives. Won't they be a little freaked out in the water already?"

"That's the point, though." Her forehead furrows in an adorable frown. "The message isn't that you're good enough to swim like kids from the suburbs. It's that you're good enough to save some-one's life. It's empowering to be told you can do something that's as difficult as it is important."

"Wow, okay. We'd better do a good job, then." Although Sylvie's competence will go a long way. "I'll do what I can, okay? My schedule is crazy, and I'm not the kind of guy you want in charge of a project like this. But when I'm there, I'll give a hundred and fifty percent."

She studies me with serious brown eyes for a moment. "I get that. And thank you."

"No problem."

"I just have one more question. Are you going to eat the rest of that chicken?"

As I pass her the platter, I think I fall a little deeper in lust.

NINE

The Tavern on Hicks

SYLVIE

ANTON GRABS the check the moment it hits the table.

My competitive streak is triggered by this show of macho behavior. "Hey! No fair. I don't need you to buy dinner."

"Didn't say you did," he says, slipping a credit card into the folder. "I'm not trying to baby you. I noticed that you hate that."

My smile is embarrassed, because he witnessed my meltdown earlier.

"But I also happened to notice that we don't earn the same salary."

"That's true," I admit. "And a problem for women's sports. But I'm not hurting like some of the girls. I'm the bookkeeper for my dad's hockey organization, so I brought my job to Brooklyn with me."

"Still," he says, giving me a confident smile. "This is my treat. You can buy next time."

Next time. I think Anton Bayer and I are becoming friends. "Well, thank you. I really appreciate it. And thank you for talking me off the ledge earlier."

"I've been out on that same ledge." He shrugs.

My new phone starts chiming with texts, and it's awfully loud.

58

"Sorry." I pull out the phone. "I'm still getting used to this thing. All the features…"

The texts are from Fiona. Some of my teammates are gathering in a Brooklyn bar. *It's on Hicks Street! Are you in?*

"Wait until you win your first game," he says. "There's a gold star that appears on the screen."

"I've heard about that. It sounds a little silly."

"Doesn't it?" He chuckles. "But, man, the Kattenbergers are onto something. After a couple of losses, you'll be missing that damn thing. I'd do just about anything for the star."

He signs the check while I read my texts. "Do you know where there's a tavern on Hicks Street?" I ask. "Is that nearby?"

"Oh, sure. I'll walk you over there." He gets up. "That's the name of the place—Tavern on Hicks. It's the Bruisers' second home, on account of being located between the arena and the practice facility. We usually walk there after home games."

He holds the door open for me, like a gentleman. And we set off down the street together. He's so ruggedly handsome that a few women on the sidewalk turn and stare.

I'm not immune to it either. It's not just his face. There's something so sexual about him, that I feel overly aware of my own body when I'm near him. I keep noticing tiny details about him, and each one is more fascinating than the last. He has golden hair on his strong forearms. And his long-legged gait is almost a swagger.

"You don't have to walk me there," I blurt out eventually. "I mean, you probably have other things to do on a Saturday night."

"Not really. Ten bucks says my friends will be there, too. And there's practically a print of my ass on one of the barstools."

"Charming," I say, trying to play it cool.

"Not that you asked, but this part of Brooklyn is safe enough. Although Bryce would probably suggest taking a taxi home if you leave the bar after ten, and especially if you're alone."

I snort, and it isn't very ladylike. "Bryce would probably like me to take a taxi all the way to JFK and fly home to Toronto."

"That isn't true."

"No?" I'm not so sure.

"No."

"How can you be so sure?"

"Because Bryce isn't insane. And only a crazy man would wish you were farther away."

My cheeks begin to burn, because I don't know how to take a compliment from a hot guy.

I'm saved from trying to think of a suitable response by the appearance of the Tavern. "This is the place?"

"Oh yeah. In all its beer-scented glory. On a weekend, both bartenders are working. Pete looks crusty, but he's actually a cinnamon roll." Anton stops to open the door for me again.

I step inside and spot the gray-haired bartender immediately. The place is more than half full, and the man looks busy.

"And then there's Petra." He nods toward a young, blond woman pouring a pitcher of beer at the end of the bar. He drops his voice even though she's pretty far away, and there's a hum of bar noise in the room. "She looks sweet, but she's made of steel. She keeps us in line."

Petra looks up, as if she's overheard. "Hey, Anton!" she calls. "Who's this? She's too pretty for you."

He puts a warm hand on my shoulder. "Just a friend who puts up with me once in a while. This is Sylvie. She's new in town, and one of the Bombshells' goalies."

Petra glances at me. And I swear her eyes narrow a little bit. "Welcome," she says stiffly. Then she carries that pitcher off without another word.

"See?" he says with a chuckle. "If you need a favor, ask Pete."

"Got it."

"If you don't see your friends yet, there's a few other things you should know about the Tavern." He gives me a serious face.

"Yeah? Like what." Anton is such a hoot.

"Hockey players carve their names into the paneling on the wall outside the men's room. You all might need to start your own spot outside the ladies'." He strokes his chin thoughtfully. "Never order the turkey burger. The fries are great, though. And the nachos are so bad that they're actually good. With that fake cheese that seems to soak up alcohol at three in the morning."

"Ah. Never knew that stuff had magical properties."

"Stick with me. I know things." He squeezes my shoulder. "You see your friends anywhere?" He glances around, and the heat of his big hand disappears from my shoulder.

I miss it. We *are* becoming friends. He said so himself. I'm grateful. It was not an easy day.

Suddenly I see a hand waving at me from a back corner of the bar. "There they are. At that funny round table." It's a C-shaped booth, just the right size for five or six women who need to gossip about their first ten days as Bombshells.

"Bummer. That's the worst table in the bar."

"Why? It's cozy. Nobody can come and bother you there."

Anton laughs. "That's it exactly. You're all stuck with each other."

"We could make room for you," I offer.

He shakes his head. "I'm going to go sit with Drake." He points at a barstool in front of a TV showing a baseball game. "You kids have fun." He gives my shoulder another quick squeeze. "Thanks for coming out to dinner with me."

"Oh, please. We both know who got the better end of that bargain." I give him a grateful smile, and those turquoise eyes smile back at me.

The effect is pretty dazzling. So I give him an awkward wave and turn away, heading for my girls.

They all shift slightly around the circle to make a space for me. "Sylvie! Sit!" Fiona waves me in. Then she leans forward and drops her voice. "Did you just waltz in here with Anton Bayer? What's up with that? Did I miss something?"

"What? *No*." As if. "He watched me lose my mind at Bryce a couple hours ago. And then he invited me out as a kind of intervention. He probably assumed it was that, or I was going to hurt some unsuspecting Brooklyn native."

"What did Bryce *do*?" Fiona asks, her eyes wide. "Did you guys have the big conversation?"

I shake my head. "No, it's worse."

"Yeah, that was some serious bullshit," Scarlet says, swigging her beer. "That man was disrespectful, and whatever you said to him afterwards, he had coming."

"It was the goalie practice," I clarify. "He was there to shoot on us. And I was struggling, so he kept sending me easy shots." When I say these words out loud, they sound stupid and whiny.

But the other women all gasp. "Oh no, he didn't," Fiona breathes.

"That *total* dick," Charli growls.

"It really was that bad," Scarlet says with a shrug. "If Bridger did that to me, I'd lose my mind."

"Wait," I stop her. "Is your husband a hockey player?"

"He was." She smiles. "He was a *terrific* college player. And we all have shitty days in front of the net, Sylvie."

I know she's just trying to be nice, but my struggles are larger than one bad practice session.

Luckily, my dreary thoughts are interrupted by a pitcher landing on the table. "Evening, ladies," says bartender Pete. "This pitcher of margaritas is a gift of those hooligans at the bar. Welcome to the Tavern, and welcome to Brooklyn."

"Thank you, Pete," I say as he sets down several glasses, too. "We sure do appreciate it. Will you tell those hooligans I said so?"

"Absolutely."

Fiona lifts herself up a few inches so that she can wave a thank you to the men at the bar. "It was your new friend, Anton, and that Drake guy. And Jason Castro."

Charli growls. "They'd better not be expecting sexual favors."

"No way," I say, flipping over a glass and pouring it for her. "Drink this and be grateful. Not everything a man does is a ploy."

"It's more like seventy percent," Scarlet says with a giggle. "But I don't mind, because my guy is the best there is."

I pour a glass for Scarlet and pass it over, wondering what it would feel like to be in her shoes—to be unafraid to say "my guy" and know that he loved you and wasn't afraid to say so.

"It was nice of Anton to send us drinks," Fiona says. "Does he have a thing for you?"

"Nah." I pass another glass across the table and then pour my own.

"He's got a reputation," Fiona whispers. "For being excellent in bed."

"Figures," I say. "His whole sex-on-a-stick thing is a little much."

"What do you mean?" Charli asks.

"Well, lots of guys are attractive. But he's just so...extra. Like, I don't know where to put my eyes, you know? Everything about him is super sexual. And super hot."

Charli shrugs. "If you say so."

"All hockey players are hot," Scarlet says.

"Sister—" Fiona puts her hand on top of mine. "—what if it's not just him? To me, that sounds like *chemistry*. Between both of you. Do you find yourself suddenly wondering what he looks like naked?"

"What? No." My face burns, though. Because during dinner I had wondered that about five different times. But it's only because he's not my usual type. He's rougher around the edges than Bryce. He wears his attractiveness differently.

But I'll *never* admit my petty fascination with Anton Bayer's incredible body. It's confusing to me. It must just be hormones or something.

"Be careful with that one," Charli says. "He's a total man-whore. Last year it became a problem—he ended up in the blogs for a hotel foursome he had on a road trip."

"A...*foursome?* That sounds complicated." Does she mean sex between four people at the *same time*? Does that math even work?

I sip my drink and try not to call any more attention to my inexperience. Not that it's anyone's business.

Charli rubs her hands together, because even she isn't immune to a juicy piece of gossip. "The trouble was that one of the women took a selfie while Anton was passed out in the hotel bed with three women around him. This woman sent it to some friends as a trophy, and it ended up on the internet. The publicity department was not pleased."

Three women in a bed with Anton. I turn my head and glance quickly in his direction. He's holding a glass of beer in one strong hand, laughing at something Drake is saying, and I feel several different emotions at once.

There's such *joy* in him, for starters. It's been a while since I laughed as easily as he does. But he reminds me that it's possible.

He intimidates me, though. Somehow I can picture each muscular arm around a different woman at the same time. I'm not sure where woman number three would be in that scenario. But still—confidence practically seeps through his pores.

I can't imagine what it would feel like to be on the other end of that dazzling smile when there were no clothes on that body. A girl could burn right up. Nothing but a little puff of smoke and a wisp of ash left to show for her.

He is really out of my league. And I really must stop staring.

I turn back to my friends and take in their happy faces. My drink is tasty, I'm full of good food, and my teammates are amusing. Life could really be worse.

And I'm enjoying this opportunity to spend time with Scarlet. In many ways, we're competitors. If she ends up starting every Bombshells game, I'll be sad. But she's smart and funny and living the life I hope to lead in a few years.

"We're in Manhattan, on the Upper East Side," she's saying. "I take a ferry across the river for practice. It's not such a terrible commute. And Lucy doesn't need us to walk her home from school anymore, because she's in ninth grade, and wouldn't be caught dead with us, anyway."

"Lucy is your...stepdaughter?" Charli guesses. Scarlet is only twenty-five, and too young to have a daughter in high school.

"Sister-in-law," she says with a smile. "Bridger is raising his little sister, and has been since she was eight. Their parents have passed."

"Awww," Fiona says, and I swear there are hearts in her eyes. "What a guy."

"Lucy is the reason that he had to quit hockey," Scarlet tells us. "He loves that I'm still playing. I run the youth hockey program at Chelsea Piers as my day job. And when Bess called about the Bombshells, Bridger brought home a bottle of champagne and told me to go for it."

There's a moment of silence at our table as we all contemplate the perfection of Scarlet's marriage. Even Charli has a soft expression on her face that I rarely see there.

And then a low voice breaks the silence.

"Sylvie."

I freeze at the sound of Bryce's voice. But I do not turn around. I'm still angry.

A warm hand lands on my shoulder. "Please. I need to apologize."

The fight seeps out of me. I don't want to make *another* scene. So I slide out of the booth and turn around to face him.

A very familiar set of dark blue eyes greets me. And they look worried. "*Désolé*, Sylvie. I am very sorry for not sending you the same shots that I sent the others. I did not mean to disrespect you."

"Thank you," I say stiffly. The hurt is still there, though. I keep attracting the wrong kind of attention from this man, and I don't know how to break the cycle.

But maybe Bryce does. He takes both my hands in his, and gazes lovingly at me. "I never want to hurt you. I love you. I'm sorry." Then, just as my heart begins melting into a puddle, he pulls me into a hug. I'm snuggled against his warm chest, and my nose lands at the collar of his shirt, where I get a whiff of the aftershave that he's always worn.

A soft kiss lands at my temple. "*Désolé*," he says one more time.

As apologies go, it's top notch. And so is this hug. *This* is the kind man I've pined for since I was a girl. Even though it was never mutual.

When his arms relax, I step back. "Did you eat dinner?" he asks. "I was about to order a burger from the bar. I could make it two."

"I ate," I admit. "But thank you."

He flashes me a rare smile. "Then enjoy your evening, *mademoiselle*."

"*Merci*." I sit back down then, to the questioning eyes of my teammates.

"Okay, that was nice," Fiona says. "But that boy confuses me."

"Sing it, sister." Confusing should be his new middle name.

"Although I might know a way you could unconfuse him."

"Really? How?" I ask a little too quickly. It's so obvious that I've spent too much time wondering how to do that.

"The black-tie dinner and dance that's coming up—let's find you a sexy dress, some killer heels, and smoky eyes."

I blink. "That's it? That's your idea?"

"Never underestimate the power of showing yourself in a new light. Men can be simple, visual creatures. You'd be activating the *other* definition of bombshell, you know?"

Charli makes a face, like she hates this plan. "Why do we have to put ourselves on display to raise money for charity?"

"You don't," I point out. "It's optional. Although the men have to put on a tux several times a year for these things. Donors plunk down a thousand dollars a head to meet the players and shake their hands."

"It's basically prostitution," Charli complains.

"It's for an excellent cause," Scarlet says. "With free food and music. Bridger and I are looking forward to it."

"Fine, but I won't be showing any skin," Charli grumbles. "I'm in it for the open bar."

"I'm in it for the new dress," Fiona chirps. "I can hear Bloomingdale's calling my name. Are you with me, Sylvie?"

"I'm in," I decide. It's been a long time since I got dressed up for an occasion. And maybe Fiona has a point. "You can help me find the dress. Bryce isn't going to know what hit him."

"That's my girl," she says, refilling my glass.

I swivel around in my seat and glance toward Bryce. He's leaning on the bar, deep in conversation with Petra the bartender. He doesn't notice that I'm studying him and trying to predict his reaction when I arrive at the party in a low-cut dress I picked out just for him.

It occurs to me that Bryce isn't very interested in dancing. But I'll convince him.

Another man catches me gazing in that direction, though. It's Anton, of course, who doesn't miss a chance to notice every silly thing that happens to me.

He gives me a friendly wink and turns back to his boys.

I pick up my margarita and raise my glass. "To teaching the men of Brooklyn a few new tricks."

"I'll drink to that." Charli raises her glass.

"Cheers!" Fiona yells as our glasses clink together. "Bottoms up, girls. I'll buy the next round."

A COUPLE HOURS later we put Scarlet in a taxi, and we walk Charli to the subway. "Where are you living, anyway?" Fiona asks her.

"I found a place. It's a few stops away." She waves off the question. "See you at practice."

Fiona and I walk home together. The cool air sobers me up.

Or so I thought. When I'm safely in my bed, I have unusual dreams. They're very sexual. A pair of hands unzips my dress. Bryce says "*Désolé*," in my ear. *Sorry*. But an apology isn't what I want, so I say, "Keep going."

He doesn't, and I wake up, frustrated.

Thanks, tequila.

When I roll over onto my back, the dream continues. There's kissing. And strong hands remove my underwear, sliding it down my body in a sensuous pass of silk on bare skin.

Those hands pass over my breasts. And then he kisses his way down my body, thrilling me. My legs are parted, and a hot, eager mouth lands exactly where I want it.

I arch my back and moan. *Yes. Finally. More.* And then I look down to watch this wonderfulness in action.

He lifts his head to give me a smoldering glance. But it's not Bryce who's pleasuring me. It's Anton, with his wicked smile, and those brilliant, heavy-lidded eyes.

I wake up with a start, sweating and turned on. I let out a quiet groan of frustration and notice that dawn has already arrived to leak pale light into my bedroom.

I sit up, grab the glass of water beside my bed, and take a gulp. My body is deeply confused. In the first place, it forgot how to lunge for pucks. But I'm working on it.

It also craves sex. I blame Bryce and his ridiculous hesitation to take the next step with me.

And Anton Bayer's appearance in my dreams? That's on me. All the man did was buy me some Chinese food and talk me out of my snit. He didn't hit on me. And he sure as hell didn't...

The image that assaults me is so vivid that I clench my thighs together, as if that would soothe the ache I'm feeling.

I drain the rest of the water. When I turn to put the empty glass back down on the table, I notice a hair pin on the wooden surface, glinting in the early morning light.

"Really, Maman?" I whisper. "What on Earth are you trying to suggest? Should I be encouraged? Patient?"

As usual, she doesn't say.

TEN

Part Mermaid

ANTON

"AGAIN!" Coach yells. "Last time!"

With sweat dripping into my eyes, I set up for the drill once more. He blows the whistle, and I carry the puck past Trevi's attempt at a poke check and make the pass to Campeau.

"Yaaaas!" Eric hollers from the bench. "That's it!"

Normally, I care a great deal what he has to say, but when Coach blows the whistle three times to signal the end of practice, I am the first guy skating for the chute. I give Eric a wave but I don't even stop to say hello.

I've got six minutes to clean myself up, or I'll be late.

After the world's fastest shower, I'm pulling my socks over still-damp feet when O'Doul stops in front of me. "Hey—can we have a quick defense meeting before tonight's scrimmage?"

In nine hours we've got a preseason matchup against New Jersey. But first, there's somewhere I need to be. "I'd love to," I hedge. "But I'm doing some volunteer work for the foundation, and it starts in half an hour."

"Dude!" Drake yells from over by the laundry cart. "It's not volunteer work if you get paid to do it!"

"Work that hourly wage!" someone else yells.

"Okay, whatever. Then call it my side hustle." I yank on my

shirt and step into my shoes. "Can I catch up with you tonight, instead?"

"Sure, man." He gives me a thoughtful nod. "I bet the organization appreciates you helping kids even on game day."

I don't deserve this praise, but I am not going to argue. "It's a cool program. Happy to do it." Clothed now, I give him a salute. I grab my gym bag and high-tail it out of there.

O'Doul might understand my zeal for charity work if he could see me a half hour later. Specifically, if he took note of where my eyes go every chance they get. Sylvie is distracting as fuck in a purple Brooklyn sports bathing suit. It's a modest one-piece, the same suit that all our female students are wearing, too.

But good grief she is spectacular. The suit hugs her strong, athletic body, showing off every ridge and curve. And every inch of her smooth skin begs for my touch.

Or I *wish* it did, anyway. I'm just a lovestruck guy in purple trunks listening to Sylvie tell these kids how to tread water. "Move your arms laterally today. But for your certification, you'll need to tread water for two minutes *without* using your arms."

"What?" one of the girls squawks. "How can we stay above the water without our *arms*. That's *impossible*."

"Today you can use them," Sylvie says quickly. "But when you've got that down, we'll practice without. Just because it seems impossible today, does not mean it will seem impossible next week."

The girl, sitting on her towel, does not look convinced.

This is our second session, and also the second time I ran in five minutes late. Morning skate always runs overtime.

Sylvie is always prompt, and now she's up there in front of a pack of teenagers, calmly explaining the skills they'll work on today in the pool.

Last session was different—with everyone wearing street clothes and learning some basic lifesaving techniques from a presentation projected onto the wall. This time, we're going to get into the pool. Even me.

"Okay, so let's take a quick poll. Who feels confident enough to swim across the pool and back again without stopping?"

More than half the kids raise their hands.

"Who can swim the crawl stroke and breathe every other stroke?"

The number of raised hands falls sharply.

"Okay," Sylvie says, undaunted. "Who is not a swimmer yet at all?"

Nobody volunteers to self-identify this way. But I notice that a couple of boys evade eye contact.

"Hmm," Sylvie says. "Let's divide into two groups like this, then. Everyone who's willing to try to swim across and back will start in one group."

"The short way across or the long way?" someone clarifies.

Sylvie eyes the pool. "The short way, but in the deep end. And anyone who isn't ready for that will go into the other group for now. Everyone strip down to your bathing suits, please. Those who are going to swim across and back, stand by the ladder. And everyone else please gather at the stairs down there." She points to the shallow end.

As the teens stand up and begin to sort themselves, Sylvie hurries over to consult me. "Hi," she says, bright eyes taking me in.

"Sorry I'm late," I say quickly.

Her forehead creases in a cute frown as she gives her head a shake. "Morning skate always runs late, no? I'm just glad you're here. It's getting real now."

"How can I help?"

"Would you mind if I give you the non-swimmers in the shallow end? I think it's mostly boys."

"Anything," I say. "My goal will be to get them to go under water, right?"

"Exactly. Blow some bubbles. Experiment with natural buoyancy. Pushing off of walls. Just getting acclimated."

"No problem," I hear myself say. I can fake this. I can take responsibility for a bunch of hormonal teenage boys who could drown. No problem. I would do anything this woman in a purple bathing suit asked me to.

"All right. Whistle if you need backup. And I'll do the same."

"Of course. Go on. We got this," I say with more confidence than I feel.

She gives me a nervous smile and pulls a nylon bathing cap over her hair, tucking the long ends underneath. A month ago, if you'd asked me if a woman could look sexy in a nylon swim cap, I would have said no.

Wrong. I was wrong. She snaps that sucker over that lush hair and then jumps sleekly into the water. Several teens splash in after her. "Come on, ladies and gents," she calls to the reluctant pair still standing poolside. "Time to get wet."

One or two of the boys over by the stairs starts to snicker.

And that's when I suddenly feel useful. I clap to get their attention. I count heads in my crew. There are seven high school boys in my charge. No girls. "Okay, guys. Let's get through some basic water skills. I don't think you're going to have any trouble, here. Please get into the pool and we'll warm up with some stationery kicking. There will be no dunking, *ever*. Got that?" I hate dunking.

"Yeah, boss," somebody says.

"However—splashing is allowed and encouraged—but you can only use your feet."

"Say what?" a kid asks. He's huge—like linebacker huge—with a baby face and brown skin. He looks formidable, which is why I'm going out on a limb to guess that he'll be my least enthusiastic swimmer. It's just a hunch.

"A good swimmer is a strong kicker. So we're going to hold the side of the pool and kick up a tropical storm, okay?" I slip over the side of the pool into the water. "Hands on the wall, boys. Feet don't touch the floor until I say so. Straighten your legs and kick hard. Like you're trying to fight off a sharktopus."

"A what?" the linebacker yelps.

"A fearsome sharktopus. Just roll with it. Let's see what you can do."

My seven students line up at the side of the pool, grab the wall, and kick like I've asked them to.

Look at me, pretending to be a swim instructor. And now I know how much water a bunch of dudes can throw into the water by kicking their giant feet.

A whole lot.

OVER THE NEXT HOUR, I learn all their names. The linebacker is Cedric, and I was a hundred percent right about him. He's a good kid, but he refuses to put his face in the water. Even though he's standing with his feet planted on the bottom of the pool in four feet of water, when I ask them to blow bubbles, he barely gets his lower lip wet.

I haven't called him on it, though. I'm working around it.

"All right. Let's float on our backs next," I say to the herd. "I'm going to time you and see how long you can do this without putting your feet down."

"Time us?" Cedric asks. "On that fancy watch?"

"Yeah, on my fancy watch." It cost a mint, but it's a waterproof diving watch, which is why I wore it today.

I don't usually wear the thing, although it's literally the only gift my father has given me since he left when I was seven. His bank sent a check every month, but he missed all my birthdays until I turned eighteen. And then he gave me a Rolex Submariner that cost ten grand. He's a piece of work.

"Who wants to start?" I ask. "Let's do this tournament style, in pairs."

Nobody raises his hand.

"Fine—we'll practice first," I say, pivoting. "Floating is basically like treating the water as your sofa. Lie back and let your feet drift upward."

To demonstrate, I lie back and show them how it's done. My ears fill, which means I can't hear what's going on for a moment. I hate that feeling. I hope they don't all get out of the pool and leave me here.

But I take a few slow breaths and let myself relax, to show them how it's done. Maybe I hate the water, but I know I can't drown in the shallow end of a pool.

When I come up again, they're all staring at me. "That's it?" someone asks. "Why doesn't your ass just sink all the way down?"

"Good question. I didn't pay enough attention in physics class to answer that one."

They all laugh, and I spot Sylvie looking over to see why. When our gazes meet, she smiles.

"But people float. You just have to relax and trust that you're not, like, secretly an alien with a different body mass."

They erupt again. I'm a hit as a comedian, but nobody is floating yet. "Okay! Everybody on his back. Leave some space between you—no kicking each other. Relax and try it."

Miraculously, everybody floats. Everyone except Cedric. He tries, but fear is preventing him from getting his feet off the ground. "It ain't working, boss," he complains. "I'm too heavy."

"You're not," I insist. "You're not still enough, is all. Here— let's do this step wise." I grab a lifesaving rescue buoy off the edge of the pool. It's like a rectangular, floating cushion. "Put your neck on this. It will keep your face above the water. Just concentrate on letting your legs float up to join the rest of you."

Shockingly, this works. After a few more thrashing attempts, Cedric is floating. Assisted, but still floating, arms outstretched.

"Ten minutes!" Sylvie calls to me.

"Got it, boss!" I call. "All right, boys. Two more skills, okay? First I want you to try treading water for two minutes. We'll move into slightly deeper water for this."

There's some quiet cursing. "With our arms?" someone asks.

"Yup. Let's move." I wade out until I'm out deeper than they are, then pull my wrist out of the water and check my watch. "Ready—*go*. Keep your head up, kick underwater, and scull your arms."

They thrash around. Two minutes feels long, suddenly. Why do people do this for fun? I like water better when it's frozen under my skates.

"I'm tired already," someone gasps.

"Slow down your breathing," I remind him. "Arms move later-ally—not up and down."

The griping stops as seven teens focus on staying afloat. But a couple of them are panting. "Is it time yet?" someone demands.

"Nope. Distract yourself," I insist. "Ask me a question. Anything."

"How much can you bench?" asks Cedric. He's actually doing it — treading water with those giant arms. I guess he doesn't mind this part, because his head is out of the water.

"I dunno. Three fifteen? Hockey players care more about squats, though. You need strong thighs and a big ass to stop players from getting past you."

They snicker at my use of *ass*.

"How much money do you earn?" someone asks.

"A lot more than I probably should," I say as a dodge. I count heads again. Still seven. I'm rocking this job.

"Is it two minutes yet?"

I check my watch. "You're almost there. After this, we'll rest for a minute. Then we're gonna try diving for those rings."

"That'll be a blast," Cedric grumbles. "You'll go first, right?"

"Um..." *Do I have to?* I check my watch again. "Let's count down. Ready? Ten...nine..."

They count with me, speeding up the seconds in order to race to zero. But we did it. Seven teens kick toward the wall and grab on, making exaggerated sounds of exhaustion.

In the farthest corner of the deep end, Sylvie is coaching someone to breathe during the crawl stroke. "It's easier to roll," she says, "rather than pick up your head."

My guys look at her like she's a mermaid. And maybe she is part mermaid. That must be why I have so much trouble looking away. There's some kind of enchantment that's stolen my brain.

I've got it bad. I can't even lie to myself anymore. Sylvie is the whole package — she's fun, she's energetic.

She's sexy as fuck.

"Arright, coach! Let us see you do this diving thing!" a kid named Javier calls.

"Yeah, it's time." I grasp the edge of the pool deck and hoist myself out of the water.

Sylvie's eyes lift in my direction. And there it is — an unguarded flicker of interest as she watches my soaking wet self cross the pool deck for the weighted rings.

She looks away again, quickly. But I swear she's thinking some of the same thoughts that I'm thinking.

Or I wish she would, anyway.

I grab the rings and jump back into the pool. I kick out into the center of the five-foot section and drop them here and there. "Let's keep it simple. Grab a ring off the bottom with your hand, then give it to me. And we're done for the day."

"Do it!" Cedric chants. "You said you'd demonstrate."

"Uh-huh. Okay." *Hell.*

"Do it! Do it!" the other kids yell, drawing the attention of Sylvie's group, too.

She looks over at me from where she's submerged in the water, helping a boy float on his back. Her eyebrows lift with an expression that says, *Really?*

So I take a deep breath and duck under the water, kicking toward the bottom. The water presses in on me. I hate that feeling. But I force my eyes open in spite of the chlorine and grab a ring off the bottom.

I put my feet down and then shoot up, breaking the surface with the ring held over my head. Just in case Sylvie is easily impressed.

The teens are laughing when I shake the water out of my ears and eyes. "Okay, your turn."

Several of them dive right under. A couple of them need more than one try to grab the ring off the bottom.

I'm afraid to tell them that their certification requires grabbing a twenty-pound weight off the bottom of the deepest part of the pool and swimming with it for a whole length.

But first things first. "Okay, Cedric. In you go."

"Uh, maybe next time," he says.

"Pussy," one of the other kids says under his breath.

"*Hey,*" I say sharply. "That's not going to get anyone a certificate in lifesaving. Cedric—talk to me. What's holding you back? Once you grab the ring, you can put your feet down and just stand up. Worst-case scenario—you get some water in your nose."

"I hate that feeling when the water is pressing on you." He shivers. "Just don't like it."

It's not like I blame him.

"But what if that was a drowning person? Huh?" one of the other kids says. "You just gonna leave her down there?"

Cedric looks uncomfortable. I don't think he's terrified of the water—he's been in it for an hour. But he doesn't seem to enjoy getting it on his face.

"Tell you what," I propose. "If you get the ring, I'll try to bench press you."

"What?" He laughs. "How you gonna do that?"

"Not sure, but you could make me figure it out. Go on."

He snorts. And just when I think he's going to refuse, he plunges his head under the water and disappears.

Uh-oh. I might be trying to lift this giant in a few minutes.

Sure enough, he pops up a moment later, coughing out a mouthful of water before grinning at me. "Guess who's gotta bench me now?"

ELEVEN

Never Forget a Woman's Name

SYLVIE

YESTERDAY, when I caught up to him at the practice facility, Anton had told me that he was a little nervous about teaching swimming. That's why I gave him the smaller crew in the shallow end.

But I've been keeping an eye on him down there, and those boys are hanging on every word he says. And he's gotten every one of them to step through various swimming skills.

And he looks mighty fine doing it, just saying. I wasn't prepared to see a dripping wet, mostly naked Anton Bayer. His sculpted upper body is luscious. And the color of his laughing eyes matches the pool tiles.

Meanwhile I'm flailing around down here trying to keep all ten of these teens occupied, trying to learn their names and make myself heard amid the splashing and the echoing acoustics.

This is more work than a two-hour hockey practice. Who knew?

I'm just dragging myself across the finish line when I see all of Anton's guys climb out of the water at once. They're very animated about something and pointing and laughing.

Anton glances in my direction, and his face looks sheepish somehow.

"Okay—everybody out," I say, climbing out of the pool to grab my towel. "Good work today!" There's still a few minutes left of our time, but I'm curious about what Anton is up to. So I head over there.

"What about those kickboards?" somebody suggests.

"Those'll break!" complains another.

"Excuse me," I say, toweling off my face. "Is there a problem?"

Anton gives me that sheepish smile again. He hasn't put a shirt on yet, and it's distracting. "Can I get your opinion about something?" He waves me over to where we can consult more or less privately.

"Sure?" And then I'm standing close to him, trying to figure out where to put my eyes.

"So, I kinda lost a bet," he whispers.

Wait, really? "With one of the kids?"

"Yup. I have to bench press him now."

I blink. That was not what I expected him to say.

"Look, I know it's kinda ridiculous, but I hope you're not too annoyed. I got him to go underwater."

Annoyed? A gurgle of laughter erupts from my belly. "Hilarious! So how are we going to do this?" I turn around to address my crew. "Does anybody want to dry off and fetch a phone out of the locker room? We're going to need some pictures."

FIVE MINUTES later we've figured it out.

"This will work better with encouragement," I tell the kids. "Give it up for Anton, maker of bets, lifter of future lifeguards!"

All the teens cheer up a storm.

Anton is lying on his back, on a couple of towels, right between two benches. There's a backboard lying across the benches—that thing they strap you onto if you injure your spinal cord.

And Cedric is on top of that board. "Ready boss?" he calls.

"Ready steady!" Anton places his palms on the underside of the board, lets out a roar, and pushes the board off the benches.

I hope he doesn't strain something. His coach will not be happy.

The kids screech as the board wobbles, but he manages to lift it into the air more or less levelly. Cedric lets out a shout of victory.

"It's up, and it's *good!*" I cry. "More reps!"

He lowers the board a few inches and lifts it three more times just for show. Cedric is laughing his ass off up there, too.

Then Anton sets the board back down on the benches, letting out a huge breath. And the cheering reaches a fevered pitch.

After the two men get up again, there's a lot of back-slapping and high-fiving that happens before the teens finally clear out.

"See you next week!" I call after them, while Anton picks up the props, grinning. "Want to ride the subway back with me?" I ask him.

"Of course." He gives me a brilliant smile.

TEN MINUTES later we emerge from our respective locker rooms more or less at the same time, because I didn't want to make him wait while I blow dry my hair.

"You know, we could get a taxi," I offer, even though I'm a fan of saving money. "It's game day, right?"

"It's a scrimmage," he says with a shrug. "Split squad." Half their team will play half the New Jersey team, and the other halves will meet in New Jersey. "At least I got the Brooklyn game. When's your first matchup, anyway?"

"Two weeks." I lick my lips. "Home game against Buffalo."

"You playing?" he asks, athlete to athlete.

"Probably not," I admit. "But I'm making progress."

He puts his hand up to flag down a yellow cab. "I'll bet you are. Spending a lot of time at the gym, yeah?"

He sees me there all the time. Our practices are at night, but during the day I use the weight room, which is mostly empty, because my teammates are at work.

"So much time. I'm doing a ton of cardio. Hey—where do you like to run outside? I asked Bryce for recommendations, but he said I should just use the treadmills." I roll my eyes. "He thinks I'm going to get mugged."

"I'll take you running," he offers as a cab stops for us. "Not, like, as your bodyguard. Just to show you the best spots."

"Would you?" It comes out sounding a little too eager. "Thank you."

"Sure. I could do early tomorrow before morning skate. Or after it."

"After," I say quickly. "If you're already tired, maybe I can keep up with you."

"It's a date," he says, and I find my face warming for no reason at all. But Anton always has that effect on me—like, I can't feel calm when he's nearby. I really don't understand it.

We get into the close quarters of the cab's back seat, which only makes things worse.

Anton gives the man directions to our block, and then sits back and smiles at me. "So that was pretty fun. I don't know what the hell I'm doing, but they didn't seem to care."

"I *thought* I knew what I was doing," I admit. "But there was more chaos than I'd hoped for. And after the girls put swimming caps on, I realized that I hadn't learned their names as well as I'd thought, because I kept getting Trina's and Theresa's names backwards."

Anton snickers. "Never forget a woman's name, Sylvie. That's a classic dick move."

"You shut up," I argue, and he laughs. "But seriously—you're good at this. There's a kind of playfulness to you that works well with teenagers. They trust you, because you don't look like a guy who's judging them."

He stops laughing and looks down quickly, like he doesn't quite know how to take the compliment. "Well, thanks, buddy. That's a nice way of saying that my childish personality is occasionally useful."

"I wouldn't say childish. I'd say fun-loving."

"Nobody cares what word you use when you end up in the gossip blogs." He gives me a tight smile. And then he changes the subject. "How's practice going? Better?"

"Sometimes." I hold back my sigh. "I coached hockey last year, but I didn't play, and I certainly didn't train for this. So while I feel sharp in the net, my fitness level wasn't where I needed to be. And the, uh, mother-dying-diet had me down twenty pounds that I somehow have to regain. In pure muscle."

"Mmm," he says, giving me a knowing look. "Yeah, I had some basic fitness issues last year, too," he says.

Bullshit, I think immediately. He's built like Adonis.

"But I spent the summer training like a beast. It was boring, but it worked. You'll get there. Lace up your sneakers tomorrow, and I'll show you where I like to run."

"Thank you," I say quietly. "I'll do my best."

TWELVE

I Just Jinxed Us

October

ANTON

IT'S A BEAUTIFUL AUTUMN SATURDAY, so I don't mind waiting a few minutes outside my cousin Eric's office while he finishes up a call. His office is directly across the street from my apartment building, anyway.

When he finally emerges from the building, he gives me a big smile. "Ready for the big game?"

"Born ready," I say, bypassing the fact that this is not, in fact, a big game. We're playing an exhibition game today at the practice rink, against the Bombshells.

His grin widens. "Uh-huh. Cool."

"What? Why are you giving me that creepy smile?"

"No reason."

"So how is this game going to work, anyway?"

"I can't tell you," Eric says. "Bess insists on complete silence until we're all assembled to hear the rules." Eric works for Bess Beringer, who started their boutique sports agency years ago. Bess is very involved with the women's team.

"Dude," I complain as we cross the cobblestone street. It's only a two-block walk to the facility. "I'm not asking for state secrets. I'm just curious, you know? Because the men are gonna *smoke* the women. What's the point of that?"

"Wait up!"

We stop for my friend Silas Kelly—the goalie—who's trotting behind us on the sidewalk.

"I have questions," he says, joining us. "How is this game against the women going to work? Are we supposed to, like, throw the game so they don't look bad?"

I wince, and wait for Eric to rip him a new one. Because I already know the Bombshells would never want that.

But Eric only throws back his head and laughs. "Sure, man. You do that. I'll watch."

Silas and I exchange a puzzled glance. Our questions are valid, though. We have years of practice playing together on a team, where the women only have six weeks. We have fifty pounds of muscle on them, too.

"The rules are going to have to change, though, right?" Silas presses. "There's no hitting in women's hockey."

"Yeah, sure," Eric says. "There's no hitting in this game. There are a few more rule changes, though. I can't tell you anymore."

"Because Bess would remove your testicles?" Silas guesses.

"Sure. But also because this is going to be *very* entertaining." Then he laughs.

That's when I feel my first prickle of worry.

AN HOUR LATER, my baffled teammates and I are assembled in all our gear, except for our skates. We've been summoned to the men's weight room, where all the equipment has been moved aside to accommodate a meeting between both teams.

The Bombshells are also suited up and ready to play. And according to the clock on the wall, the puck drops in less than twenty minutes.

Bess climbs up on a weight bench to address the whole crew.

"Okay, sports fans! The Battle of the Sexes starts in just ten minutes."

"I thought we were just playing *hockey*," Drake whines.

"There are several rule changes you need to know about. First of all, you can't make any body checks. Absolutely no hits. And the ref will give you a five-minute penalty if you break this rule."

"Got it. No hits," Trevi says. "Wouldn't want to hit a woman, anyway."

"That's what you think," Castro breaks in. "But what if she steals your action figures and decapitates them?"

Fifty people turn and give him a weird look.

"What? I have two sisters."

Bess goes on, ignoring him. "There are a few more rule changes you need to know about. We'll play six games of ten minutes each. No shift changes during the game, but a *full* shift change for each new game, including goalies."

I can't help it. I glance over to the women's side and spot Sylvie. She's smiling ear to ear, her cheeks glowing. And I feel the same damn pull I always feel when I look at her.

It's safe to say that we've become good friends. We run together all the time. We're strangely well-paced for running together. It's almost eerie. And I've never had so much fun sweating for ten miles, as Sylvie tells me about her childhood in Montreal, and I tell her all the dumb things that have happened while I'm traveling with the team.

Not *all* the dumb things. I tell her about missing the jet and how much teasing I took for that. But I don't tell her about that stupid photo of me in bed with those women. That's just too embarrassing, and I want Sylvie to think highly of me.

Yup. My crush rages on.

But my attention is snared by Bess, who's now holding a remote control in her hand. "In a moment I'm going to show you a live view of the rink. You'll notice several things—the first one being the thousands of fans on hand to watch. We're raising almost a hundred thousand dollars for Brooklyn youth sports today. Also? Take a look at the ice, kids. It looks a little different."

"Uh-oh," Trevi grumbles.

"The moment I show you the ice, the fifteen-minute countdown to play begins. There will be no on-ice warmup. But you can consult with the members of your coaching and training staff to strategize. Since the Bruisers have more men on staff than the Bombshells have, we're lending Heidi Jo to the women."

"Oh shit," whisper half the men around me, because Heidi is an ace at all kinds of games.

"And you won't be using your regular sticks," Bess says.

"Wait, what?" Castro bleats. "Not my lucky stick?"

"You'll be fine, honeybunch," Bess says cheerfully. "Now take a look at this." She pushes a button, and the screen resolves to show our practice rink, where *all* the new seats are taken up by fans. It's a sea of purple out there.

But spread all around the familiar ice are eight big purple... things.

"What are those?" I call out.

"They're *bumpers*," Bess says gleefully. "If you collide with them, it won't hurt. But if a flying object collides with them, it will bounce. So please realize that your ordinary team tactics and positions are not going to be effective in this game."

On the men's side of the gym, there's a stunned silence. While on the women's side, they begin to whisper among themselves.

"Okay, wait," somebody says. "This is like bumper pool. Who's good at billiards?"

"Me!" Across the room, Heidi Jo throws her arms up in the air.

"We are so dead," Castro grumbles. "Who usually wins at pool —besides my wife?"

"Baby Bayer beat me that time in Tampa," O'Doul says. "Give us some tips, man. How should we play this?"

"Um..." I think about a pool table, and then I look back up at that screen. "Guys, I don't know. Maybe I can only play pool when I'm drunk."

Everyone groans.

Across the room I hear Heidi say, "Just picture the ninety-degree angle. If the puck hits the bumper here, it will bounce in this direction."

The men turn their heads to try to see what she's doing, but the women's team blocks us with their bodies.

"Bess!" I yelp. "Tell us more about the equipment we're using." I figure if we can't win with geometry, at least we'll have more experience on the ice.

"Why sure," Bess says, clapping. "The first two games will be played with a broom and an inflated rubber ball."

"What?" Drake yelps. "A broom?"

"You're up first," Coach says, touching Drake on the shoulder. "I want to see the finest broom-handling in all of Brooklyn. Whoever scores the most goals today gets a guaranteed starting spot in the game against Toronto next week."

"I think I jinxed us," Silas whispers.

"How?" I whisper back.

"When I said that thing about letting the women win."

"Sounds pretty stupid now, doesn't it?" Eric says, barely concealing his chuckle.

"I've never defended the net against balls," Silas says.

"Better get stretching, then," Coach barks.

"Yessir."

THIRTEEN

Some Saves are Guesswork and Prayer

SYLVIE

THE TRUTH IS that I didn't upend my life to move to Brooklyn just to play in a somewhat ridiculous exhibition game. And on one level, it makes me crazy that my Bombshells game jersey is getting its first and only real action during today's publicity stunt.

I still haven't played a single pro game, because Scarlet is having the season of a lifetime. And that stings.

On the other hand, I have never had as much fun as I'm having right now. After five of six games, the women are up four games to one.

I'm guzzling water, waiting until it's time to guard the net for our very last game—and the only one where I'll be holding an actual hockey stick.

The first two games—the ones with brooms—were hilarious. Just as the players on both teams had begun to adapt their game to the strangely exuberant equipment, Nate Kattenberger and Rebecca Rowley Kattenberger had begun flinging *more* balls onto the rink.

I watched, wide-eyed, as every player on the ice tried to shoot a big ball at the net, *at the same time*. The result was chaos. Players got in each other's way. I watched as Bryce accidentally bounced a shot off Castro's padded ass.

And then one team was the first to solve the quandary of how to score efficiently. And that team was the Bombshells! My girls formed a sort of bucket brigade, funneling balls in turn toward two shooters, who bombed goalie Mike Beacon in *pairs*, forcing him to choose which shot to defend.

We won the first game with a score of fourteen to nine. And when I skated out for game two, we kept up the good work. I learned to use my broom sideways to defend the whole zone at once, and again we won, this time by eight goals to six, since the men had also learned a few things in the meantime.

Games three and four had been even weirder, with every skater wielding a giant rubber spatula. That's right—spatulas. They looked like the kind you'd see at any kitchen store, except they were five feet tall, and the rubber spatula part was as broad as a snow shovel.

The "puck" was a rubber object shaped a lot like an egg. It was slippery, which made everything more complicated. And it refused to roll in a straight line.

Once again, whomever could adapt the fastest would win. And again, that was the Bombshells. We won games three and four by narrow margins.

And I really enjoyed the look of consternation on Anton Bayer's face as he tried to score on me with that unwieldy spatula. The egg went spinning away from him, and I have never seen a man look more confused.

The fans are *loving* this, too. Every crazy ricochet and error is cause for cheers and shrieks of laughter.

Finally they've put hockey sticks back into our hands, and the playing field has leveled out very fast. Those crazy bumpers positioned around the ice make passing a perilous experience, though, causing far more turnovers than in a regular game.

But the men have learned to negotiate them as quickly as the women, and they end up taking just as many shots on goal. Scarlet fought her hardest in the first game, but she let in three, while Beacon only let in two. The Bombshells lost by a nose.

And now it's my turn to defend the net for our very last game. When the whistle blows, I vault over the wall. Bryce gives me a big smile and a thumbs up as I head for the net, and it warms the center of my chest.

He and I used to argue over hockey all the time. It had been fun. We don't squabble like that anymore, and I miss it. Maybe that's why I got so mad at him when he took it easy on me during that goalie practice. Because he used to treat me like an equal.

I push that thought out of my head, though, because I have a job to do. I edge my blades all over the crease, roughing up the ice just the way I like it. The whistle blows, and Fiona sets up for a faceoff against Leo Trevi.

Those bumpers make it hard to see the puck, and a goalie's job is to see the whole ice when my teammates can't. So I have to rely on other visual cues. You can tell who has the puck by the set of their shoulders, and the tension in their arms.

"To Castro!" I shout to Charli. "Wing! Incoming!"

Charli anticipates him, getting right in his way. He passes toward Bayer, but the bumper interferes, and Fiona intercepts it.

The next nine minutes are a sweaty blur. I deflect a couple of squeakers. And my girls take several good shots, too, but Silas denies them.

Castro eventually gets another shot on me. But since Charli's already in his face, he can't run it in as far as he'd like, and the puck is airborne long enough for me to set up for a beautiful glove save.

Fans are screaming as I toss the puck to the ref, and he sets up another faceoff. I know in my gut that the clock is running down, and somehow we're scoreless.

Sure, it's only a ten-minute game, but I'm earning my weekly five hundred bucks right now against an NHL team that has made it to the playoffs the last three years.

Fiona loses the faceoff, and the men take control. They've figured out the bumpers, too, and they execute a series of nice passes as I call out instructions to my teammates.

"Cover left! Charli—man on!"

Unfortunately, Charli gets stripped by Anton Bayer. And suddenly the big defenseman is barreling toward me, stick-handling around the last bumper to rush the net.

And this man—my friend, my running buddy, and the man I told under no uncertain terms that I would *never* want anyone to take easy shots at me—is about to let the puck fly from close range.

Given my centered stance, he'll have to choose left or right at the last moment. I hear him connect with the puck, and our gazes lock for just a nanosecond. Those ridiculously bright blue eyes are full of intention as he fires a missile at me.

Now, some shots can be planned for, if there's time. But some require only gut instinct and prayer. This shot falls into the latter category.

My body chooses to go right. Maybe it's something in his stick action that sends me in that direction, or maybe it's just dumb luck, but my lunge puts my glove in the path of the puck, and when it lands, my hand practically vibrates with the force of it.

But I've done it. I stopped the shot. And the buzzer rings as I'm staring at the puck in my glove.

I let out a whoop of victory as my teammates speed toward me, shoving Anton out of the way. When I glance over Charli's shoulder, he's smiling and shaking his head.

"WINNERS...BOMBSHELLS!" the announcer calls.

And I can't stop laughing.

THAT EVENING, while I'm having a celebratory drink with my teammates, Anton texts me his congratulations.

Anton: Nice work today. It's a good thing I don't have a fragile male ego.

Sylvie: Thank you. Your ego seems pretty durable to me. Look! I got a gold star on my phone. You're right—it's the best feeling.

Anton: For you, maybe. I'm drowning my sorrows in a cupcake while I wait for my order of spicy chicken.

Sylvie: There are many things wrong with this scenario. You're having spicy chicken without me? And you're eating the cupcake first?

Anton: There is nothing wrong with eating present. And I'd share if you were here. Feel free to swing by.

Honestly, I almost get up and head for the door. It's a strange impulse, given the fact that I'd already decided to eat a Tavern burger for dinner, and all my teammates are here, too.

Anton is at home, though, making good on his vow to avoid late drunken nights this season. They have a road trip in the morning, too.

Besides, he was just teasing me. He knows how I feel about spicy chicken. I'm so gullible.

Sylvie: You eat that chicken and beat Arizona. We're playing Stamford tomorrow.

Anton: Make 'em cry. Hey—are you going to the black tie next month?

Sylvie: Yes!

Anton: Good. Becca throws a good party.

Sylvie: So I've heard. Dressy parties aren't really my thing, though. they always sound fun until the minute it's time to get ready.

Anton: Get out of my brain. But I always show up for these, because management likes to see our faces. And I like to make management happy.

Sylvie: You make a few good points. I guess I'll see you there!

"Who are you texting?" Charli asks. "You're smiling like you just won a puppy lottery."

"Are puppy lotteries a thing?" I ask, ducking the question. I don't want to explain. Anton and I are just friends, even though he still makes me feel tingly inside.

"They should be," she says. "But who were you texting?"

"Oh, just Anton." I shrug.

"You guys are tight lately," Charli observes. I think she's fishing for gossip.

"We're workout buddies," I insist. Although it's more than that. We're friends, too. He's a good listener and a fun guy. And he has a kind of sunshiny self-confidence that's rare in professional athletes. He's a great athlete, but he doesn't have the ego to match.

There's no bluster. No bragging. It's refreshing.

Anton: Save me a dance. And see you at the pool next week, too!

He signs off with a smiley face.

And now I'm wearing one to match.

FOURTEEN

You Could Do This Professionally

November

SYLVIE

TWO WEEKS later I find myself seated on a sofa at the Colorbox salon, waiting for my manicure to be declared officially dry, when Charli blows in through the front door. Then she removes her coat, and I almost swallow my tongue. "Wow, Charli! You look..." I actually run out of words. After all her complaints about tonight's benefit party, I thought she might bail completely.

But here she is, dressed in a body-hugging, forest-green sheath dress with translucent sleeves. There's no skin showing, but it's so beautiful. That dark color makes her pale skin and hair practically glow.

"That bad, huh?" Charli says, snapping her gum.

"Stop. You look *magnificent*. Wow."

"Thanks, babe. Not to make this weird, but are you going to this party? Not sure the sweatpants are your best option. At least level up to jeans, maybe?"

"She's stalling!" calls Fiona from behind the curtain that was put up just for us tonight.

Rebecca threw us a glam-you-up pre-party at her nail salon. I just had my first manicure in a year.

"Sylvie, put on the fucking dress already," Fiona calls. "It's time."

"Okay but…" I gulp. "I don't know if I bought the right thing."

Fiona sticks her head out from behind the curtain. "Put that *damn* thing on, or I'll make the whole team do a bag skate tomorrow morning."

"Whoa." Charli's head snaps back in shock. "She's not fucking around. Put the dress on, already."

"Fine." I get up off the sofa and walk back behind the curtain, where my teammate Samantha is adjusting the ruffles on her dress.

"It's all yours," she says. "I'm going to do my makeup in front."

Fiona tries to hand me my dress bag, but first I have to shimmy out of the sweatpants. I sit down on a stool and pull the sheerest stockings I've ever owned in my life over perfectly shaved legs and sexy panties.

"Somebody better see that lingerie tonight," Fiona says, clucking her tongue. "Somebody besides me, I mean."

"Dream on," I grumble. I've hoisted my boobs into a black lace strapless bra, too.

"I might have left a condom on your bedside table," she whispers.

"What? Why?"

"Because this dress is magic. As a woman who's sometimes into women, I'm here to tell you that you don't know its power." She thrusts the dress at me again.

"All compliments are welcome," I tell her as I drop the little black dress over my head. I bought it last week at Bloomie's, with Fiona's encouragement.

Too much encouragement, maybe. The dress is cut from black velvet so soft that it feels like butter in a fabric form. It has a circular, halter-style neckline that doesn't show any cleavage. But it's *short*. The hem style is called an "ellipse" because the back is longer than the front.

Maybe this was a bad idea.

I put it on anyway, and then—holding the neckline closed so I can see how it drapes—I look in the salon's three-way mirror.

And then I remember why I bought this dress in the first place. It just *fits* me. The velvet clings to all the right places. The hem skims across my thighs in a flattering spot, and then drops elegantly down a few inches to sufficiently cover my rear.

It's not scandalous at all. Not on the face of it. But it makes me look more sensual and sexy than anything else I've ever owned.

I take a deep breath, step into the heels that Fiona lent me, and consider the whole look. My hair is clean and shiny. I'm wearing makeup, and I've dabbed a bit of Fiona's perfume at my pulse points. The whole effect was designed to make Bryce Campeau's jaw drop.

But now I find I'm losing my nerve. "Fiona!" I bark.

"Yes? Need me to pin that dress?"

"No! I'm not going."

"What?"

Charli yanks the curtain aside, and now she and Fiona are staring at me. "*Damn* girl!" Charli says. "I'd fuck you. Holy hell."

Embarrassed, I laugh. "One vote of confidence, then?"

"Two!" Fiona adds. "You look so beautiful. So what's this bullshit about not going?"

And now I guess I have to explain myself. "I just don't see the point. I'm trying to get over him. Why would I try to seduce him?" Not to mention that I've never seduced *anyone*. The odds of failure are high.

"You're trying to get over him," Fiona repeats. "But how's that going? Are you still mad?"

"Yes," I say quickly. "Of course I am."

"So he's still on your mind?" Charli clarifies.

"Sometimes," I admit. "Okay, often. But that's just because I spent years thinking about him. And my mother thought we'd end up together."

"But you're letting him off the hook," Fiona presses. "He owes you a real conversation about his feelings. He keeps ducking that by telling you he's waiting for the right contract extension or what-the-fuck-ever!"

"Yes," Charli agrees. "Exactly."

"And this dress is going to make him see that?" I ask, waving my hands in front of my scantily clad self.

"Men can be simple, visual creatures," Fiona says. "One look at you in this dress and the man will not be able to treat you like his little sister. Because he will realize, on a gut level, that the *other* men at this party will all start drooling when you walk through the door."

"If I had those cheekbones…" Charli sighs.

"Or those legs." Fiona shrugs. "This is about messaging. And waking that man out of his stupor. Whether you seduce him or not is beside the point."

"It's a 'Come to Jesus moment,' with your tits and your ass," Charli finishes. "If he doesn't want to dance with you—vertically or horizontally—he'll understand that you're moving on without him."

I do like the sound of that. Thinking about Bryce all this time hasn't done me any favors. "All right. I get it. I'll go."

"Yay!" Fiona claps her hands together. "Can I pin it, then?"

"Sure. Thanks."

At the store, we'd realized this dress had one flaw, which was that one half of the hook and eye at the back of the neck was missing. Fiona had suggested to the saleswoman that the flaw deserved a discount.

To my surprise, the saleswoman had agreed on the spot. "I think I could take thirty percent off," she'd said. "You can take it to a dry cleaner and ask them to repair it."

The price cut got me over my indecision, and I got out my credit card on the spot. There wasn't time to fix the hook and eye, though, so Fiona promised to pin me in to the dress. "Come here," she says, wielding a tiny safety pin.

"And then let's do your eyes," Charli says now, opening her bag.

"I already did," I argue.

"Let me," Charli says. "Please?"

Oh dear. I've never even seen Charli wear makeup. And now she wants to paint my face? "Um…"

"Let me show you," she says. "If you don't like it, you can

96

remove it and I promise not to be offended." She opens a compact with several shades of brown, gray, and gold shadows. "Sit down out here on the sofa."

I follow her back out front, because it's easier than arguing. And makeup is removable, right?

"Close your eyes. Keep them closed."

I obey, if only to prevent getting stabbed with the applicator. Charli goes to work on me in short, confident strokes of the brush. Then I feel an eyeliner pencil and a mascara wand in action.

"Open," she orders.

I'm treated to a close-up view of Charli's serious green eyes as she does something to my bottom lashes.

"There," she grunts. "If you don't get laid tonight, then it's a truly hopeless situation."

"Harsh," Fiona says. "Let's see—" She blinks. "*Whoa*. Hot damn."

"Should I be afraid to look?" I ask.

"No," Fiona insists. "You look incredible. Charli! *How* are you a wiz at makeup? I've never even seen you in lip gloss!"

"I don't like to attract male attention." She shrugs. "But that doesn't mean I don't know how."

Rising from the sofa, I walk over to the mirrors. I'm greeted by someone far more sophisticated than the girl I was a half hour ago. My eyes look bigger and bolder. She dramatized me without piling on the makeup.

"Whoa!" I call out. "You could do this professionally."

"Thank you. Now I'll do Fiona, if she wants."

"Only if you also do yourself," Fiona says. "Let's knock 'em *all* dead."

THE EVENT IS HELD at the Green Building, a renovated brick warehouse deep into Brooklyn. We hand over our coats in the little lobby before entering a big, brick-walled room with rustic wooden doors and iron beams on the ceiling. There are vintage chandeliers, and tiny lights clinging to birch branches "planted" along the walls.

Thousands of colorful autumn leaves twist overhead on invisible threads. It's like stepping into a fairy woodland.

"Wow, is this funky or what?" Charli gasps. "It must cost a mint to throw a party like this. I don't understand rich people."

"Hush," Fiona whispers, because Nate and Rebecca Kattenberger are just inside, receiving guests. Rebecca is wearing a dark red velvet gown in a vintage mermaid shape. She looks like a 1920s movie star.

"Well, hot damn!" she crows. "Look at you three. Thank you for coming out on your night off."

"We wouldn't have wanted to miss this spectacle," Fiona says.

"Grab a drink. There's food, too. I highly recommend the pork meatballs. There's a silent auction, and the band starts playing dance tunes in a half hour."

"Right after I make a boring speech," Nate puts in.

Rebecca makes a face. "You're really selling yourself, baby."

"It won't be boring on *purpose*," he says. "It's just the nature of speeches. I'll keep it short."

I think I like Nate Kattenberger.

"All you have to talk about is my winning streak," Rebecca says sweetly. The Bruisers are in the midst of an unprecedented early-season winning streak. They've had four shutout victories in a row, and all the pundits are wondering how long it can last. "Just stick to the facts."

"Yes, dear," he says, waving us into the party. "Have fun, Bombshells."

I quickly spot Bryce and his pals near the bar.

What is it about a man in a tux? I swear, every guy is doubly handsome when he puts on that pleated shirt. I love the way the crisp white color stands out against Bryce's rugged jaw, and the bowtie looks so dapper.

I once believed that he would wear a tux for me on our wedding day, and that I would pull a bow tie off him on our wedding night. My rusty heart gives a little lurch. I've reached the point where I can no longer tell if that reaction is love, or just stubbornness.

He's right in my path, so this is for all the marbles. I can't rock another dress any harder than I'm rocking this one, and it had better do the trick. I need to give Bryce a little electric zap—to wake him up and see me.

Bryce finishes shaking hands with a man I don't know. A donor, probably. The man moves off, crossing in front of the hockey players, and Bryce doesn't see me coming until the path is clear again.

Then I see when it happens—he notices me. His eyes widen, just like I'd hoped they would. "Sylvie. Wow. You look…" He seems unable to finish that sentence.

Someone else finishes it for him. "Smashing," a sultry male voice says. It's Anton Bayer. "Who invited three goddesses to the party?"

"Oh, you're a smooth one," Charli grumbles, although her smile says she's pleased by the compliment. "And I hate myself a little for noticing how well a hockey player can rock a tux."

"Which hockey player?" Anton teases.

"Oh, I meant it in a general sense." She rolls her eyes.

Bryce finally seems to shake off his stupor. "You look beautiful tonight, Sylvie. Can I make a trip to the bar for you ladies?"

"Absolutely." I step forward into his personal space and place a hand on Bryce's chest. His eyes widen again. "Do you think they'd make me a whiskey sour?"

"I'll check," he says immediately. Then he takes a half step backward.

Okay, this is *excellent*. I've rattled him. Fiona is obviously a genius.

"Anyone else?" he asks. "Fiona? Charli?"

"I'd love a glass of red wine," Fiona says. "Thank you."

"A beer would be great," Charli says. "Ale, if there's a choice."

"Coming right up." But before he turns away, he locks eyes with me, giving me a strange, curious glance. After a quick head shake, he heads for the bar.

"Interesting," Fiona whispers under her breath.

"Let's see what's up for grabs in the silent auction," Anton suggests, herding me and my friends toward the displays lining one brick wall.

"There won't be anything reasonable to buy," Charli points out. "Overpaying is the point of these things."

"That doesn't mean we can't have some fun." Anton rubs his hands together, a boyish gleam in his eye. "What are you bidding on, Heidi Jo?"

"Hi, Anton. Bombshells," the assistant to the Bruisers' general manager greets us. She's also married to Bruisers winger Jason Castro and is the most bubbly human I've ever met. "My honey just got outbid on this weekend on Nantucket."

"Too bad," Fiona says. "That looks like fun." There's a photo of a spectacular house overlooking a rocky beach. And another photo of the private plane that will deliver you there. Wow.

"I've never been to Nantucket," Heidi Jo muses. "I think it's time to change that, don't you?" Then she leans over and writes *Jason Castro* on the next line, with a new bid, for three thousand dollars.

"Ooh!" Fiona laughs. "That's one way to handle it."

Heidi Jo shrugs. "We probably still won't win, so I won't have to explain myself. But it's good for the charity, right?"

"I like the way you think," Anton says.

"Oh, this sounds nice," Fiona says, reading another item's description. "A week at a Vermont cabin. Donated by retired player Dave Beringer. Nobody has bid yet."

"What's the minimum?" I ask.

"Five hundred dollars."

"I bet Bryce would enjoy Vermont," Anton says. "Don't you?"

"Well—" I'm not about to write his name down.

"Guess we'll find out," Anton says. He picks up a pen, and a moment later Bryce Campeau has bid seven-hundred-fifty dollars on a weekend in Vermont.

"You are such a prankster." I chuckle.

"Actually, I've given up pranks this year." He smooths the lapels of his jacket. "Except if it's for charity."

"Very noble of you." Fiona giggles.

"Look at this," Charli says, rolling her eyes. "Neil Drake bid on a golf club. Who would have guessed?"

"He's not winning," I point out.

"We can fix that." Charli grabs the pen out of Anton's hand, and with an evil grin, she adds another bid to the sheet.

"Charli!"

"He can afford it," she says. "With a name like that?"

"Neil?" I ask.

"His full name is Cornelius Harmon Drake the third. His grandpa made a fortune leasing private jets."

"And you know this how?" Fiona asks.

"Google." She puts down the pen. "Now let's get our drink on."

Bryce reappears with a tray full of drinks a few moments later. I help him pass them out, and then I take my chance to get him alone. "Would you take a walk with me?" I whisper. "I'm curious about what's outside." There's a set of double doors open to some kind of patio. I see firelight and deeply cushioned sofas.

I turn toward the open doors, hoping my ploy works, and Bryce follows patiently. It's quieter out here, which is good, because I have things I need to discuss.

But *wow*. The patio is walled with brick and topiaries in interesting shapes. It's lit with torches, hanging strings of mini bulbs, and a wood fire burning in a giant hammered copper bowl. As I take it all in, the first strains of jazz music begin to play from inside the building.

My cocktail is ice cold against my hand, but in spite of the cool night air, I feel warmed from within. Tonight is such a welcome shift in my life. I have friends. I have my hockey team, where I may eventually make a contribution. I have a glamorous party in a bustling city.

And I *feel* beautiful. Fiona was right that dressing up could make a difference. I must be a simple, visual creature, too. Because I feel alive with possibility, whether Bryce can see it or not.

"Shall we sit?" I ask. "That looks cozy." I point to a sort of hanging hammock chair that seems designed for couples.

"That? Is that *furniture?*"

Ah, Bryce. My cute little traditionalist. *Some men need a push*, Fiona had said, and I agree with her. But falling out of a hammock chair might not have been what she meant.

So I abandon the hammock thing and turn in the other direction. "Isn't this a cool spot for a party?"

"Yes. But are you cold?" He eyes my bare shoulders, and I have to hold back my smile. *Finally!* The man isn't blind after all.

"Not cold at all," I say. "This is fun." We continue our slow circuit of the patio together, as other partygoers also spill out of the building, drinks in hand, talking and laughing.

"How was practice this week?" Bryce asks. "Better?"

"Much," I assure him. "I'm getting back in the swing of things. Coach told me yesterday that she was impressed with my work ethic."

"Hey!" His eyes light up. "That's great."

"We scrimmaged today, and I only let in one to Scarlet's three."

"*Magnifique!*" Bryce is animated now because I'm speaking his love language—hockey.

"But that's not what I wanted to discuss with you."

"No? What, then?"

I take a deep, measured breath. "Us. I want to talk about us."

"Us?" he repeats, as if he's forgotten the word.

"You and me, together," I add, just to clear up any ambiguities.

"You want to have that conversation right now? In this busy place?" He glances around, incredulous. We're standing near the open doors, where the party rages inside. The band is playing, and people are dancing already.

"It doesn't *have* to be here," I say with a shrug. "We could go back to my place right now. It's *very* quiet there."

He stares. "Right now."

"Right this very second," I say, dropping my voice into a sultry register. I'm daring him. It's childish. But he's the one who sent me all the mixed signals. He has it coming.

Bryce looks conflicted. His cool eyes do a slow trip down my body.

Yes!

Then he sighs. "I do not think it is a good idea."

My heart crashes. *Why?* I nearly shout. Why does Bryce need to overthink it?

But goalies don't panic. "Look, you're very confusing to me. We

102

did have a conversation once about us. As a couple. I didn't dream that, right?"

He looks down, and shakes his head. "No. That was a mistake, Sylvie. I should not have said those things to you. And we should not have another big conversation now."

A *mistake*. Wow. Okay. "Thanks for clearing that up." I set my nearly empty cocktail down on a ledge. "Sorry to be your *mistake*."

"You are *not*." He makes a noise of frustration. "All the mistakes are mine."

So here we are again. I know better than to be surprised, I guess. What I am is frustrated. Inside, the band is playing a fast song now—a swing tune. I can either stand here and argue with Bryce, or redirect all of my frustrations. "Dance with me, then," I say, holding out my hands. "That's all I ask."

"Have you ever seen me dance?" he asks, an embarrassed smile forming on his rugged face.

"No, Bryce. But that doesn't mean you can't."

He takes my outstretched hand, and my heart lifts as he brings it to his lips and kisses it.

But then he drops my hand. "*Je suis désolé*, Sylvie. I am sorry to disappoint you." Then he turns away, and disappears into the crowd.

FIFTEEN

The Twist

ANTON

AT SOME POINT in their conversation, Sylvie and Campeau switch to French, so I can't understand what they're saying. But I don't need to know French to understand what's just happened. Sylvie entreated him to go home with her. And then she asked him to dance.

And that damn fool said no. *Twice.*

The look on her face makes me want to punch him. I'm not kidding. I have never hurt a friend, or even wanted to. But there's a first time for everything, apparently, because the pain in her eyes is not okay.

Fiona makes a beeline for Sylvie. Their heads bend in conversation, with Fiona's eyes darting toward Campeau and then back to Sylvie.

"Excuse me, ladies." I approach them both. "I have a couple items of business with you two."

"Really?" Fiona asks. "But Baby Bayer, this is a social occasion."

I pull my wallet out of my back pocket. "First, I owe you twenty bucks. Three goals in three games, minus the goal I got this week."

"Aw, shucks," she says, taking the bill I offer her. She folds it in thirds and then tucks it into her bra. Fiona is a hoot. "Thank you for the timely payment. And congratulations on your goal."

As we joke around, I watch Sylvie take a deep breath. Then she straightens her spine and lifts her head, replacing her defeated posture with her game face.

"The second thing is, who wants to dance?" I hold out a hand to Sylvie, and then I have to shout because the band has just begun playing a Chubby Checker classic. "Can you do the twist?"

"How hard could it be?" she asks, grasping my hand like a lifeline. "Let's twist."

"Fiona?" I ask, not to be exclusive.

"You two go ahead," she says with a bright smile. "I'm going to mingle."

I lead Sylvie onto the dance floor, and start to move my hips. Dancing is one of my specialties, although many athletes are excellent dancers. Sylvie is no exception. She knows how to move. The twist is a somewhat silly dance, and I'm a somewhat silly man, so I twist with enthusiasm.

It isn't long until she's smiling, and the color is back in her cheeks.

Sylvie could bring a man to his knees. My crush on her was already a rager, but tonight it's an inferno. The black dress she's wearing is made of soft, touchable fabric. And the way it's cut, showing off her smooth shoulders, and her long, kissable neck...

Unngh.

And don't even get me started on her legs. In those heels, they look long enough to wrap around me twice. And I'm the lucky guy who's dancing with her.

How *could* a man say no to her? It boggles the mind.

When the song ends, and the band moves into a slow song, I don't even think, I just pull her a little closer and put an arm around her waist.

She looks at me with those big brown eyes. I've got a couple inches on Sylvie, but she's wearing killer heels. We're nearly nose to nose, and I take a long breath of her perfume and feel several inconvenient emotions at once.

"Thank you," she breathes.

"For what?"

Her eyes soften. "For asking me to dance when I got shot down."

"Like it's a hardship," I whisper. "I am not the kind of guy who criticizes his friends. But I will say that I just don't understand some people."

Her eyes dart to the side. "I'm mad at myself for caring. Did you ever carry a habit too long in your game?"

"My game." I blink. "You mean hockey?"

"Yes, hockey." Her eyes flash with humor. "Follow along, Bayer."

I grin, because this girl kills me. "You mean, like, hesitating on the pass?"

"Exactly," she says, patting the lapel of my tux. "You realize the hesitation is wrong, and you know you need to fix it. But you've been doing it so long that it's hard to stop."

"Sure? Of course. All the time."

"That's me and Bryce. I thought we would end up together. And I do love him. This has been a difficult year for me, though. So even when it began to be clear that he doesn't feel the same, I still held onto it. I pictured our future together. It got me through some difficult things."

"I see."

"It's a habit now. I even tried making him jealous. I went on dates with men that were not interesting to me." She rolls her eyes. "But in the back of my mind, I was still stuck on him. And—" She frowns.

"What?" I ask, turning her in a slow circle. Dancing with her is the best thing that's happened to me all week, even if she is talking about another man.

"This will sound crazy. But my mother thought we would be a couple."

"She did?"

Sylvie nods. "Yes. And that made me hold on against reason, *non?*" A bit of French creeps into her accent when she talks about her mother. "It's hard to let go of the past."

"Maybe he just needs time," I hear myself say. "And maybe he needs a push."

"You sound like Fiona." She rolls her eyes. "But I don't think they make dresses any shorter than this one. He didn't even notice."

"Put him out of your mind," I whisper. "Just for a few minutes. And put your arm around my neck."

Sylvie doesn't ask why. She slips a hand higher on my shoulder, bringing us closer together. Her other hand is clasped in mine, her palm warm and steady.

I slide a hand up the buttery velvet of her back. And as the music swells, I dip her carefully toward the floor as a big smile breaks out on her face.

When I ease her back into a vertical position, we're nose to nose. "You are a ridiculously good dancer," she whispers.

"The party boys always are," I say, shrugging off the compliment as if it doesn't matter. But it does. I feel a sharp awareness of everywhere we're touching. And I can't help the way I'm looking deeply into her eyes.

Sylvie stares right back at me. And then her hand finds the back of my neck, where her fingers sift through the short hair at my nape. Maybe she's trying to make Campeau jealous. But my body doesn't know that. Every nerve I possess sits up straight and sings hallelujah.

"Any man could lose his heart to you," I whisper. "So easily."

"Just dance with me," she whispers back. "I'm done talking about him."

I hadn't been talking about him, though. I'd been talking about me. We're slow-dancing in the midst of a sea of people. This party is huge. But as far as I'm concerned, there's only one other person in the room, and I'm holding her in my arms, the way I've wanted to do since the first day I saw her.

Sylvie never breaks our gaze. She's either a terrific actor, or she's feeling a tiny shred of what I'm feeling. I hope nobody is watching, because there's no way to hide how I feel right now, my hands full of velvet, my body swaying with the slow beat of desire.

She leans in, her soft cheek brushing against mine. "You're doing it," she whispers.

"Hmm?" I ask, my voice too thick to speak.

"You're looking at me the way a man is supposed to look at a woman."

"Mmm," I say, turning her slowly, in our own little world. She's right, but I don't know how to stop.

"I think I'm done with this party. Take me home, Anton," she says quietly. "Would you do that for me?"

My heart skips a beat. "Sure."

SIXTEEN

A Little Safety Pin

SYLVIE

I WATCH Anton's slow blink when I ask to be taken home. He isn't sure if I mean *escort me home* or *take me home to bed*. But I have a hunch he'd be good with either scenario.

I'd meant the latter one. I'm tired of carrying a torch for a man who doesn't want me. And I'm *really* tired of being the only girl in Brooklyn who goes to bed alone every night.

Anton accompanies me to the small lobby of the building and asks me if I have a ticket for the coat check. I hand it to him silently, and he retrieves my coat, tipping the attendant, and then slipping it on me like a gentleman.

Outside, he summons a cab with a sharp whistle, then politely waits for me to get in, before seating himself a respectable distance away from me on the seat. "Water Street and Bridge, please. In DUMBO."

The cab glides away from the curb, and I look out the window at all the happy people out on a fine autumn evening. I'm tired of waiting to live my life, and I'm not going to do that anymore. I'm going to have to be clear about my intentions.

Without glancing his way, I slide my hand across the seat until I find his.

He takes mine without hesitation, flipping it over, and then tracing a sensuous circle around my palm.

I close my eyes and just appreciate the sensation. Anton is a true friend, and I don't want to wreck that. I also know he's a player in every sense of the word.

But if he's in the mood to escort me into my bedroom and remove this dress, I'm in the mood to experience it.

Even though we hit every traffic light, it's only a ten-minute ride. As the driver loops around to turn onto our street, I remove my hand from Anton's and dip into my coat pocket for the credit card I have zipped in there.

"No, I got it," Anton says, pushing a bill through the slot toward the driver.

I let him pay and slide across the seat to get out of the cab. My heart is thumping with expectation. He's waiting for me on the sidewalk. "I'll walk you to your door," he says.

"Actually, would you mind coming up?" And then I remember something crucial. "Fiona had to pin me into this dress. I could use some help with the safety pin. There's a glass of wine in it for you."

His eyes darken, and then his forehead creases with uncertainty. I can tell I've caught him off guard. He's not sure if I mean what he thinks I mean.

I let a beat of silence pass between us, while I hold his exceptional gaze. "Please," I say in a low voice.

"Okay," he says in an even lower one.

Wordlessly, he takes my hand in his. We're both afraid to blink, maybe. That must be why we stare at each other for another long moment.

And then Anton makes his decision. He looks away, checks for traffic, and then leads me across the street. With my free hand, I pull my keys out of my zipper pocket, and open the outside door. A moment later we're both climbing the stairs toward my empty apartment.

The mood is solemn as I open my apartment door. It's dark in our little living room, and I switch on only the dimmest lamp.

"You've done some decorating," Anton says, glancing around as he removes his tux jacket and lays it over the arm of the huge sofa. "Looks nice."

"Thank you." Fiona and I have added a coffee table and pillows. There are vintage posters framed on the walls. It's a nice little home.

But none of that matters right now. I'm a woman on a mission. I don't offer Anton the glass of wine that I mentioned. Instead, I march over to him before he can sit down. "It's a little safety pin. Right here." I touch the back of my neck.

"Of course," he says in a silky voice.

A big hand sweeps the hair off my neck. I'm so primed for his touch that even this makes my breath hitch. The heat of his palm on my body gives me a sudden case of goosebumps, and I close my eyes, concentrating on the sensation of a powerful man's gentle fingers on the sensitive nape of my neck.

He hums under his breath as he locates the safety pin tucked under the fabric, and carefully frees it from the dress.

"There," he says quietly as the velvet begins to slip against my skin. "Ah, careful." He pauses, holding the dress in place, because that narrow circle of fabric is the only thing holding up the top of the dress. It wants to slip down my body.

I don't make a move to help him. I don't reach back, and I don't let him off the hook. Instead, I reach for his free hand, and wrap it around my hip. And then I lean back against him, taking in the heat of his hard chest through his tuxedo shirt.

I hold my breath. Because I want this. No, I need this. I'm so tired of waiting and wanting. And Anton's nearness has always done swoopy things to my stomach.

Why not now? Why not him, and why not me?

"Sylvie," he whispers, and it sounds like a prayer. Then he drops the collar of the dress, and it slides like a silky waterfall down my upper body, until stopped by the zipper.

Then? I reach back and tug the zipper down slowly.

Cool air hits my skin. Anton makes a low groan of protest as the dress continues to slide, exposing my lacy strapless bra. Then soft lips slip across the back of my neck. "Is this what you're asking me for?" He kisses the juncture of my shoulder.

"Yes."

"And this?" His tongue darts out to taste my skin, and my goosebumps redouble.

"*Yes*," I gasp.

He kisses me again, his mouth growing bolder and less gentle. Wet, open-mouthed kisses swirl against my skin, and then he taunts me with his tongue.

Hell, I feel it in my nipples. I feel it *everywhere*. And I tilt my head to give him better access. He groans again, tasting my skin, tongueing each new inch, sucking lazily where it suits him before moving on.

It's absurd how quickly I get wet. I had no idea a man could get me so hot by kissing my neck. I want more, so I try to turn around.

But Anton tightens his arm around my waist, fighting me. He pins me in place, my back to his chest, and he continues the erotic assault on my bare shoulder.

My breasts feel achy, and I've started to shake. The brace of his hard body makes me sweat. "Please," I beg. I'm in a hurry now. More. Hotter. Faster.

"Slow the fuck down," he hisses. "If we're making this trip to the land of reckless decisions, I'm gonna enjoy the ride. Now hold still."

I stand quietly on loose knees, while Anton locates the zipper where it's trapped at my hips. He eases it down at a torturous pace. I fight off a shiver as he drags his fingertips down my bare back, past the lace of my bra, and all the way onto my lacy black panties.

My dress falls into a silky heap at my feet.

"Jesus, Mary, Mother of God," he whispers, as one big hand massages my ass cheek. "You're stunning, Sylvie."

No one has ever paid me such a compliment, in such a reverent tone. And nobody has ever run his hands over my ass the way he's doing now—his touch a mixture of wonder and ownership.

This is exactly what my life has been missing.

Again, I try to turn around, and this time he lets me. I look up into that incredible gaze. "Take me to bed now, Anton. You know you want to."

He swallows roughly. I see a flicker of something dark cross those bright eyes. "If this is really what you want." He lifts his chin toward the bedroom. "Lead the way."

"It is," I assure him. Then I step out of the circle of my dress and lean down to pick it up, wearing nothing but see-through black lingerie and my heels.

"Jesus fuck," he mutters in a voice that sounds almost angry. The moment I'm vertical again, he yanks my hips toward his body as his mouth crushes mine.

I wasn't expecting the kiss, but I *am* a professional goalkeeper, and pretty damn good at catching things flying my way. So it only takes me a split second to adjust to the friendly assault of Anton's aggressive mouth. His lips stroke mine urgently. I lean in and kiss him with everything I've got.

He tilts his head and brushes his tongue across the seam of my lips. His roughened hand cups my jaw, his thumb sliding over my cheekbone. It's possessive in a way that makes my heart stutter.

It doesn't matter that I'm in way over my head. It doesn't matter that I've never actually been naked with a man before. When I chose this one, I chose well.

This was *exactly* what I wanted. As Anton's tongue pushes inside, I feel even luckier than I had before. This man has always made my heart beat a little too fast. Call it chemistry. Call it luck. Call it intuition. But why have I been ignoring the possibility of *this*?

A naughty hand slides down my thigh, lifting my leg to wrap around his body. And then I'm balanced on one high-heeled foot, braced against him in a wanton pose that would be ridiculous if it weren't so hot. My bare thighs slide against the smooth wool of his trousers. And, hello, there's a *very* hard cock bumping between my spread legs.

I moan into his mouth as his kisses continue to destroy me. Our teeth click as he tilts his head, searching for an even more thorough way to torture me.

This seduction was my idea, but there's no mistaking who's in control right now. And it's not me. My mind turns to a static fuzz as I hold tightly to his body and allow each plundering kiss to roll through me.

I'm not even surprised when he manages to slip his other arm down to scoop me completely off the ground. Then I'm airborne for a short time while he maneuvers into my bedroom, kicking the door shut behind him.

He sets me down carefully beside my bed. Drunk from his kisses, I put a steadying hand on his shoulder as I make a move to remove my shoes.

"Don't," he rasps. "Leave them on."

"Okay?" It had never occurred to me to leave them on, but I'm prepared to do whatever this man says.

I can't resist reaching up to tug one end of his bowtie. The satin gives way, and I unravel it, sliding it all the way out of his collar. I toss it on the bed, and then reach for the buttons on his shirt.

In the darkness of my room, the white buttons are a little hard to spot on the white shirt. I get most of them, though, before Anton gets impatient. With one quick yank, he snaps the last two buttons off, and one of them hits the wall with a pop.

Did he just...?

"Lie down," he says. "On your back."

I reach behind my body for the clasp of my bra. "Should I—"

"Leave it," he says.

"Yessir," I say, meaning to make a joke. But his eyes flare. There's that look again—like he's half desperate, half angry.

I don't know why I like it, but I do. I lie down on the bed, my heart thumping wildly. My bra feels too tight, and the scrap of lace serving as my panties are soaked. I just want them gone.

Luckily, the view keeps improving. Anton works his way out of his tux trousers and toes off his shoes. His body is lit only by light leaking in from the street lamps, but it's enough to make a girl crazy. Those strong shoulders flex and pop as he leans down to discard his socks and underwear. A dusting of sandy blond hair glints across his pecs.

And when he stands upright again, I can only stare. No man has ever stood at the foot of my bed, his thick cock jutting proudly forward, ready for sex with me.

I'm not afraid. Although the mechanics of how I'm going to accommodate *that* are not a hundred percent obvious.

He puts a knee on the bed, and I wait for him to kiss me again. But that's not what happens. Instead, he leans down to my breast and tongues my nipple through the lace fabric.

"Oh," I gasp, because it feels so good. My nipple is hard and achy, and then he actually bites me gently. It's so unexpected that I have to squeeze my thighs together against my desire.

I hear a chuckle. Then he tugs the bra down a couple inches until I spill over the top of it. This time, the first swipe of his tongue makes me moan shamelessly. And the bra is really a problem. I want nothing between us at all. So I reach back and give it a tug. It releases on the first try.

"Naughty," he breathes, flinging the bra away. "I was enjoying that."

"But—"

He presses a sudden kiss to my lips, shutting me up, as he grabs both my hands and hoists them overhead. His body covers mine. Finally. The hard heat of him is everything I ever wanted.

"Did you know?" he mumbles into my mouth as we kiss, fast and messy.

"What?" I pant, threading my fingers through his. I flex my stomach muscles and roll my hips, just to feel more of him rubbing between my legs.

"How much I've wanted to fuck you?"

"No," I whimper, lifting my knees to wrap my legs around his ass. "Maybe you could get on with it, then."

He actually snorts. "You'll wait until I'm ready. And I'm not nearly ready." Then he lowers his cock between my legs and grinds down until I whimper.

We fall into more of those soul-deep kisses that I've waited far too long to taste. I'm ready for him to take me completely apart.

And I doubt I'll ever want to be put back together again.

SEVENTEEN

There's Nowhere to Hide

ANTON

I'M ON FIRE, kissing Sylvie like a man possessed by the devil.

For two months I've had fantasies about her. But none of them unfolded like this—with Sylvie luring me up to her apartment and bidding me to remove her dress.

Take me to bed, she'd said. I'm not a strong enough man to turn her down, no matter the complications.

This is a fluke, and I know it. In fact, I'm probably going to wake up in a minute to find that I've fallen asleep in front of the TV with a half-eaten Dorito on my chest. Because this resembles a really good dream far more than it resembles real life as I know it.

Either way, this is probably my one and only chance. And you'd better believe I'm going to make it last.

Pulling back, I break our kiss, only to kiss my way down her throat while she shivers. Her hands ruffle through my hair, and I groan against her skin.

Trailing my lips down her body, I pause and tease her tummy with my tongue.

"Anton," she pants. "Please."

Pinch me, already. I never thought I'd hear her moan my name. And I really want to hear it again, so I slide even farther down, until my feet hit the floor, and I can lift those long legs over my shoulders. Dipping my chin, I breathe hotly against her pussy, which is still trapped in lace.

"*Oh* God," she pants.

I spread her thighs and lower my mouth to the lace. I'm a little rough, a little dirty. Usually I'm sweet with Sylvie, but I was so confused when she invited me upstairs that I lost my manners. I dropped the facade of indifference that I usually carry when we're in the same room. What's left is a hungry animal.

The sweet scent of her is making me insane. I lick and tease her through the lace until she's riding my mouth and nearly sobbing. Her heels are digging into my back, and I'm practically rutting against the bed.

And the soundtrack running through my head is *mine mine mine*. And *finally*. I've never been so turned on, because I've never wanted anyone as badly as I want her. When I can't take it anymore, I lift my head and look up at her. She grips the comforter with long fingers, and her exquisite chest rises and falls rapidly.

"Condom?" I pant.

She gestures with a shaky hand toward the bedside table. The packet is waiting right there on the surface, at the ready.

I feel it like a punch in the gut. That condom was waiting there, but not for me. I'm just the backup plan.

Fuck. That stings. But not enough to give up this chance.

I reach over and take the packet in hand, then slowly tear it open. Sylvie watches me with hungry eyes. She chose me as her backup plan for a reason, right? I'm the player who's good in bed. Always up for a good time. She's heard the talk.

I give my cock a slow stroke, putting on a show, and then roll the condom on. The truth is that I *am* an excellent lay. She won't be disappointed. I'm going to make sure she remembers this for a long time.

Stretching out beside her, I prop myself up on one hand. "You're so lovely," I whisper as my other hand coasts down her sleek body. I pause to roll one of her nipples between my thumb and forefinger, and she gasps in surprise.

"Kiss me, darling," I murmur. And she doesn't need a second invitation. She pulls me in for a kiss that's both hot and sweet.

My hand skims farther down her body, between her legs, until I finally reach beneath her panties and sample the slick evidence of her desire. She moans into my mouth, and then reaches down to free herself of that last scrap of lace.

I tug them off and fling them across the room. I might as well be flinging my heart across it, too. This girl is already under my skin. I didn't ask to fall for her. It sure isn't convenient. But as I slowly pleasure her, teasing her opening with one blunt finger, I know there's no place I'd rather be.

Sylvie lets out a soul-deep moan. Her hands are everywhere now. They're skimming across my pecs and coasting down my abs. Her tongue is in my mouth, and those sexy shoes finally hit the floorboards with matching thunks.

This is it. There's nothing left between us except a condom and my evaporating sanity. I stroke her until she's close to the brink, but I'm too selfish to let her go over without me. I want her staring into my eyes as she comes.

Abruptly, I roll on top of her, position myself, and slide home. Heat grips me tightly. Sylvie takes a startled breath that echoes my own shock.

So tight. So good. I'm afraid to breathe, because it might wake me from this exquisite dream. We blink at each other for a long beat, and then I spread my body over hers, because I need to feel more of her skin against mine.

Bracing myself on my forearms, we come nose to nose. Her color is high, and her breathing is rapid. I didn't intend to slow things down, but I find that I can't pass up lingering over this moment of our joining. She stares back at me—as if we're both surprised that the evening brought us here.

Then Sylvie reaches up and puts both hands on my face. "Anton," she breathes.

"Sylvie, darling," I say with a reverence that probably gives me away.

She doesn't say anything more. She arches her neck to kiss me, and I can't resist. I fall into her mouth like I fall into the sweetest dreams.

Long arms wrap around me, and then I'm really doing it. I'm

fucking the girl that I'm falling for, in slow, deep thrusts. Those long legs I've been dreaming about hug my ass.

It's heaven. A sweaty, urgent heaven, where the angels have strong thigh muscles and moan on every stroke.

The sounds she makes are beautiful, too. I pick up the pace, just so I can hear more of those breathy moans. It kills me the way her brown eyes soften with a lusty haze.

My stamina is always on point, but this is a big moment for me. I'm approaching the edge of my control. It's all the soul-deep eye contact. There's nowhere to hide.

She gasps with dismay when I pull out. With movements that are eager, bordering on rude, I urge her onto her hands and knees. She drops her head on a happy moan as I fill her again, her hips in my hands.

Having put a little more space between us, I calm down and do some more of my best work. My hands are free to touch and rub and tease.

Since my mouth is also free, a string of sweet and dirty encouragements pour forth. Words like *darling* and *gorgeous* and *need you* and *yes yes omigod yes*.

I don't know half the things I say, but I mean all of them.

My body is many things. On the ice it's a lethal weapon. Off the ice it's a delivery vehicle for laughter, hunger, and pleasure. But as I strain in the dark against the most amazing woman I've ever met, it's also a font of panting, overwrought emotion. I've never given more than I am right now.

I've never needed so badly to be seen by anyone. But I faced her away from me, so that she wouldn't notice.

"Give it to me," I whisper in the dark. "All of it. Are you going to give it to me?" I babble.

"Yes," she pants.

"That's my girl," I croon. I push her down on the bed, my hand wedged between her legs. My next thrust causes her to grind against my palm.

She lets out a moan of pure excitement.

"Who's making you come?" I whisper. "Say it." I give her another slow thrust, and her thighs shake and quiver.

"Anton!" she sobs. "Please. Harder."

My body flashes even hotter, and I give the lady what she wants. More of me. More of the ache I feel when I hear my name on her lips.

I'm shaking now, letting out a brutal grunt with each stroke. We're wrapped together in a knot of skin and muscle and need. And then she lets out a deep moan of victory, and her body pulses around mine. She buries her face in the pillow and sobs.

I can't hold back any longer. I break as if on command, following her lead, spilling the last shred of my sanity into the condom before collapsing beside her.

She rolls immediately into my embrace, her arms around me, her hair wild.

Even now I can't stop my words of praise. *Yes* and *sweet thing*, and *so beautiful*. I kiss her eyelids and her mouth and her chin.

Breathless, she parks her forehead against mine, and I stare into those brown eyes. And at least for this moment I have everything I ever dreamed of.

EIGHTEEN

Ice Ice Baby

ANTON

IT'S LUCK, really, that my phone wakes me up at all.

But at some point, when one of us was returning to bed in the darkness, Sylvie's bedroom door was left open a crack. And in the depths of my dreams, I hear my phone in the other room, blasting "Ice Ice Baby," the alarm tone I use for waking up for a road trip. After a few bars of Vanilla Ice's one-hit wonder, my eyes fly open in alarm.

I'm still not over the humiliation of missing the team jet that time last year. I sit up and quickly realize that I'm naked in Sylvie's bed. She's passed out cold, face down in the pillow beside me.

Whoa.

I slide quickly out of the bed, dart into the living room, and locate my tux jacket on the couch. Quick as I can, I silence Vanilla Ice.

That's when her roommate's door opens a crack, and Fiona's head pokes out. Her eyes widen comically as she catches me standing there, obviously naked, even if the tux jacket is shielding the important bits.

Her face breaks into a big smile. Then she withdraws into her room and shuts the door again.

Fuck. I really don't want to become the next gossip nugget on the women's team. I promised Eric that I'd be the least interesting player on the Bruisers' roster this year.

I promised myself, too.

I'll have to worry about that later, though, because I have a plane to catch. My apartment is just across the street, but my morning routine is still going to suffer.

I tiptoe back into Sylvie's bedroom, where she's still sleeping like the dead. I pull on my clothes, except for my bow tie and one sock which does not want to be found. Then I perch on the edge of the bed to say goodbye to Sylvie. I run a hand down her hair.

She doesn't move. So I lean down and kiss her shoulder. She sighs contentedly, but does not roll over.

A real man doesn't slink out of a woman's bedroom, so it's time for Plan B. I glance around until my gaze lands on a pack of sticky notes on her bedside table. I grab one, but there's no pen, so I burn a couple more minutes locating one on the coffee table in the living room.

I dash my thoughts on a note and leave it for her to find. It's not Shakespeare, but it will have to do. I *really* have to go. So, after patting my pockets for my phone and keys, I get the heck out of her apartment and run down the stairs.

I probably look frightful in last night's untucked shirt and tux, wearing one sock, no less, as I dash across Water Street and into my building.

I'm on the verge of calling out a greeting to Miguel, my favorite concierge, when the elevator doors open. I move on instinct, darting behind the big wooden desk where Miguel runs the world, crouching low as a pack of my teammates shuttles out of the elevator and towards the front door.

"Morning, boys," Miguel says calmly, while I crouch like a loser beside his trouser-covered legs. "Your car is outside."

"We missing anyone?" Castro's voice says. "Where's Baby Bayer?"

I drop my head, wondering how I get myself in these jams. This was supposed to be the year that I acted like a grownup. But if my teammates saw me like this, they'd want to know where I was last night, and I'm not willing to say. I haven't quite processed it yet.

"You know, he's running a little late," Miguel says. "He asked me to get him another car and said you shouldn't wait."

"Thanks, man."

I hear the shuffling of feet as my teammates roll their suitcases out the revolving door. Finally, I stand up with a sigh.

"Rough night?" Miguel asks.

"Not really. But I didn't want to answer questions." Even as I say this, I'm ducking around the desk. "You're my rock, Miguel. Can I have a car in—?"

"Eight minutes," he says, poking at his phone. "Sprint, boy. You got a plane to make."

I run for it.

I SET a land-speed record for showering and shaving. And because I really *am* capable of learning from my mistakes, my suitcase was already packed and waiting near the door of the generously sized studio loft apartment that I rent from my cousin Eric.

It only takes me ten minutes to get back to the lobby, where Miguel is holding the car. I pass a twenty-dollar bill into his hand as I hurl my bag into the back of the car.

He closes the door on me and off we go.

It's all looking good until we end up behind a fender bender on the BQE. Each of the nine minutes that we inch along takes a year off my life. By the time we're back up to speed, I've sweated through my shirt.

I end up doing a comical sprint into the Marine Air Terminal with my suitcase, locating the right gate by the sight of Heidi Jo's blond hair near the jetway.

Thank the good lord. I made it.

"You're the last one," she says cheerily as she crosses off my name on the flight manifest. "Close call."

Wasn't it ever. A baggage handler takes my suitcase from me, and I step onto the jetway. My heart is still pounding, but I reach the damn plane a moment later. A few of my teammates raise an eyebrow at my tardiness, but Coach Worthington is near the middle of the plane, tucking his suit jacket into the overhead compartment, looking unconcerned.

If he hasn't noticed my late arrival, then I'm good. No harm, no foul. I just need to put this ass in a seat before he sees me. There's only one near the front of the jet.

Right beside Bryce Campeau.

Oh fuck.

He looks up as I hesitate, then moves his magazine off the empty seat. I have no choice but to sit down quickly, tucking my bag under the seat in front of me.

"Good morning," he says.

"Morning," I grunt. It's just sinking in that I'm going to spend the next couple hours trapped here beside him. At least we're side by side, because I don't think I could look him in the eye.

This. This is why I spent the last several weeks trying to ignore all the things I feel for Sylvie. Because I never wanted this moment to arrive.

And yet here we are.

The flight attendant gives her safety spiel, and I listen as though I haven't heard it a million times before. *Bear in mind that your nearest exit may be behind you.*

If Bryce knew what I did last night, I might need an emergency exit.

When she's finished, the jet takes off. I feel the plane lift and then bank toward the south.

As we climb, I close my eyes and try to relax. But the first thing that comes to mind is Sylvie. The taste of her, the softness of her hair between my fingers. The heat of her skin...

My eyes fly open. What the fuck had I been thinking? Now I'm *that* guy—the one who fucked a teammate's... Well, she's not his girlfriend. But they're complicated.

And I just made it worse. I tug at the knot in my tie, loosening it so I can breathe.

"Thank you," Bryce says, dropping his phone into the seat-back pocket.

"For what?" I say, nearly choking on the words.

"Last night I made Sylvie unhappy. She walk away from me

mad. Then I worry she won't be able to get a taxi home from that place. And somebody said you took her home to Water Street. She got home okay, no?"

My skin flashes cold and then hot as he speaks. Of course someone saw us leave together. I wasn't exactly subtle. Christ almighty. "She got home okay," I mutter.

"Good." He sighs.

"But I don't get it," I hear myself say, even though I know I should just shut up. "She came to the party last night looking for you. Why didn't *you* take her home?"

In the silence that follows my question, I can actually picture it, like a movie in my head. Sylvie putting on that dress, thinking of him. And Campeau taking one look at her and leading her out onto the dance floor. It would have been his ass in that cab on the way back to DUMBO. And it could have been him in Sylvie's bed.

I feel sick just picturing it.

I have never *ever* been so confused.

"Let me tell you a story," he says.

"Okay."

"I don't know my father at all. And my mother dies when I am seventeen years old. The last thing she say to me is, 'Buy me some cigarettes you worthless piece of shit.'"

"Jesus." I don't even try to cover my shock. Campeau doesn't open up much, even to his friends.

"Last year, Sylvie's mother dies, too. The last time I see her was during the season—we all have dinner together when we play against Toronto. At dinner, I'm worried about our game. And Marie says to me, 'I am forever proud of you, *mon grand*. No matter what.'"

"Oh," I say stupidly.

"Sylvie is not just any girl," he continues quietly. "She is the daughter of my trusted coach and of the mother of my heart. She is like family."

"So...you don't find her attractive?" I guess that's probably just wishful thinking.

He snorts. "I would have to be a dead man not to find her attractive. But I cannot treat her like a hookup." The word sounds

125

different in his accent. "There is no tryout contract for Sylvie Hansen. There is no walking away. If I say yes to her, I say yes to her forever."

The flight attendant stops beside us. "Coffee and a bagel, gentlemen?"

"Yes, please," I croak, and Campeau also nods.

After she's passed over our provisions, I butter my bagel and try to push Sylvie out of my mind. It's hard to sort myself out when I'm sitting next to Campeau.

But apparently some kind of dam has broken with him, and he can't shut up now. "I don't even know my own father. But Sylvie's father taught me all the best things I know. In hockey and life. I would do anything for that man."

I realize the pickle he's in now. It's not just his relationship with Sylvie that's at risk. It's his relationship to his own past, and to a man he respects. "You think Mr. Hansen would be upset if you were a couple?"

Campeau shrugs. "Maybe not. But I do know that Sylvie is still grieving. She doesn't know what she wants. And I will not toy with her. Christ, she's probably a virgin."

All my circulation stops. And the bagel turns to glue in my throat.

NINETEEN

The Whole Catholic Thing

SYLVIE

LONG AFTER DAYLIGHT ARRIVES, I lay stretched out in my bed, my eyes shut, fighting off the reality of morning.

My thighs ache, probably from yesterday's workout. But I'm also deliciously sore in some places I didn't know I could be sore.

Behind my shuttered eyelids, the night isn't over yet. If I stay in this dreamlike place, I can relive each thrill that Anton gave me. Each stroke of his magic hands across my bare skin.

As first times go, I realize I've hit the jackpot. His obvious skill and devotion to female pleasure make me a very lucky girl.

But that wasn't last night's biggest surprise. It wasn't just the thrills and chills. It was the heady emotional journey that we seemed to take together. His kisses tasted as hungry as mine. His touch was reverent, his words desperate.

Maybe it's all in my head. A girl can imagine a deep connection that isn't really there.

I'm a pro at that, actually.

But it felt so real. Even after the last groan and gasp had passed, Anton's kisses didn't stop. As I floated down from the extreme high of sexual pleasure, his lips continued to trace my neck, and gentle hands smoothed over my hips and down my back.

That part—the aftermath—was just as beautiful to me. I'd never wanted it to end.

Eventually, he'd gotten up to visit my bathroom. I'd heard him running the sink and washing up. Then I'd braced myself for his departure. His team began an eight-day road trip this morning. It's not like he had a lot of extra time to share.

But he hadn't thrown on his clothes and left. Instead, he'd come back to the bed, straightening out the covers we'd tossed around during our sex fest.

Then he'd lifted the covers and slid in beside me.

Feeling blessed, I'd rolled to meet him in the middle, where strong arms wrapped me into the sweetest embrace.

We hadn't spoken much. I'd felt too dreamy for casual conversation. And I don't know what I would have found to say besides *wow* and *thank you* and *please feel free to do that again.*

My silence had also prevented me from blurting out the news that the whole experience had been a first for me. That's nobody's business but mine. And Anton doesn't need the burden of dealing with my strange life choices.

I didn't want him to know, because it would have changed everything. He didn't baby me. His brand of aggressive, bossy, emotional lust was a real eye-opener.

But only metaphorically, because I refuse to open my eyes.

Although I'd already cheated once, when I'd rolled over to discover that Anton had left me a note—short and sweet and just as perfect as our night together.

Sylvie—you are a sleeping beauty. There aren't words to describe last night. Except maybe "Wow." I will call you tonight. —A.B.

And there was a smiley face. When I'd read the note, that smiley face had matched my own.

"Sylvie," comes Fiona's voice through the door, followed by a knock. "Are you still in bed?"

"Yes. So?" I cover my eyes with one arm, as if the extra barrier could prevent the day from arriving.

"Get up. We have to go to brunch."

I search my memory for anything related to brunch and come up empty. "Why? Shouldn't you be at work?" I stretch lazily.

"It's Sunday. Get up. You have twenty minutes to shower and get dressed."

"Or else?" I do not understand the urgency.

"Or else I will combust from all the questions I have for you."

Uh-oh. Fiona seems to know that I wasn't alone in my bedroom last night. Maybe she heard Anton leave. But I'm not about to tell the whole team about my wild night. "It's just going to be you and me at brunch, right?"

"If you don't get up, I'll start inviting other people."

"No!" I throw off the comforter. "Fine. I'm getting up."

"Twenty minutes," she repeats.

Grumbling, I sit up slowly. The daylight pouring through my windows is unwelcome. I have failed to hold onto the night, and now I'm faced with the reality of wild sex hair and Fiona's spike heels askew on the floor.

After easing my naked body off the mattress, I make the bed without changing the sheets. Maybe the bed will still smell like Anton's skin when I climb in again tonight. He'll be in a hotel somewhere, and I'll be here, thinking delicious thoughts.

I lean over to pick up the shoes. *Leave those on*, he'd said. It makes me shiver just hearing his voice in my head.

When I open the closet to grab my bathrobe, a glint catches my eye from the windowsill. Slowly, I belt the robe and then take three paces to the other side of my tiny room. But I already know what I'm going to find there.

It's a hairpin. Copper-colored, this time. And suddenly I have goosebumps again, but not the fun, sexy kind.

"Mom," I whisper. "Maybe there are things you don't want to know."

She says nothing, of course. It's just like my mother to drop in on my life and make a comment, without letting me defend myself. That's exactly what's happening here. I took the wrong man to bed, and she has opinions. She thinks I should be patient and wait for Bryce to love me.

But I'm not doing that. In fact, I'm never doing that again. I am done pining for that man. So, so done.

I toss the hair pin in the box in my top drawer, grab a clean towel, and head for the shower to wash the (excellent) sex off my body.

And I'm not sorry. Not one bit.

FIONA DOES NOT ASK me any questions as I sip my mug of strong diner coffee. And when the pancakes and bacon land in front of me on the table, I think maybe she isn't going to pry.

But then she pounces.

"So... tell me how a very naked Anton Bayer ended up in our apartment last night?"

"Shh!" I glance around the diner, looking for Bombshells. But we're the only ones. "It was just... a happy accident. I was frustrated with Bryce. Anton asked me to dance. I enjoyed it. A lot." He's always gotten a strong reaction from me. It's just that I used to be better at ignoring it.

"Was it his idea?" Fiona asks, leaning forward in her seat, eyes bright.

"Nope." I cut off another bite of fluffy pancakes. "I told him that you'd pinned me into that dress, and that without help I'd be playing hockey in it this evening."

Fiona snorts. "And that's all it took? I should have asked Anton Bayer to remove a pin from my collar ages ago."

My stomach twists unpredictably, which is ridiculous. Anton isn't mine. Still, the idea of Fiona staring into Anton's bright, lust-filled eyes makes me unaccountably queasy.

"It was just a joke, Sylvie," she says gently. "I wouldn't really."

I hide behind my coffee mug. "He doesn't belong to me."

"But he could," she argues. "He's really into you."

"What? No he isn't." I take another fortifying gulp of coffee. "Why would you say that?"

"Because he looks at you the way you looked at that bacon when the waitress set it down."

"They have really good bacon here, though." I pick up a strip and bite off the crumbly edge. "You're confusing me. I thought Bayer only played the field. You said it yourself."

"Well, he's well-known for that." She looks thoughtful. "And men who are afraid of commitment will avoid it even when they really love someone. But he seems to really like you."

"That's ridiculous." Isn't it?

"It's just a feeling I get. But what about you? And how was the sex?"

My cheeks burn. "You ask a lot of questions."

"That good, huh?" She steals a strip of bacon off my plate.

"It was the best of my life," I say, which is obviously ridiculous, since it was the *only* sex of my life.

But Fiona doesn't know that. And somehow I suspect that it will remain true. I'll probably be eighty-one years old and playing cards at the retirement home. And I'll still be able to picture Anton's hungry expression as he hovers over me and...

I pick up my glass of ice water and drink half of it in one go.

"Would you like my ice water as well?" Fiona asks with a knowing smirk. "We could ask for a whole pitcher of ice. Excuse me, miss?" She pretends to look around for the waitress.

"Stop." I give her a kick under the table. "It's warm in here."

"If you say so." She tosses her hair. "So what made it so amazing?"

"Just everything." Even if I were accustomed to talking about my sex life, I still wouldn't be able to explain how completely overwhelming the experience was. From the moment he touched me to unpin my dress, the *intimacy* of it all came as a surprise.

It was so much more than skill and nerve endings. I have such tender feelings for Anton this morning. I don't know how to describe them. But I doubt he feels the same way about me.

"I think Anton is out of my league," I confess.

"What? That's ridiculous. Nobody is out of your league. And, PS, if he thought so, he wouldn't have taken a shot on your net."

I giggle like an idiot at the innuendo.

"And why are you so convinced that he wouldn't like a rematch?"

"Because we're just friends? Or I thought we were? I'm pretty confused. I haven't wrapped my head around it yet."

"Hmm. So if Anton called you tonight and said, 'Hey Sylvie, I can't wait to spend more time with you,' how would you feel?"

"Lucky." And delighted. Like a helium balloon floating upward towards a blue sky.

"Well, that's revealing." She plays with her fork. "And what if it was Bryce who called right this second, apologizing for his stupidity, and asking you to date him seriously. How would you feel?"

"Stunned," I grumble. "I'd ask if he had the wrong number."

"You're angry at him," Fiona says. "Too angry to shout at each other for a while before some sweaty make-up sex?"

"I am still angry," I say slowly. "But anger fades." The problem is that I can't picture a reality where Bryce and sweaty make-up sex belong in the same sentence. When I pictured us together, it was always kind of sweet and quiet. And maybe just a little boring.

You wouldn't think that a single one-night stand could change my life's trajectory. But you'd be wrong. Last night was a real education.

"Are you going to tell Bryce about your hookup?" Fiona asks.

"*Hell* no!" My vehemence startles the old lady at the table next to me, so I drop my voice. "It's none of his business."

"Would he be upset?"

"Yes," I say immediately. "But only out of concern for me. And I'm so tired of his concerns. He doesn't love me, except as a friend. I think I realized it the minute he spotted us in the tunnel that day after our first practice. There was no joy."

Fiona sips her coffee, a thoughtful expression on her face. "That man isn't easy to figure out, I'll give you that. Joy doesn't seem to be part of his vocabulary."

"He can be joyful." It's funny how quickly I will jump to his defense. But I know Bryce very well. He's a wonderful man. It's just that I'm no longer sure if he's wonderful for me. "I don't want to be anybody's project, you know? I want a man who loves me so desperately that it hurts him to be apart. Bryce is not that man."

"Not so much," Fiona says gently.

"And—let's face it—Anton probably isn't that man, either. Am I asking too much?"

"No," my roommate says, pushing her plate away. "I want the

same thing. Except it doesn't have to be a man. It could be a man or a woman. I'm not picky like *some* people."

I laugh.

"Can I ask you a serious question? Does it freak you out that I'm bisexual?"

What? "No way. Why would you think that?"

"Well, it's the whole Catholic thing? The candles? The daily prayer?"

"Oh, please. That's not the kind of Catholic I am."

"What kind are you?"

"The kind who goes out for brunch with you on Sunday instead of going to Mass. The kind who loves everyone. So did my mother, by the way. She considered herself Catholic but she didn't believe the church's teachings about homosexuality, or birth control."

"What about premarital sex?" Fiona asks, eyebrows arched.

I let out a long breath. "I'm not exactly sure."

Fiona signals for the check. "Good thing she doesn't have to know."

Oh, but she does, I think. "I found a hairpin on my windowsill this morning. Do you use those? The U-shaped kind?"

"Never." She gets out her credit card and waves it toward the waitress. "Brunch is on me. You can buy next time, and maybe I'll supply the juicy gossip."

"Gossip that stays between us, no?"

"Absolutely."

IN THE AFTERNOON, as usual, I light a candle for my mother. I say the familiar prayer. And then I sit quietly, watching the flame and wondering if she's judging me right now.

She told me that she thought Bryce and I would be together. And she was rarely wrong.

"I'm sorry, Maman," I whisper into the stillness. "But nobody's record is perfect. And I got tired of waiting."

It comes as no surprise when she makes no answer.

She's not the only one who's silent. I'm also waiting to hear from Anton, of course. His note said he'd call me, but my phone doesn't ring before practice, or after.

And then he's busy playing Ottawa. I watch the game on TV, and whenever the camera pans the bench, I look at the players' determined faces. There's Bryce, his concentration fierce. And there's Anton, his bright gaze fixed on the game.

The announcer spends so much time yapping about the team's current, unprecedented winning streak that I have to mute him just to hear myself think.

When the game is over, the Bruisers have won again. Beacon allowed a single goal, though, so technically their shutout streak is over. But everything is still going well for the Bruisers. I'd love to congratulate anyone who happens to call me tonight.

Nobody does, though.

When I finally turn in for bed, I'd swear that my pillow smells like Anton's aftershave, but it's probably just wishful thinking.

I lie here missing him, feeling unsettled.

TWENTY

Rescue Attempt

ANTON

AT THE CONCLUSION of our week away, I'm at the front of the line to board the jet home. The rest of the team straggles along behind, looking weary. Road trips are always exhausting, but after three wins and a tie, much celebrating was done last night in Detroit.

But not by me.

In the aisle, I toss my carry-on into the overhead bin. Coach Worthington settles into the seat across from me and then dry-swallows two Advil. "I would offer you some. but you look twice as perky as any other man on this plane."

"That's because he went to bed *early*," scoffs Drake, who nudges me out of the way so he can take the window seat beside me.

"Alone, I hope?" quips Danny, the publicist who's traveling with us. "Or, at the very least, with someone who doesn't know how to use the camera on her phone."

"My ass is safe from further publicity," I mumble even as my neck begins to burn at this familiar dig. I'm basically famous for that photo of me asleep in a bed with three women. And I won't ever live it down, apparently, even though Danny knows that only *one* of those women was present when I had my fun.

Her friends had thought it would be hilarious to stage a photo to show they'd had some kind of orgy with the hockey team. They had thought nothing of embarrassing me, and I'd learned a very potent lesson.

That photo is still circulating on the internet. It doesn't matter how many takedowns the reputation-management company serves —it will always be out there somewhere for people to see my sleeping face and my bare butt crack.

"At least she says you were good in bed?" Campeau had said at the time.

I hadn't been flattered. The only good thing about the incident is that it served as a constant reminder that a man can sacrifice his credibility by stepping out of line.

I'd like to say that I no longer needed those reminders, but my behavior last weekend suggests that I still deserve my reputation.

Although I'm working on it.

More hungover hockey players shuffle past us. When the aisle clears, coach reaches across and briefly lays a weathered hand on my forearm. "Jokes aside, I see your seriousness," he says. "You've had your head down this whole trip, thinking nothing but hockey. And I do note it."

"Thanks, Coach."

He picks up his news magazine, and I buckle my seatbelt. Drake is already dozing against the window on his travel pillow.

Coach is only half right, though. I *have* kept my head down on this trip. I turned up promptly for every meeting and every bus ride to the stadium. I made every team meal and even yesterday's yoga class.

But he's wrong to think that my mind has always been focused on hockey. I spent much of the week chastising myself for making such a terrible mistake with Sylvie.

It can't happen again, no matter how badly I desire her. It's too complicated for both of us. And I'm just going to have to live with that.

The problem is that I haven't called her. She probably thinks I'm the kind of dick who forgets about a woman the moment I leave her bed.

I am a dick, but I'm the kind who never should have been with her in the first place and who can barely be trusted not to do it again.

_____

EVEN WHEN WE GET HOME, I still don't call. Her phone number is burning a hole through my phone, and I'm right across the street, but I don't text, and I don't go over there.

Instead, I hit the gym with Drake and Campeau. When they ask if I want to get some beers at the Tavern later, I make vague noises and then fail to show up.

Sylvie might be there, and Lord knows we need to talk, but not at the bar in front of all our teammates. I stay on my couch and watch Dallas play L.A. This is what I need if I'm going to succeed —more focus and calm.

It's easy enough until the following afternoon, when I'm due to show up at the pool for lifesaving class. And, yup—the moment I see her sitting on the edge of the pool, her long legs dipping into the water, smiling at one of our students, I feel my facade start to crumble.

It only gets worse when she turns her perfect chin and looks in my direction. Her expression grows serious as she stands up to cross the pool deck to meet me.

I feel so many things as she walks toward me in her bathing suit and a sporty little Bombshells coverup. Desire. Sorrow. Tenderness. Sylvie just disarms me. One look, and my heart shifts, my internal thoughts changing their rhythm.

All week I've been marching myself around, ruling my consciousness with words like _focus, dedication,_ and _resolve._

But now I look at her and all I can hear is _yes, this,_ and _more._

I am a fool. And it isn't just the sex, which was spectacular. It's _everything._ I want to kiss her hello and ask her about her week. I want to invent a new Frankenword and make her laugh.

But I can't. This is not the time or the place. Her expression is cool, and I know that's my fault. I could have called, but I was too busy feeling like a guilty ass.

Which I am. So now I give her a vague smile. "Hey. How was your week?"

"Quiet," she says crisply. "The Red Cross sent us a stand-in for you." She gestures towards an attractive young man at poolside, holding a training manual. "And I asked him to come back today, because I wasn't sure you'd show."

"Why?" I ask before I think better of it.

Sylvie just gives me a *look*. Like maybe if I'd called her, or replied properly to her text, she wouldn't have to wonder.

"Okay, right. Well, I'm here."

"I see that," she says drily. "Let's do some warmups and then teach some rescue techniques. Fineberger is going to lead them."

She turns away, and it takes me a beat to realize that I've been dismissed. So I shake myself and go over to greet my crew of teen boys.

"Okay, guys!" I say, feigning cheer. "Let's see what progress you made last week. I want four laps for a warmup. Crawl stroke, please."

There's some minor grumbling. But every kid hauls his butt into the pool and starts swimming. It's astonishing how much progress everyone has made with his swimming in just a week. Even Cedric can do a passable crawl stroke now.

"Whoa," I say as he returns after his last lap. "Look at you go."

"I practiced," he says with a shrug. "Where were you, anyway?"

"Road trip. Canada and then Detroit."

"You win?"

"Yeah," I say simply.

The buzz about our season continues to grow. It's dumb to call a team invincible in November, but some of the pundits have already begun. They don't mind piling on the pressure, I suppose. If we crack, they can write something breathless about that, too.

"Cool, cool," Cedric says. "How can a guy score tickets to watch you play?"

"Oh, well..." I'm about to offer him my comp seats, but I realize that I don't have enough to go around. I get two tickets for every home game, but half of those are promised to various people and organizations, and there are seventeen kids in this pool.

Those tickets have a face value over a hundred bucks, and they're scarce. So I can't just hand them to Cedric, even if he is my favorite.

"Tell you what," I say. "Whichever of you gets the two highest scores on the written lifesaving test gets a ticket to an upcoming home game." That's fair, right? It's a contest. I know I have at least a pair of tickets available to give away.

"What if we all tie?" someone asks. "Cause I'm planning to ace it."

"Then I'll be scrambling to find some more seats." In the meantime, I've got another idea. "Hey, Sylvie?"

She turns in my direction, smooth shoulders swiveling toward me. I have a very inappropriate, yet vivid, memory of rolling her over in bed to take my cock from a new position.

Jesus. I have to take a breath before I ask my question. "When are the next two Bombshells home games?"

"Friday and Saturday," she says before turning around, dismissing me again.

Friday and Saturday are too soon to pull this off. I'm away on both of those days, and I don't have the rest of my schedule memorized. "Tell you what, crew. I'm gonna find a date to sponsor a hockey night at the Bombshells game. Everyone in this pool will be welcome. I'll cover a block of tickets and food."

"Cool!" Cedric asks with a grin. "You can get those tickets easy?"

"Yeah, it's a newer team," I say quickly. The Bombshells are selling out sixty percent of an arena that's a tiny fraction of the size that we play in. But that means I can get the seats.

"I'm in!" he says.

"Me too!" yells one of the girls who's treading water nearby. "I want to see Sylvie play."

Sylvie gives her a tight smile, and I realize that she might *not* see Sylvie play. And now I feel like a dick again.

I guess I'd better get used to that feeling. It doesn't seem to be going anywhere.

"You *might* see me," Sylvie says. "There are two goalies, and so my teammate Scarlet might be playing. But come, anyway. It will be fun. Now let's get back to work, okay? We're learning how to save a drowning person today. Everybody out of the pool. Get your towel if you're cold. You need to listen closely to Mr. Fineberger."

The Red Cross guy stands at the front of the group, manual in hand. I hover at the back, half listening as he walks through rescue techniques with a pole, a shepherd's crook, and a flotation device.

He asks Sylvie to be the victim, and I wake up as she peels off that coverup and dives gracefully into the deep end.

The kids practice saving her, while I practice not letting my tongue hang out of my mouth whenever she looks vaguely in my direction.

"Now, what if you don't have a flotation device?" the Red Cross dude asks. "It's much more dangerous to swim out for a drowning person without a float. What's a terrified person going to do when you reach them?"

"Grab your ass," a kid offers.

"That's right. An average of five people die every year while trying to save a drowning person. And most of those fatalities happen when there's no flotation device."

Every face looks serious, and there are no snarky comments coming from our teens now.

"So we're going to show you the right technique for assisting a swimmer who needs help, in a way that keeps you safe." He looks directly at me. "Would you mind rescuing Sylvie?"

"Oh." I clear my throat. "Sure. Not at all." I toss my towel aside and glance into the water where she's treading water with minimal effort. "Incoming."

I leap, gathering my knees to my chest and cannon-balling it right in. The teens are laughing as I pop back above the water, and Sylvie is wiping her face.

"Mr. Bayer would use a split-stride entry if he was guarding a swimming pool," the instructor says sternly. "It's bad form to splash the person you're trying to save."

In other words I've already fucked it up.

"But then again, he'd also use a flotation device. So we have to pretend this is a risky ocean rescue. Now Mr. Bayer, I want you to approach the subject from behind."

Of course he does. And if I hadn't already *approached her from behind*, this would be far less awkward.

"As we said a moment ago, if Miss Hansen is panicked, she'll grab ahold of him."

Sylvie's face grows stony, as if I'm the last man she'd ever reach for during an ocean rescue.

"So if Mr. Bayer wants to keep use of his arms and legs, he should approach from the rear and hook his arms under hers. Don't be shy, Mr. Bayer. Approach the victim."

Call me crazy, but I'm positive my ass is in more danger right now than hers.

TWENTY-ONE

Dumplings as Collateral

SYLVIE

OH, so *now* Anton is shy?

I can feel his hesitation as he swims up behind me. It takes effort not to roll my eyes. If I'd known that Anton would start treating me like a leper, I would have never...

Okay, that's a lie. I would have had the sex anyway. It was phenomenal. And let's face it—if our friendship was so flimsy that it couldn't survive one wild night, then I guess there was never much there worth saving.

Now there's a depressing thought, though. I like Anton. A lot. More than I should.

But he still hasn't saved me from a fake drowning. "Come on, Bayer. I'd be dead already."

All the teens snicker.

Suddenly, two spectacular forearms hook me under my armpits. He gently grasps my shoulders with those strong hands.

"Now put your hand under her chin," the instructor says. "To keep her face above the surface of the water while you swim to safety."

Holy heck. Anton's broad palm cups my chin, his fingers stretching gently across my throat. And then he tips me backward against his bare chest.

I realize two things at once. The first is that I'm still angry. The second is that I enjoy the feel of his hard body anyway. I still crave it. Every night I lie down in my bed and feel turned on just thinking about our night together.

I hate my life.

"Tow her in now," the instructor says. "Kick your feet and do a back stroke or a side stroke. But don't let her go."

As if. We both know he can't wait to let me go.

AFTER CLASS, I tell myself I'm just going to grab a cab and get out of here before he does. There's no way I'm going to stand around looking pathetic, like I'm trying to snag his attention.

It almost works. But when I reach the building's vestibule, I spot him on the sidewalk outside, surrounded by a handful of our students. He's tapping someone's email address into his phone by the look of it.

I walk fast in the other direction, but a student blows my cover.

"Hey, Miss Hansen! We got a question." It's Trina, and she's waving me over.

Anton looks up and—*smack*—that turquoise gaze clobbers me.

"He didn't know if you have a whole list of our emails? For planning our hockey night?"

"That's right," Anton says, looking sheepish. "Do we—by which I mean you—have a way of contacting everyone once I sort out the ticket situation?"

"Sure," I say stiffly. I wish I didn't feel so brittle. The man is doing a nice thing. "I've got a full list. I'll forward it to you."

"Thanks." His smile brightens, and I feel it like a sunburn.

Even before I saw him naked, his attractiveness was hard to ignore. Now it's blinding.

Ow.

I manage a friendly wave goodbye to Anton and his admirers. I glance up the street and see a yellow taxi stopped at the traffic light just a block away. I raise my hand, and the cab starts to roll toward me as the light changes.

Hurry! It can't arrive soon enough. The moment he pulls up beside me, I grasp the door handle and prepare for a fast getaway.

"Hey, Sylvie! Wait up!" Anton calls as I open the door.

Crap.

He's near enough that I can't pretend deafness. And a moment later he's sliding into the taxi beside me. The door shuts with a click, and I'm trapped with the man I can't stop thinking about.

"Hey," he says softly after giving the cabbie his address. "I need to talk to you."

"Now? Did you lose my number?"

He sighs. "I didn't call," he says, stating the obvious. "Because I wasn't sure what to say."

That's certainly not what a girl wants to hear. "Is it really that difficult?"

"Yeah, it really is."

"Why?" I ask, and it comes out sounding more anguished than I'd like.

"Because…" He scrubs a hand over his face. "Because I really liked spending the night with you. Really. A lot. But now I have all kinds of guilt. Like I took, uh, advantage of a situation."

This is not the speech I wanted him to give. So now I'm looking for an out. "You want to do this here? With an audience?" I wave a hand toward the cab driver who's sharing the car with us.

"I guess not," he says levelly. "Fine. You can come over to my place."

"What? No."

"But I ordered lunch—a double order of spicy chicken."

My stomach gurgles without my permission.

"We can talk for a minute."

That sounds awkward. "Did you also get the dumplings?" I hedge.

His smile grows wide. "As a matter of fact I did." And then his phone starts playing a loud ringtone. It's the Bruisers win song —"No Sleep Till Brooklyn."

"Christ. What now?" He pulls out his Katt phone, and I notice the edges are glowing red.

"Whoa. I've never seen that before."

"That means an urgent call from the team," he grumbles. "Usually means I've fucked up somehow."

"Guess you'd better answer." It's not like I'm in a hurry to hear his silly apology, anyway. Not unless he tells me that the reason he didn't call was because our night together was so perfect that he couldn't form words.

"Hey, Heidi," he says after answering.

Even from a couple feet away I can hear her animated voice. "Anton! Why is your father blowing up my phone with a request for free tickets?"

"My father?" Anton asks. "Tickets for when?"

"Tonight."

He groans. "That asshole. I'm sorry, Heidi. He is *not* your problem."

"We are in agreement about that. Unfortunately, tickets are tight tonight. We set aside a block of seats for the Bombshells team. I don't know if they're all planning to attend, but I don't have the time to sort that out."

"I understand," Anton says. "My dad is a piece of work. Not every Bayer is as cool as me and Eric. Those genes sometimes skip a generation."

Heidi Jo laughs. "Just make it stop. He wants five seats. Good luck with that."

"How did he even get your number? Wait—never mind. It doesn't matter. Sorry. See you tonight." He hangs up and scrubs a hand across his face. "So now I get to deal with that."

"Is your father local?" I ask, curious about Anton even when I know I shouldn't be.

"No. He shows up in New York once or twice a year, always expecting a hero's welcome. He's exhausting." He scrolls through his messages and sighs. "Yup. He wants four seats, with eight hours' notice. *Good seats*, it says. One for himself and a client, and two for his kids."

"His kids? Aren't you his kid?"

"Only when it's fun and convenient." His thumbs move over the screen as he shoots off a text. Then he shoves the phone into his pocket as the taxi pulls up in front of his building.

I shove a twenty through the pay window, planning a quick escape.

"Come on, now," he says, seeing right through me. "I wasn't done apologizing." he says.

"What if I'm done being apologized to?"

"Then think of the dumplings. Will you let me feed you lunch and explain myself at the same time?"

"If you keep the explaining to a minimum."

"I'll try." Those beautiful eyes look so sincere that I find myself caving.

"Okay," I concede. Besides—even if I don't like what Anton has to say, I want to stay friends.

Plus, dumplings.

So I follow him into his building. And wow—what a difference crossing the street makes. Anton's lobby is vast, with plush sofas and grand carpets on the marble floor. "Afternoon, Mr. Bayer," says a uniformed concierge from behind a formidable desk. "Should I put in your lunch order?"

"Already done, Miguel. Just send him up when he gets here?"

"No problem, man."

I follow Anton into a shining elevator for a short ride up a couple of stories. "I guess men's hockey pays pretty well."

"True enough," he says. "Although I'm renting from my cousin, Eric. And he doesn't charge me top dollar."

"That's handy."

"You know it. I didn't even need furniture because Eric left everything to me when he moved into his girlfriend's penthouse in Manhattan."

He leads me out of the elevator, down a lovely carpeted hallway and into an apartment that's nothing like I expect it to be. It's one big room, with tall leaded-glass windows set into a red brick wall. At one end is the living area, with a big comfy couch and a TV.

At the other is a sleek kitchen, above which is a loft bedroom. An industrial metal staircase climbs up to a broad landing, where I can see a giant, low-slung bed with a fluffy white comforter and blue velvet cushions.

I realize all of a sudden that I'm staring at Anton's *bed*.

Whoops!

I turn around to find him watching me, a solemn expression on his face. "Can I get you a cherry seltzer?"

"Sure. Thanks." I clear my throat, feeling suddenly uncomfortable. The truth is that I can't seem to stamp out my attraction to Anton, even if I'm mad at him.

In his tidy kitchen, he pours two glasses of seltzer, then squeezes fresh lime and a splash of some kind of high-end cherry syrup into each one. After giving the drinks a quick stir, he brings them to the sofa and sets them onto the coffee table.

"Thank you," I say, taking a fruity sip. "Your place is really nice."

Those blue eyes study me. "Can I grovel now? I'll make it quick."

"If you must. Unless it's some kind of bullshit thing about how you took advantage, or something. Because that's ridiculous."

I get a quick smile for that. "Look, I'm glad to hear that you don't regret me. But I feel like I complicated your life. You have unfinished business with my teammate."

"No way," I scoff. "Not true."

"But you were upset about him just one hour before we…" He clears his throat. "You were, Sylvie. You said so yourself."

Well, crap. He has a point. "But only because I'm stubborn," I point out. "And rejection is never fun. Even before I came to Brooklyn, I already knew how things stood. But I'm the kind of person who likes things clarified. So I sort of forced him to reject me the other night. And—sue me—I didn't like being shot down. But it wasn't actually news."

"Yeah, okay. But there's still a lot of history between you. And he…" Anton sets his glass down and shakes his head.

"He what?" I demand. "Did you *discuss* me?"

"Just for a moment," he says quietly. "He, uh, thanked me for getting you home safely."

"*Oh*." That sounds like Bryce. And I can only imagine how Anton felt receiving this bit of thanks. A snort of inappropriate laughter escapes me, and I clap a hand over my mouth.

"Yeah…" Anton chuckles uneasily. "I was trapped on the jet

next to him. So I asked him why he didn't, uh, deliver you home himself."

My smile dies. "Do I even want to hear what he said?"

"It's not my place to broker information between you." He doesn't meet my eyes. "That's what I'm trying to say—that I can't be the guy who's in the middle of your complications. It's not fair to anyone, and it's not good to keep secrets from my friend and teammate. I can't be that guy, Sylvie. No matter how much I—"

"How much you…?"

He shakes his head. "It doesn't matter. You two have things to say to each other."

"Not really. I thought he cared about me. But I was wrong."

"You're not, though." His voice drops into a husky register, and out comes a whole lot of words at once. "Bryce isn't like me. He doesn't shoot first and ask questions later. There's a lot going on in that guy's head. You have years of history together, and I felt like some dick who just barged in, okay? And here's Bryce—the kind of guy who takes *everything* slowly and carefully, and..." He lets out a frustrated sigh and runs a distracted hand through that same golden hair that felt like silk under my fingers. "Christ, I was a brute."

I almost argue the point, because a brute had been exactly what I was looking for, and I hadn't even known it.

When he lifts his eyes again, they're full of remorse. "I just didn't know what to say to you afterwards," he whispers. "I hope you'll forgive me."

"For not calling?"

"For everything." He gulps, and his regret seems a little over the top if you ask me. Although genuine.

What on Earth did Bryce say to this man unless…

No.

Oh *hell* no. I level Anton with a stare. "Hold on. What did he say about me, exactly?"

Anton shakes his head.

"Did he..." I swallow hard at the horror of it. "He didn't tell you that…"

Anton winces, and that's when I know the ugly truth.

"Oh my God."

When Bryce decided to pour out his conflicted heart, my lack of a sex life might have come up. Which is dumb, Because Bryce doesn't even *know* that I'd never had sex before that night with Anton. He might assume it. But he really has no idea.

And *no right to discuss it with his teammate on the goddamn jet.*

"I'll *kill* him," I thunder. "I'll roast him alive. That's none of his business! And it's also none of yours."

"Sylvie." Anton has his head in his hands. "You're right. And I'm sorry. Bryce was kinda word-vomiting. He isn't the kind of guy to invade your privacy like that."

This is probably true, but I'm still upset. And then I have a brand new horrible idea. "*Wait.* You didn't *tell* him, did you? About us?"

"*No!*" Anton yelps, looking up at me. "Not a goddamn word. I just sat there feeling like the world's worst human."

"For what?" I gasp. "Dancing with me? And then making me feel like the only girl in the world? *God.* It was the best thing to happen to me in a *long* time."

His eyes flare. But I'm not done.

"So if you can't live with yourself, spare me the details. That's so sexist, Anton. You're no better than Bryce installing a lock on a door that doesn't need another lock. You're making decisions about me without considering my point of view. Let me just ask you this —did you enjoy it?"

"*Fuck* yes," he growls.

"But now you regret it? Nobody asked you to do that. I've just spent the last eight days wishing you'd show up at my door and do it again. I *truly* do *not* understand what it is about me that has this effect on men. Where did I go wrong?"

"Nowhere," Anton says. His hands are fists. "You didn't do a thing wrong."

"You say that. And yet you feel this weird need to protect me. When all I want you to do is pin me down and shut me up."

"Sylvie," he groans. "Jesus."

"Maybe we shouldn't have lunch together." I stand up suddenly. "I'm happy to be honest with you, but you don't seem to like what I have to say. And you obviously didn't spend the last week thinking about me as much as I thought about you."

I blow out a breath, and then I make myself turn around and walk toward the door. It takes tremendous willpower, though. There's so much fire in his eyes right now, and it makes my skin feel hot.

And now I'm walking out on spicy chicken and dumplings, damn it. But sometimes a girl has to make a point.

I'm reaching for the door handle when Anton grasps my free hand and spins me around to face him. "Sweetheart, wait."

My stupid knees go a little squishy when I look up to find a whole lot of heat in his expression. "What?" I breathe.

"It's not true," he says in a pained voice.

"What isn't?"

"That I didn't spend the whole week thinking about you. Because I absolutely did."

I swallow hard.

"I just feel really caught."

"Because of Bryce?" I ask.

"Partly. But that's not the only thing. Just like Bryce, I made promises to myself this year. To focus on my team and my game. And then there's the fact that you're a good friend. You're important to me. And I'm not boyfriend material. If you don't believe me, you can google it."

Good grief. I'm going to be friend-zoned again.

"But then there's this thing between us. It's pretty hard to ignore." He scrubs a hand across his face before leaning against the door.

We're just inches from one another as he studies me with those unbelievable eyes. And they can't hide how conflicted he is. Whoever says Anton is a shallow party boy is wrong, damn it. And it only makes me like him more.

"Fuck," he whispers. And I can tell he wants to kiss me. He wants it almost as much as I do. And—

Someone knocks on the door, and we both startle.

"Hell," he whispers. "Food delivery."

I hop away from the door, and Anton answers it. The delivery guy hands the bag to me. Anton thanks him, and then closes the door.

We're alone again, but the moment is broken.

"I want to stay friends," Anton says.

"Friends." Of course he does. Now I'm mad all over again. I open the bag, pluck out one of the dumpling cartons, and shove the bag at him. "Fine. But if you ghost me completely, I'm going to be pissed. I'm keeping these dumplings for collateral."

"Oh sweetheart. I wouldn't ghost you."

"Better not," I snip. And then I leave before I say anything I'll regret.

TWENTY-TWO

The Universal Cures for Heartbreak

SYLVIE

I HEAD HOME and apply the universal cures for heartbreak—a sexy Netflix series and junk food.

Fiona comes through the door at four o'clock. "So Anton didn't show at the pool?"

"Oh, he did," I grumble. "He wants to be *friends*."

She cringes. "I'm sorry. That makes no sense to me."

"Me neither. But I gave up trying to convince men to love me, so…" I hit pause on my show and sit up. "Are we really going to the Bruisers game tonight?"

"Free third-row seats? Hell yes, we are. Don't let two men put you off hockey, Sylvie. You could always root for the other team."

I laugh for the first time in hours. "Yeah, good point."

"I have a text from Anton about the game," she says. "He asked me very politely if there were any Bombshells who couldn't use their tickets. He has family in town."

"Oh, yeah. I heard something about that. His dad sounds like a real tool. Maybe it's genetic." I feel instantly bad for saying this. Because I know in my gut that Anton is not a tool. He's just not ready for me.

Maman is right to warn me away from him. She is always right, damn it.

"I found him two seats," Fiona says. "Can I ask you to meet Eric Bayer in the lobby before the game and hand them over?"

"Sure," I grumble. "No problem. I'll admit that I'm a tiny bit curious about his father."

"Let's face it, he's probably a fox." Fiona gives me a silly smile. "The Bayer family gene pool is spectacular."

"Probably."

She gets out a fat ticket envelope and hands me two of them. "Oh, and here's yours, too. Don't worry about the seat numbers—we have the whole section. You don't have to sit next to Anton's foxy dad if you don't want to."

"Small mercies."

"Want to go running?"

"Not really?"

Fiona gives me a patient stare.

"Okay, sure. Let's go."

THE LOBBY of the arena is mayhem on game night. The Bruisers' winning streak means that every game is sold out, with extra tickets trading for hundreds of dollars on resellers' sites.

I watch the fans stream in, faces bright, tickets in hand, heading for the turnstiles. There are so many Brooklyn jerseys that the lobby is a sea of purple.

I'm watching for Eric Bayer and also, I suppose, for Anton's father, if I'm able to recognize him.

And then I see them both at once. There's Eric, with his business partner, Bess, and they're moving toward a handsome man in a dark suit coat. It's so easy to recognize him as Anton's father. He's every bit as handsome, although his golden hair is turning a bit gray at the temples.

I could be imagining it, but he looks colder than Anton could ever look, even if he was encased in ice. The elder Bayer waits for Bess and Eric's approach with the bearing of a visiting dignitary who's used to people coming to him, and not the other way around.

I see Eric's features harden, as if he might share Anton's opinion of the man.

Interesting. I weave between groups of fans, crossing the lobby to meet them.

"These four are in section six," Eric is saying as I approach. "And—oh, here she is." Both Eric and Bess break into a smile when I approach. "This is Sylvie, a member of the Bombshells team. They scared up two tickets for you as well. Those are in section four."

I smile in greeting, although it's just hitting me that this is a little awkward. As I glance between Eric and Anton's dad, I can't help but think: *I just had relations with your relation...*

"Those two seats are separate?" says another voice. "We'll take those."

I glance behind Mr. Bayer and spot a skinny young teenager, another unmistakable member of the Bayer gene pool. He's got bright blue eyes like Anton's, with a mouth full of metal braces.

His father barely glances at me, and does not introduce himself. "Rudy, you want to sit with the girls' team?" He lets out a snort. "Sure, pal. Thanks for that."

"*Women's* team," Bess corrects under her breath.

"We don't mind," Rudy's brother says. The other Bayer teen is older than Rudy—maybe fifteen or sixteen years old.

"Awesome," their dad says, peeling off a hundred dollar bill from a wad of cash in his wallet and handing it to his older son. "I can sit with my clients. And hey, Eric—would you mind hanging onto them after the game for an hour? A lot of business gets done at the bar after a good game."

Eric's eyes narrow for a split second. I can almost see the thought bubble over his head. *Oh, and I'm your babysitter now?*

But he agrees, anyway. "Sure. We'll walk over to the Tavern on Hicks. You can meet us there. I'll text you the address." He delivers this instruction with no room for argument. "All right, boys. Let's watch your brother make Philly cry."

I END up seated beside Rudy, who's thirteen and very chatty. Eric and Bess are on the other side of Rudy's stoic older brother, Paul.

"This is awesome," Rudy says. "Hey, Paul! Can we buy those foam fingers?"

"The money is for food and drink," Paul mutters.

"Okay, popcorn? Hot dogs? We never go to hockey games. There's going to be a new team in Seattle, right? I want to go. But Mom hates hockey and Dad travels a lot. So I don't know."

"But you've seen Anton play before, right?" I ask, even though it's none of my business.

"Not in person," he says. "Only on TV. But we don't have the channel with all the hockey games. Dad goes sometimes, I think. On business trips. Where is Anton, anyway?"

"Right there," his big brother says, throwing him an elbow. "Look." The players are skating out for the anthem now, and Anton lines up, the word BAYER visible on the back of his jersey.

"Oh. Duh."

"Please rise for the national anthem," the announcer says. "Sung for us tonight by Grammy-winning singer-songwriter Delilah Spark!"

"Well, that's really freaking cool," Rudy says, clapping as the lights dim.

I feel a swirl of excitement in my belly as the music starts. Two lines of hockey players put their hands to their hearts, and the anthem is sung. The place is packed, and I heard Bess say that ticket sales were rocking all the way out for the duration of the regular season.

Their record is still on fire. It's only November, but they already have more points than any other team in the league. *This is our year*, Bryce keeps saying. *I can feel it.*

When he's said this, I've also heard a subtext that says: *so I couldn't possibly have time for you.* But I have to admit that standing here with nineteen thousand hungry, cheering fans makes that feel more plausible. Those boys down there have a lot of pressure on them.

I wonder if Anton will say the same thing to me, too. Am I

selfish for wanting more of his attention? Is this really the year of greatness?

Am I just the needy distraction that Bryce (almost) said I was?

"GET HIM!" Screams Rudy two hours later. He's gotten up and down more times than a guy at a Catholic Mass. "SMASH HIM! HULK SMASH!"

I think Rudy likes hockey. And in his defense, it's a *very* exciting game. Philly is determined to break Brooklyn's winning streak. The score is four to three in favor of Brooklyn, but Philly is angry and the pace of play has picked up to the speed of machine-gun fire as the third period wanes.

Our boys are not going to give it up easily. They're fighting hard. Bryce and the other forwards have forced the other goalie to practically stand on his head this period. And our defense is rough and tumble.

"No wonder my mother hates this game," Rudy says with obvious glee, as O'Doul smashes a Philly sniper into the boards. "It's awesome."

His brother is quieter, but enthusiastic in his own way. He's shoving handfuls of popcorn into his mouth.

Rudy glances at the scoreboard clock. "What happens if they tie?"

"Don't jinx us," his brother grumbles.

"But what happens?"

Paul shrugs, and they both look at Eric. "Overtime," Eric says. "But let's not let it come to that."

Even as he says the words, Philly gets a breakaway past O'Doul.

"Noooo!" Rudy screams. "GET 'EM, ANTON!"

Fiona chuckles from the seat beside me. "Good lungs on that kid."

And then Anton does what's necessary. I'm gripping my seat, white-knuckled, as he steps on the gas, burns the skater, and pokes the puck away. Fiona lets out as squeal as Trevi receives the puck and fires it at the upper right corner.

The lamp lights, and I gasp. But the loudest shout is from Eric. "That's my BOY!" Then he puts his hands together in the prayer position and pins them against his lips. As if he has so much joy that it might just spill out.

Down on the ice, Anton looks momentarily stunned, as if he doesn't trust his eyes. But the stadium is erupting with glee, and so he spins in a tight circle, a big smile on his face. And Trevi skates by to cuff him in a celebratory back slap.

"Goal to Leo Trevi! Assist by Anton Bayer!" the announcer shouts.

"They said his name!" Rudy hollers.

"Yeah, he gets credit for that assist," I explain. "A point on his stats."

"That is awesome. And *we* saw it."

"Yes, you did," I say, and I sound far more invested than I have a right to be. But the more I get to know Anton, the more I like him.

I'm not boyfriend material, he'd said. And then I told him I didn't care.

Maybe I lied.

AFTER THE GAME, Eric leaves with the two teens, and I hang back with Fiona and Scarlet.

"Care for a drink?" Fiona says to both of us.

"Sure," I agree immediately. "The Tavern should be fun tonight, after that win." Plus, I can stare at Anton like a lovesick creeper.

Maybe I should have picked a different spot.

"I was going to suggest the Tavern," Scarlet says. "It's not too far from the subway."

So, it's really not my fault that we walk into the place twenty minutes later, right? The Tavern is rocking, just like I predicted. There are several tables full of Bombshells enjoying a night off together.

Fiona and I drift around, saying hi to everyone. And then the Bruisers eventually begin to trickle in, causing a new shout of congratulations every time the door opens to admit a hockey player in a suit.

I watch that door like a hungry dog waiting for its master to return from work. And when Anton's smiling face finally appears, I feel fireworks go off in my tummy.

The things I did with that man...

"Your tongue is hanging out," Fiona whispers.

Chastened, I make myself look away.

"I think we need another pitcher of beer," she says. "And it's your turn to buy." She hands me our pitcher and gives me a little shove toward the bar, where I'll obviously encounter Anton, since his young brothers are perched up there eating wings.

I weave my way through the crowd toward the bar. Anton can't reach his family yet, since he's beset by bargoers offering their congratulations.

Our eyes meet, and he offers me a smile so big that I feel it everywhere. I offer him a thumbs up, and those blue eyes sparkle back at me.

"Hey, Anton!" Rudy's squawk cuts through the bar chatter.

Anton turns his head, and when he picks out Rudy's metallic smile, his beautiful eyes give a slow blink of astonishment. "Hey! Look who it is!"

"Great goal!" Rudy chirps.

"*Assist,*" his brother grunts.

"I know that, but it was *part* of a great goal," Rudy insists.

"Thanks, man," Anton says, lifting his hand for a fist bump. "So you enjoyed the game, and now you're hitting the bar for some brewskis?" He looks utterly delighted by this development.

"It's soda," Paul says.

"And a dozen wings," Eric adds, lifting his own fist for a bump. "*Great* play tonight. That was one for the highlight reel."

"Yeah?" Anton tries to bury his smile, but it doesn't quite work.

"Hey, who's this?" Castro asks, handing Anton a beer. "You're recruiting 'em young for your fan club?"

"Castro, meet my brothers, Paul Jr. and Rudy," Anton says, his smile goofy. "They're usually in Seattle, but they came to the game tonight."

"Your…" Castro looks gobsmacked. "You have two brothers?"

I'm watching this little drama unfold, so I don't immediately notice that the bartender — Petra — is glowering at me. "Are you just holding that pitcher?" she asks. "Or do you actually want me to put something in it?"

"Oh, sorry," I say, handing it over. "The lager, please."

She practically yanks it out of my hands. I don't know what I ever did to offend this woman. The few times I've been in here, it's always the same.

She takes her time, too, setting the pitcher down and then busying herself with other bar tasks before actually filling it.

I really don't get it.

So I'm standing here, cooling my heels, when the door opens again. Everyone in the bar looks to see if another hockey player has joined the party.

But, nope. It's Anton's father, strutting in like he owns the place. The crowd moves out of his way, too. Maybe he off-gasses Important Guy pheromones, or something. He walks right over to his sons. "Everyone have fun tonight?" he asks like he's the host.

"Did you see Anton's assist?" Rudy crows.

"Sure did." He glances at Anton. "Next time shoot it in the net, son." He guffaws. "The goal would look better on your stats than an assist, no? Thought I taught you to go for broke."

"You motherfucker," I say under my breath.

TWENTY-THREE

Hit Me With Your Digits

ANTON

HERE WE GO AGAIN.

It's always like this. My father has never been able to say anything nice about me. I've learned from an early age to shrug it off. I had to.

The problem is that other people don't know what to do when he's rude. My brothers are blinking at their father, like they don't know if he's kidding. My friends are staring. And I feel all kinds of tension radiating off Eric beside me. "You son of a…" he says in a low whisper.

Instinctively, I reach for his forearm and give it a squeeze. *Leave it alone*, the gesture says.

My father grins, like he's gotten away with something. "Saddle up, kids," he says to Junior and Rudy, because apparently thirty seconds with his oldest son is plenty.

"But you just got here!" Rudy points out, and Junior actually winces.

"Yeah, but it's late. Thank your cousin Eric for hosting you tonight."

"Anytime," Eric grinds out. "But the seats were a gift from the Bombshells," Eric says. "They deserve the gratitude."

"Oh yeah, thank the girls' team for me."

"*Women's team,*" a female voice says. Heads swivel toward Sylvie, who's standing by the bar, a pitcher of beer clutched in her hands. Two bright pink spots stand out on her cheeks, and her eyes are flashing with anger. "Your sons are lovely, by the way," she says to my father. "So I'd do it again. But you are a very impatient, unpleasant man. So don't bother asking for another favor unless you're bringing Rudy and Paul Jr."

Holy fuck. And here I didn't think she could get any sexier.

My father turns toward her, a sneer on his lips. He gives her the kind of up and down glance that you'd give a mangy dog if you're hoping it won't put its muddy paws on your Valentino overcoat.

"Well, then," he says, and I brace myself. "I guess hockey is the right sport for you, honey. Gotta get that aggression out somehow. 'Night, guys!" He raises a hand in the direction of Eric and me. "Rudy. Junior. We're going."

Then he stomps past Sylvie and heads for the door.

"Wow, Sylvie," my brother Paul says, thrusting out his hand to shake. "I'm gonna stay on your good side."

"Sorry," she squeaks. "I shouldn't have yelled at him."

He shrugs. "Somebody should. 'Night. Bye, Anton." He turns around to give me a serious wave as he goes.

"Bye." There's a lump in my throat. I've spent more time with the teenagers at the pool than I ever have with him. I was in the third grade when he was born, and I spent a lot of time trying not to think about him. Every year I got a Christmas card in the mail— the kind with the posed, professional photo on it. My father was always holding one of those boys—his upgrade children—in the photo.

Rudy doesn't follow his brother, though. Not yet. He takes a leisurely last sip of his soda, and then he sets it down on the bar. "Thanks for the wings, Eric."

"My pleasure, kid."

Then he turns to me, and I'm startled when he throws his arms around my chest. "Great game, Anton. Super cool."

"Thanks," I say, giving him a squeeze. What a strange night this has become.

"Hit me with your digits," he says, releasing me.

"Sorry?" I glance toward the door, where my father's glower is visible. He's waiting for his son.

"Your number. I have my own phone now." He pulls it out.

I gather my wits and rattle off my phone number. Then I give the kid a smile and a shoulder squeeze. "Later, Rudy. Thanks for coming to my game."

"It was awesome!" Still grinning, he grabs his jacket off the barstool and heads for the door.

"People," Eric grunts a moment later. "I don't understand a lot of 'em. Your dad is such a tool. But that kid is a ray of sunshine."

"Weird, right?" I take a swig of my beer and glance around the bar, wondering where Sylvie went.

I don't see her anywhere.

"DARTS?" Castro prods me a little later. "Heidi isn't here, so we might actually win if it's men against women." His wife has creamed every one of us at darts at some point. And pool. And cards.

So I'm tempted. But my one beer for the evening is empty and we have a plane to catch tomorrow morning. "I gotta pack and get some sleep," I say instead.

Castro gives me a thoughtful glance. "Okay. You do you. I'm not the kind of friend who complains that you used to be more fun. So long as you're not the kind of friend who draws Sharpie mustaches on his hungover friends who are sleeping it off on the jet tomorrow."

I chuckle, because this is something I used to love to do. "Have you seen me with a Sharpie this season? Have I put a fake spider on your lucky sandwich? Have I turned off the hot water in the locker room when you were in the shower?"

"No," he says, licking his lips nervously. "But it just makes me think you're saving it up for something major, you know?"

"Uh-huh. Your problem is that you're a bullshitter, too. He who lives by the Sharpie knows that he will someday die by the Sharpie. But not tomorrow, my friend." I give him a fist bump.

"Good to know. You have a nice night. Great play, by the way."

"Thank you, man." After that, I loosen my tie, say a few more goodbyes, and walk Eric out to his waiting Uber.

Then I head home on foot, which is easier when you're sober, I have to admit. Except I'm a little too stuck inside my head tonight.

Hit me with your digits, Rudy had said. I wonder what kind of a man he'll grow up to be. I wonder if I'll get a chance to know my half-brothers, or if we'll always be orbiting each other, like distant moons around a cold, ugly planet.

It's always like this. No matter how infrequent they are, visits from my father leave me feeling sideswiped.

But tonight it's really not so bad. That point I just added to my stat sheet cushions the blow by quite a bit. And then there was that outburst from Sylvie. That made me smile, even if my heart is achy breaky.

I look both ways before crossing the street and then pull out my phone to text her a good-night message. It's imperative. I promised to be a good friend, and I'm not going to break that promise.

When I check my messages, she's already beat me to it with a series of texts.

Anton I'm so SORRY I sounded off at your father. First I yelled at you. And then your family?

It's really none of my business.

God, you must think I'm a crazy person.

PS: Great play tonight! We were all screaming, including your cute little brothers.

The message is only fifteen minutes old, so even though it's late, I tap her avatar and dial her.

"Hello?" she asks, sounding sleepy. "Is this the man who made a Philly sniper cry?"

A grin like a fool. "Hey, sweetheart. Thanks for the props."

"You're welcome. And I'm sorry about the bar—"

"Don't be," I break in. "You're hot when you're fired up." And then I want to kick myself for saying she's hot. Because what kind of dickhead sends a woman mixed signals like that?

She's quiet for a second. "I have a bit of a temper."

"My dad is a first-class tool, Sylvie. He could make anyone lose her cool. Get this—when I showed up in Brooklyn two years ago, I barely even knew Eric. My father alienated Eric's side of the family a long time ago."

"Ouch."

"Yeah. It is what it is." It took me a good decade to learn to use that phrase when speaking about my dad. His bad behavior is not my fault, even though I spent more than half my life thinking it might be.

"I'm sorry."

"Don't worry about him. He barely exists to me. But that's not why I called you. I just wanted to say goodnight, and tell you that I can't wait to go running with you later this week. I get back on Saturday."

"I'm in Providence then. We always have weekend games."

"Ah, right. Sorry. Monday, then?" She's quiet. I can sense her hesitation. "Look, I know I fucked up. And I know I'm confusing as hell. But that's because I'm confused. But it won't stop me from trying to be a good friend to you."

She sighs. "Thank you. You're not the only one who's confused."

"I know that. Goodnight, sweetheart. Pleasant dreams."

"You, too," she says softly.

"You know I will." My voice rasps, because I'll probably dream about her.

We hang up, and I walk the last part of the journey. I stop on the sidewalk on my own side of the street, and look up at her darkened windows. She's up there, probably in bed, her silky hair spread across the pillow.

All I want you to do is pin me down and shut me up, she'd said today. And I don't doubt her sincerity, or her right to do whatever—and whoever—she pleases.

But this afternoon I'd walked into my locker room and sat down on the bench next to Campeau. He'd asked me if I'd seen Sylvie at the pool today.

"Sure did," I'd said. "We practiced some open-water rescues for the kids, and then took a cab back to Water Street."

He'd frowned at me. "I called her earlier and she did not pick up."

"Try again, man," I'd said, looking him right in the eye.

I'd meant it when I'd said that I didn't want to be their go-between. And I sure as hell didn't want to be put in the position of ducking my teammate's questions.

I'm still frozen here on the sidewalk, looking up at a certain third-floor apartment. If I buzzed Sylvie's door right now, she'd let me in. And hell knows I want to.

But I can't be that guy. Because of my teammate, and because of *me*. My father takes what he wants and doesn't care who he hurts.

I won't, though.

So I turn around and head toward my own building. The doors open automatically, because one of the staff has seen me coming. "Evening, sir," he says as I enter the lobby. It's Borek, the new guy.

"Evening, Borek. Did anybody arrange a car to the airport tomorrow?"

He picks up a sheet of paper on the counter. "Leo has room in his."

"Sign me up, would you? Thanks."

"My pleasure, sir. Good night."

I head to the elevators alone. This is how discipline works, right? I go to bed on time. I sleep alone. I skate like the devil is chasing me.

I won't fuck this thing up again.

TWENTY-FOUR

A Dudevorce

SYLVIE

MAYBE HEARTACHE IS good for my hockey game. Because I am on fire this week at practice. My stamina is back, and I feel strong for the duration of every practice. And when Friday comes, I head to Providence with my team, knowing that I'm finally playing at a high level.

Meanwhile, Anton keeps up his campaign to stay friends. My phone is full of funny, chatty texts from him.

It's harder than I thought it would be, though, to step back into the role of sidekick and workout buddy. Not after all that we shared. That night meant something to me. But it didn't mean the same thing to him.

I'm just setting my gear down in the Providence locker room when he texts to wish me a good game.

Anton: Smash Providence, Bombshells!
Sylvie: We'll do our best. They had the worst stats last year, so I think the girls are feeling good about this one. What are you up to?
Anton: I'm on a bus to the arena in San Diego. Castro and Trevi are having a vicious argument in the seat behind me. It's bad. I think they might end up getting a dudevorce over this.

Sylvie: A dudevorce? That's another one of your strange words. What are they fighting about?

Anton: By *strange* you mean excellent, right? They are fighting about book three in Game of Thrones.

Sylvie: Oh. You had me worried for a second. I thought you meant actually fighting.

Anton: I think you underestimate the emotions on both sides. I hope neither of them gets traded over this because our win depends on team unity.

"Sylvie?"

I'm still wearing a silly grin when I look up to find Coach Sasha Marshall standing in front of me. "Yes? Sorry." I put the phone down in a hurry.

"Scarlet is experiencing some muscle soreness. And I'd like to put you in the net tonight."

"Yes! Of course," I say immediately. "I'm ready."

She smiles. "Excellent. Get warm and limber. You've got two hours."

"Right." I pop off the bench, phone forgotten, and start stretching.

This is an *excellent* development. Providence was the worst team in the league last year. And our next game is against the top-ranked Philadelphia Fillies, so Coach probably wants to rest Scarlet for that tougher matchup.

But that's fine with me. All that matters is that I'm playing in my first pro game.

I close my eyes and think of Saint Sebastian, the patron saint of athletes. *Let me not screw this one up*, I ask him. *Pretty please?*

I stretch, warming up my body with everything I've got. Skating out for the pregame warmup, I feel awfully jittery. It's unlike me to be so nervous, but there's a lot riding on this. If I can't make a good showing against Providence, Coach Marshall might look around for another goalie.

And Bess Beringer is here too, along with Rebecca Rowley Kattenberger, in the front row, armed with a huge camera, the lens as long as my arm.

But no pressure.

My hands are sweating as I watch the first faceoff. Fiona wins it, and from that moment on, I'm a hundred percent in the game. I'm calling out plays to my girls and deflecting everything that comes my way, like I was born to it.

To be fair, Providence doesn't put up much of a fight. Their right winger is terrific, so I have to keep an eye on her at all times. But their defense is overmatched, and the puck spends much of its time in our attack zone.

In between periods, I guzzle fluids and get encouragement from Coach, and from Scarlet, who's just as gracious as ever about my fine performance.

By the middle of the third period, it's four to zero, in our favor. With just four minutes left to play, our defense has a bad couple of minutes. There's a penalty against Charli that isn't called, and then a shot bounces off the post, producing a rebound opportunity for Providence.

Their sniper finds it, and I'm scored upon, damn it.

But we win the game, four to one, and Coach is full of smiles.

And so am I. I grin like a crazy lady all the way through my shower. It's so gratifying to put up a win in my first pro game, with a save average in the high nineties.

My dad is going to be so pumped. I didn't get the chance to tell him I was playing tonight. And my mother would be thrilled for me. I choke up, knowing that I can't call her with the news.

"How are we going to celebrate?" Fiona asks, toweling off her hair in the locker room beside me.

"Not sure we have many options," I point out. We're staying at a Holiday Inn near the highway, and it's ten o'clock already.

"Pizza and TV it is, then!" Fiona announces. "Hey Sylvie, don't sit on that thing. You'll poke yourself in the ass."

"Hmm?" I turn around to try to figure out what she means.

"On your towel. Look out." She points.

Sure enough, on the towel I set down a few minutes ago, there's a shiny hair pin.

I let out a squeak of surprise and pick it up. And then I turn away from Fiona because my eyes get wet, and I don't want to explain why hairpins make me cry.

My mother was the mystic in the family, but these days I'm a believer, too.

———

LATE THAT NIGHT I pick up my phone and find a selfie of Anton wearing an exaggerated frown. Its caption: *You didn't answer. And now I have a bad case of textpectation*.

Please tell me you beat Providence, he adds.

I look back over our conversation and see all my cheery responses to him. Even though I'm sad about being friend-zoned, I can't help myself when it comes to him. I want his attention.

So of course I'm going to reply. Especially because I can't resist telling him my news. I take a screenshot of the gold star on my phone, and text it to him with: *And guess who guarded the net?*

My phone erupts with congratulatory gifs. Monkeys beating on their chests, movie stars clapping. Fireworks. But his words mean even more to me. *That's the best news I've heard all week. Well done, Sylvie. Way to show them all*.

———

WHEN THE NEWS GETS OUT, everyone is thrilled for me. My dad sends a dozen roses to my Brooklyn apartment, and Bryce leaves me two phone messages.

The glow hasn't worn off at all by Wednesday, when I'm sitting in One Girl Cookies, waiting for Fiona, and texting—yet again— with Anton. He must have found the cache of photos that Rebecca took in Providence with her giant lens. He's taken a series of photos of me and photoshopped them.

In the first shot, I'm obviously yelling something to a teammate, but he's put a golden crown on my head and labeled it, *The Queen*.

The second photo has me diving for a puck, and he's put a super-hero's cape fluttering from my shoulders. That one is my favorite.

There's one more of me making a save with my stick, and there's a thought bubble overhead, announcing, *Not today, Satan.*

It's cute and thoughtful, and it gives me a big old heartache. Anton Bayer is a catch. But he doesn't want to be caught by me.

Fiona pulls out the chair opposite me just as another photo appears on my phone, and I say, without looking up, "Omigod, he is so hilarious."

"Who is?" asks a deep voice.

I glance up fast, and it's not Fiona who is sitting down across from me. It's Bryce.

"Oh," I squeak. "Hi."

"Hi." He gives me a funny smile. "You look happy. Care to share?"

I put my phone face down on the table, and I take a deep breath. I'm still annoyed with him for discussing me with Anton. But I don't want to explain why, so for once in my life I'm not going to let my temper rule me.

"Sylvie, what's the matter?" he asks. "You don't return my calls."

"I've been busy," I say in a voice that doesn't offer further discussion.

He tilts his rugged chin, inviting me to give more details. "You are still mad at me. About the party. I am sorry."

I do not want to talk about that, either. "Look," I say, tracing the edge of my phone with a finger. "I really have been busy. I'm kind of seeing someone."

His eyes widen immediately. "Oh." He swallows. "A guy?"

"Yes."

He avoids my gaze. "You met him here in Brooklyn?"

"Yes."

"Who is it?"

I wait until his cool blue eyes wander back to mine. And I wonder what I should say.

TWENTY-FIVE

The New Guy on Jeopardy

ANTON

IT'S GAME DAY AGAIN. I'm lying on the bed of a hotel room in Calgary, fingering the strings of the travel guitar that I always bring with me on road trips.

An hour ago we ate lunch in a hotel banquet room, and now it's time to rest up before the game. But I'm too bored to go to sleep.

I didn't even know that was possible. But here we are.

This season is turning out exactly like I planned. My stats are good. All mentions of me in the sports news are for points, not shenanigans. Management likes me again.

In other ways, it's a total letdown.

I honestly believed that if I worked out every day, went to bed early, skated hard and drank one or fewer light beers every day, that I would come to exist on some higher plane. I thought that mastering my baser desires would be so satisfying that I wouldn't miss late nights, drunken pool games, and bad decisions.

Don't get me wrong—it feels good to show up for practice well-rested and headache free. And as we roll toward December, I've already got three goals and four assists.

But God, I'm boring. I've binged every single decent TV show. I've finally learned the guitar part to "Every Breath You Take." And I've called my mother every week just to say hello.

I pick up the phone and dial her again. At least I'm a good son.

"Are you okay, Anton?" she asks when she picks up.

"I'm fine. Why?"

"I never hear from you this often. Is there something you're trying to tell me? You have a gambling addiction? You witnessed a murder? You're gay?"

"No! Jeez, Mom."

"I was pretty sure that last idea was far-fetched. But I'd love you no matter what."

"Thanks," I grunt. "I'm just twitchy."

"So… is it meth?"

"Mom!"

She laughs. "Sorry. I know that's not funny. And I guess that means you're having girl trouble."

"Nah. Not exactly." The moment I say it, I know it's a mistake.

"Aha!" she pounces. "What's her name?"

"There is no girl. I mean, there is. But it's not going to be a thing."

"Why not?" she presses. "And you forgot to tell me her name."

"It's Sylvie."

"Sylvia?"

"No, just Sylvie. It's French. She was born in Quebec."

She makes a sound of pure delight. "So what is it about this *Sylvie* that's got you so tied up in knots that you're willing to call your mother all the time?"

"I'm not tied up in knots," I grumble. "I'm just sick of my own company. I promised myself—no women, no boozing, no scandal. I don't know what's left to do."

"My baby is lonely! Now, is this Sylvie a scandalous boozer?"

"Not hardly."

"Then I fail to see the issue. Rules are what you make of them. You could spend time with this nice girl if you wanted to. Unless she rejected you." She takes a startled breath. "Wait. *Did* she reject you?"

"Well, no. But I'm not looking for a relationship. And it's complicated because she has some history with my teammate. With Bryce Campeau, Ma. And he'd freak out if I started seeing her."

"Ooh. Well, Bryce is a bit intense. Are you sure they're done with each other?"

Mothers have a way of getting to the heart of the matter. "That's just it. I think he's still carrying a torch. And I can't do that to my teammate. He's the best kind of guy, you know? Think of the uproar if two guys in the dressing room are fighting over a girl."

"That Bryce is a wild man," my mother says. "Always making a scene."

"No, he's not, Ma," I object. "He's more of a silent, broody type."

She cackles. "I know, sweets. That's my point. If necessary, you two can talk this out like gentlemen. But Lord knows you have a complex about being anyone's second choice."

"What? I do not."

"Oh honey. You do! You hate your team nickname."

"Would *you* like people calling you Baby Bayer?"

"Baby bears are cute. Everyone likes them. But you don't like the implication that you're the inferior Bayer. This is all your father's fault, of course. May he rest in peace."

"He's not dead, Ma. I just saw him."

"Well, he *should* be. That man wrecked us both. I was his starter wife and you were his starter son, and he made it freely known to both of us that he'd moved on to bigger, better things."

"What does any of that have to do with my woman troubles?" I grumble.

"It has *everything* to do with it. I watched you break up with your girlfriend from Denver about a week after you left, because she said your replacement was cute."

That is *not* what happened. "I broke up with her because I didn't want to do long distance. I didn't love her. Besides—she and Mr. Cute are dating now."

"That just proves my point," my mother insists. "You broke up with her because you couldn't stand the idea that she might break up with you first."

I lie back on the pillow and close my eyes. "Mom, are you trying to get me off the phone? Is *Jeopardy* on, or something?"

"Baby boy, you will *never* be second place in my heart to

anything. Certainly not *Jeopardy*, even if the new guy is kind of cute."

"Mom."

"Do you think he worries about being everyone's second choice?"

"What? The new guy on *Jeopardy*? I can't follow this conversation."

"I think you're following just fine." There's a pause, and then she lets me off the hook. "Did you really see your father recently? How was that?"

"Dreadful. As always. But he brought his boys. They're little men now."

"Are they just like him?"

"No, although it's kind of a miracle. They were cool, though."

"Why do you sound so surprised?"

"Well…" I chuckle. "He's such a shit."

"You're nothing like him, you know."

"Of course I'm not. I know that."

"Do you? I hope so. You're *nothing* like that man. Even if you fall head over heels for Bryce's ex, that does not mean you're anything like your father. Because you're the best there is, honey."

"Thanks, Mom." There's an actual lump in my throat now, even if my head is spinning. "Thanks for the pep talk."

"Any time! Beat Dallas!"

"We play Calgary next."

"Then beat Calgary. Whatever. Now that we've got that settled, *Jeopardy* is on. Watch with me?"

"Nah. I'm supposed to be napping."

"Sleep tight!"

In the silence after she hangs up, I check my texts to see if Sylvie has responded to my latest.

Nope.

I can't text her again, because that's just pathetic. So I find my little brother's name, and I tap out a text to Rudy. *Hey man. How's it going with you?*

Rudy: Not good. I forgot to unload the dishwasher and so Lana changed the wifi password.

Anton: Bummer. Who's Lana?

Rudy: The babysitter. Guess who's going to unload the dishwasher next?

Anton: You?

Rudy: Yup. What are you doing?

Anton: Sitting in a hotel room. Kinda bored.

Rudy: Does the hotel have a pool?

Anton: I'm not sure.

Rudy: Well find out! What are you waiting for?

I smile, because suddenly I can remember feeling *exactly* the same thing—that an unexplored hotel pool was the most exciting thing in the world.

Rudy: Something the matter, Anton? You don't usually text me.

Anton: Nah. Just wondered what you were up to.

Rudy: So it must be girl trouble?

Holy crap. Am I that transparent? *Well there is a girl. I like her. But it's complicated. I suspect she still likes this other boy.*

Rudy: Story of my life.

I crack up. And while I'm laughing, Rudy keeps typing.

Rudy: If you're not sure, tho, that means you have a chance.

Anton: I suppose you're right.

Rudy: Hey, is it Sylvie? Because she was FIRE. He follows this with the drool emoji.

Jesus Christ. Precocious little shit. *I'm afraid to answer this question, because you might try to ask her out first.*

Rudy: Ha! I knew it. Do you want me to tell her you like her?

No! I type immediately. I've survived middle school already. I don't need to go back.

Rudy: Just say the word, man. I could thank her for the tickets and then just casually mention that you think she's cute.

Anton: That's a nice offer, but I got this.

Rudy: You better. Don't let that other loser get there first. You're a professional hockey player FFS.

I type through my laughter. *So is he, Rudy.*

Rudy: Oh dang. Don't wait then.

Anton: I won't thanks.

Rudy: I better unload that dishwasher. Or no Fortnite. You want to play sometime?

Yes, I say immediately.

Rudy: Do you have good gear?

Anton: I've never played.

Rudy: Oh man. Okay. Can you practice first? I don't want us to die because you're a noob.

Anton: Sure. I'll make an account.

Rudy: Sick. We'll play this weekend.

Anton: Perfect.

I toss my phone onto the bed and smile up at the ceiling.

Then I get up to find my laptop so I can learn to play *Fortnite*.

TWENTY-SIX

Suckitude

ANTON

A FEW HOURS LATER, however, I realize that boring times in my hotel room aren't the worst thing in the world. Because the game against Calgary is a total shit show.

Things start going wrong right away in the first period. Campeau misses a beautiful pass, then Castro gets a two-minute penalty for no reason at all.

Then we give up a goal in the tenth minute of the game.

These things happen. But somehow we all get rattled by it, which doesn't help. Castro chirps at Campeau over the missed shot, and Campeau snaps back.

Coach is getting grumpier by the minute. I'm skating with Tank tonight. We hold it together pretty well, although we have to watch our forward lines fall apart.

At the center of all this suckitude is Bryce Campeau. The dude is having an off night to put it mildly. He still can't put his passes in the right places and he can't find his line mates' rhythm. It's ugly.

He's not handling it well, either. Anytime someone offers a word of advice or encouragement, he practically bites their head off.

Calgary scores on us again in the second period. It turns into a very long game. Trevi pulls off a beautiful fast-touch goal, but then the minutes tick down, and we're still losing. And somehow it feels inevitable. No winning streak can last forever. And for no good reason—since we're only down by one—the loss seems fated.

Coach tries to rally us, and we fire on the keeper a few more times. Castro gets a breakaway and manages to ship the puck to Campeau. And, man, he *almost* makes it work. Campeau finds his opening, but not before the same jerk who tripped him earlier in the game trips him *again*.

Then those fuckers score, and the ref doesn't call the delayed penalty.

"What the *fuck*," O'Doul barks, before skating off to argue the call. But even from twenty yards away I can see the ref giving him the universal shrug for *I didn't see it*.

Meanwhile, the Calgary fans cackle while Campeau fumes.

We line up for another faceoff, and the game that started rough and then turned bad, jumps the rails all the way to ugly. Because Campeau skates right over to his opponent, throws off his gloves, and slugs the guy.

I should mention at this point that Bryce Campeau is a fine hockey player with a bright future. He has many enviable qualities. Fighting, however, is not his strong suit. So the minute he picks this fight, every other dude on my team groans.

"Fuck, I can't watch," Trevi says, giving me a worried glance as we wait awkwardly in front of the bench for the fight to be over. "How bad is it?"

"Bad," I mutter as Campeau's helmet flies off after a punch to the jaw. "That's gonna leave a mark."

"He should never have taken this fight," Crikey says from the bench.

"At least it will be over soon, right?"

"Uh-huh," I say with a sigh. "Right about...*ouch*." The Calgary heavy lands two more meaty blows—one to the chest and one to the face, and my teammate finally falls down hard on his ass.

The refs jump in, haul the Calgary dude away, and help Campeau up.

My teammate is clutching his ribs. He doesn't even stop to pick up his helmet and gloves, or his stick. He just skates for the bench, cursing to himself and looking defeated.

The Calgary fans are laughing their butts off, and there's one minute left in the game.

"All winning streaks end eventually," Trevi says with a sigh.

"Man. I really deserve my light beer tonight."

Trevi laughs and shakes his head.

EVERYONE'S MOOD after the game is somber and quiet, except for Coach, who is blazing mad. On the bus back to the hotel, I can hear him up in front, reading Campeau the riot act.

He started with words like "ridiculous" and "short-sighted," and his criticisms only got more colorful from there.

Coach is pissed because Campeau managed to injure his ribs, and probably will miss a few games, *"for no fucking reason,"* as he put it.

Ouch.

I close my eyes and try to relax. The first thing that pops into my head, though, is Sylvie. I wonder if she had practice tonight. I wonder if she saw our shitastic game.

And I wonder what she thinks about Campeau's fight. Is she worried about him?

"Psst," O'Doul says as the bus pulls up at the hotel.

I open my eyes fast. "Yeah?"

"It's Jimbo's birthday. I'm throwing him a little party in the lobby bar. One hour from now. Don't miss it."

"Oh, Christ. Yeah, man. I'll be there."

"Bring your guitar," he says. "We're gonna need a lift."

I've still got that reputation—the guy who can make you laugh after a rough night. The guy who shows up for the birthday cele-bration.

I guess there's worse things to be famous for. So I get off the bus and head upstairs to get my guitar.

"OUR LITTLE MAN is all grown up!" Castro crows as he passes out bottles of Corona with lime—Jimbo's favorite.

I take one even though it's not technically a light beer. But it's close enough.

"To another year of keeping us in line!" O'Doul says, and we all raise a bottle, while our twenty-two-year-old equipment manager shoves his hands in his pockets and ducks his head. The kid can't take a compliment, but we don't care. We're going to razz him anyway and buy him a bunch of drinks.

Jimbo is a Brooklyn local who started working for the team right after high school graduation. He'd never been on a plane until he started traveling with us, but now we couldn't manage without him.

Of course we tease him about his hair gel and his personal life and every other damn thing. He's used to it. And now I'm going to sing about it. Once a party boy, always a party boy. Even if I'm changing my stripes this year, I can't let Jimbo down.

After a swig of beer, I set the bottle down and pick up my travel guitar. "All right, boys. I've got a new one just for Jimbo."

"I hope it's Fall Out Boy again," Trevi says.

"Lady Gaga?" someone else suggests.

"Nah, I went old school this time," I say. "Barry Manilow."

There are a few chuckles. And when I strum the opening, everybody shuts up right away to hear what kind of spectacle I'm willing to make of myself tonight.

Jimbo's special birthday tribute is sung to the tune of that "Copacabana" song. I'm proud of it, honestly. Not bad for an hour's notice.

HIS NAME IS JIMBO... He keeps us moving
  And when the bus is running late, he always gets us to the gate

THE LAUGHING STARTS UP IMMEDIATELY.

. . .

HE KNOWS OUR SKATE BLADES....AND our cup sizes
  Just don't mess with his hair — he'll lose your luggage at O'Hare

THE ROOM ERUPTS WITH LAUGHTER, and even as I sing the second verse, Jimbo is blushing behind his dark scruff.

Then I hit the bridge, and the laughter only gets louder.

HE WORKS from eight to four
  He's the last guy out the door
  He's a man of style and class
  Our schedule's tattooed on his ass

AND SO ON. I'm a man of many talents. By the third verse, beer has already come out of Drake's nose, so I know I've done well.

There's only one man who isn't smiling by the time I play the last chord. That man is Bryce Campeau. He's watching me with a steely gaze, a Corona clutched in one hand, and an ice pack held to his face with the other.

It looks like he has a split lip as well as a shiner. Just ouch. And if a guy can't laugh at a Barry Manilow remake, there is something seriously wrong. So after wishing Jimbo a happy birthday, I take my beer and head over toward my beat-up friend.

Unfortunately, Bess Beringer gets there first. It's just Campeau's luck that his agent witnessed the whole thing, and is ready to yell at him, too.

Ouch. Bad night for my teammate. Maybe I can head Bess off at the pass. "Hey guys. Everything okay?"

"Not really," Bess says tightly. "Doc says he's missing two games at least. And tomorrow they're going to check him for costochondral separation."

I shudder, because I know what that is. It hurts, and it's nasty.

"And then there's the *photo shoot* you were supposed to do the day after tomorrow.

"Fuck," he whispers. Then he hangs his head. "I can't be in those pictures like this."

"Probably not," she says with a sigh.

When Campeau goes off to the men's room, Bess turns to me. "Anton—can I offer you as a replacement?"

"For…what?"

"The photo shoot. It would be your first endorsement."

"Oh, heck. What's the company?" I can't hide my interest.

"It's for Brooklyn Outfitters, they make—"

"—sporty clothing," I say for her. "I've got some of their stuff." Seeing as I spent the whole summer in various Brooklyn gyms, it's not a big surprise.

"The shoot was supposed to be Castro, Trevi, and Campeau, with some of the Bombshells, too." She pulls out her phone. "I arm-twisted them to have six models. And now I have to pull one of them. Could you make it, Baby Bayer? The pay is really decent."

There's that nickname again. "Yeah, sure. But only if Bryce can't do it."

"Thank you." Bess puts a hand on my shoulder. "It's not a Cartier sponsorship, but it's something. They're rolling out a line of cobranded T-shirts with the Bruisers and Bombshells logos. It will be fun, I promise."

"Sure. Thanks. Just send me the details."

Then it hits me. Look who's second choice again? This guy. And my mom was totally wrong. It doesn't bother me.

Not much anyway.

Okay, sure. It bugs me a little.

Damn it.

Campeau comes back, with Drake tagging along. "Need more ice, buddy?"

"No," says our surly friend. "But scotch would be nice."

Drake blinks, because Campeau never touches the hard stuff. "Hmm. Okay, sure. Let me see what single malts they've got."

"I'll do it," I offer, and head for the bar. I order a Talisker for Bryce, and when the bartender slides it in my direction, I take a deep inhale of the caramel scent.

"Something else?" he asks.

I hesitate. There's no reason I can't have a shot. I don't have a problem with alcohol. Except I promised myself that this year would be different. And here I am ready to break that promise for no good reason.

"Just a Coke," I say.

"You got it."

By the time I get back to Campeau and hand him his drink, Drake is working hard to unpack whatever is bothering him.

"Just got a lot on my mind. I never let this stuff distract me."

"What stuff?" Drake chuckles. "Women stuff?"

"Yeah," he grunts.

All my blood stops circulating.

"Camps, I never see you with a woman," Drake points out.

"And you never will," he says. "Sylvie tells me this week that she is seeing someone."

Holy shit. My soda glass suddenly becomes fascinating to me. I don't even dare look up.

"Oh hell," Drake says, his voice hushed. "That was fast. Why did she tell you, anyway?"

"I see her at the coffee shop, and she's laughing at something on her phone. And I ask why. She was not expecting me, I think. I catch her off guard."

Drake leans forward. "So who is this guy?"

"She did not say."

I practically sag with relief, even though I can't be sure that Sylvie meant me.

"Is it, like, serious?" Drake asks.

"No," Campeau says abruptly. "I asked, and she said no. Not at all."

"Huh." Drake looks thoughtful. "Sorry, man. You don't look happy about this."

"No, well..." He gazes into the distance. "The thing is? She looked so *happy*. Like this text was better than a dozen roses. And I only want Sylvie to be happy. I am just surprised."

"You want me to find out who it is?" Drake asks. "I could ask around, you know? If you're worried."

"No." He holds up a hand. "That's, like a stalker." When I look up to check his expression, it's worried. "I just hope he's a good man, you know? Not some oversexed boy. She deserves the best."

I am wildly uncomfortable now. I am surprised by Sylvie's confession to Campeau. And I'm surprised by how strangely he's taking it—blowing up a game, picking a fight, and then telling us that it doesn't really matter. When it sure looks like it does.

And I'm also dying of curiosity. Whose text was Sylvie reading, anyway?

What if it was mine?

I wander a safe distance away and check my texts. There is nothing from her. And now it's past midnight in New York, so even if I were going to indulge my curiosity, I can't.

I only want her to be happy, he'd said. Either it's true, or he's very dedicated in his martyrdom.

"Play us another one, Bayer!" Crikey shouts. And I look around for my guitar, because my public needs me.

TWENTY-SEVEN

Tough Act to Follow

SYLVIE

"HOW DID you make my hair smooth like that?" I ask Keyanna, the hair and makeup person who—in the space of five minutes—has turned me from a jock into some kind of glamour queen.

"It's this," she says, holding up a pricey-looking bottle of something called *hair finisher*. "I'll text you the label. And I just used a round brush." She shrugs.

"Round?"

Keyanna holds up the kind of brush where the bristles go all the way around the handle. "You own one of these, right?"

Slowly, I shake my head.

"Oh, honey." She makes a tsk sound. "When you dry your hair, just bend the ends around the brush. It's easy-peasy."

"That's what you think."

She laughs in a big, throaty voice. She has gorgeous dark skin and curly hair piled into a glamorous heap on top of her head. I already have a girl-crush on Keyanna, and on this whole photoshoot experience.

"I can't believe I'm getting paid for this." In fact, the paycheck will equal a third of my Bombshells salary for the whole season. I'm making that money in three hours.

Best. Scam. Ever.

185

"Girl, you are so pretty, those cheekbones are a work of art. There's nothing surprising at *all* about picking you for this boondoggle."

There are three of us, including Charli and our teammate Samantha. "It's us three because I'm half Chinese," Samantha had said with a snicker. "Sylvie's Canadian and Charli is a redhead. That's what counts as diversity in hockey."

Either way, I feel a twinge of guilt about earning thousands of dollars to stand around in this brightly lit studio in tight black jeans with a sporty satin stripe down the side of the leg.

But not guilty enough to turn down this job.

"Okay, girls," Bess says as soon as the hair and makeup people are done with us. "This is the moment when I give you my stump speech about photo shoots—you can always say no to a photographer's request. You can say you're not comfortable with a pose, or that something feels wrong to you. Except there's very little chance of you feeling squicky with Asher behind the camera." She points at a very cute photographer, who's bent over the monitor where his assistant is reviewing the shots they already took of the men.

"Asher never hits on women," Keyanna says with a grin. "You all are not his type."

"That may be true," Bess says. "But I meant that Asher is a real professional behind the camera and a retired athlete himself."

"And he's dreamy," Samantha whispers.

She isn't wrong. Asher has shaggy, dark-blond hair that's carefully styled to look careless, and beautiful hazel eyes. He has the kind of face that belongs at the other end of the camera, not the back of it.

"Does anyone have any questions?" Bess asks.

"I do!" Charli raises her hand. "Do I get to keep these clothes?"

"Yes," Bess says firmly. "They said you could keep everything except that leather jacket they're putting on Sylvie. Now go mug for the camera. Asher is ready for you."

Keyanna fits the jacket over my shoulders as Asher beckons us toward a green-screen backdrop ablaze with fancy lighting. "All right, ladies. Join me on the set," he says. "We'll start in front of the taxi." He waves a muscular arm toward the edge of the vast room. "Let's have the taxi, gents!"

I don't know why I'm surprised when a garage door opens in the far wall and a vintage cab rolls slowly to the center of the set.

Asher struts up to the rear door and opens it with a flourish. "All right. What's your name, gorgeous?" he asks my teammate.

"Samantha."

"Samantha, please come this way and put a foot up on the running board of the cab. That's it," he praises her as she takes the position. "And you, miss? Is it Charli? That charcoal color is hot on you. It makes your skin glow."

"Thank you," she says smiling in spite of herself. Asher is so charming that even Charli can't resist him.

He positions her in the shot. "Now you, Sylvie..." He pronounces my name in a French accent, like my mother used to. "With those cheekbones that could etch glass. You're the tallest, and I need you leaning against the bumper." He beckons me toward the rear of the car.

I feel self-conscious as I place my hand on the shining paint, my hip braced against the car.

"Yes! Now turn your shoulders a few degrees toward me. There! Drop your left hand to your hip. And lift the crown of your head... *Yes.*"

He chuckles to himself and positions the camera, which is suspended on a sophisticated mechanical arm. "You three are making this easy for me. I want a smile from Samantha. Now Charli—give me a coy smile. Like you know a secret. Yeah, baby! You do coy really well. And Sylvie—I want attitude from you. Like there's somewhere else you need to be."

Oh boy. I feel a little out of my element as I gaze to the side and try to look put out.

"Good, good," the photographer encourages. His camera shutter fires rapidly. "Now please take a step forward and move closer together. Charli—arms around the others. Samantha, another half step forward please. Look this way."

I line up with my teammates as the lights blaze at us. It's like high noon in the desert. But what's a little sunstroke? I'm making thousands of dollars right now.

"Sylvie," Asher says. "Look over my shoulder into the distance. There it is. Yes!"

When I focus my gaze over Asher's shoulder, though, I happen to spot a man in the shadows against the brick wall, staring hotly at me. Anton Bayer, in all his bright-eyed glory, is watching every move I make.

My heart gives its usual flutter at the sight of him. I shouldn't be too surprised—I'd heard the men were shooting earlier in the day for this same company.

But that's the thing—I always feel a little stunned when Anton enters the room. No other man has ever made me feel this way—like I'd walk through fire for just one more kiss. Maybe it took me a while to realize, but from the first time I ever set eyes on him, I felt that pull.

He feels it too, damn it. He's over there, arms crossed over his delicious chest, leaning ever so casually against the wall. But there's nothing casual at all about his expression. There's so much heat and tension in it that I can practically hear the sizzle all the way over here.

"That's *fierce*, Sylvie," Asher says. "Lordy lord. Turn it up, hon. I can take it. Lengthen your neck, and show me that heat."

Two can play this game. As I swivel slowly, I stare right back at Anton. It was his choice to walk away from me.

The camera clicks on. Asher adjusts my teammates, too. Then he comes back to me. "I want you up against the hood of the car. This isn't the monster truck show, so you don't have to drape yourself on it. Cock your hip. You're a busy, important woman about town in your three-hundred-dollar jeans."

"Three hundo?" Charli yelps. "Are they spun gold?"

Asher chuckles. "All right. We're going to get rid of the taxi, and I have another set piece for Sylvie. You two will be back in a few minutes. Capische?"

The taxi backs up the way it came and disappears. Two men push a platform across the floor, and on it is mounted a single carousel horse.

"Really?" I laugh. "What am I going to do with that?"

"Hop onto the platform," Asher says. "Hit the fans, boys. And we also need some tunes."

Asher's assistant goes skating off to plug in an extension cord. A moment later, a breeze begins to blow in my direction, lifting my hair away from my face. And the soul-deep thump of house music begins to emit from hidden speakers.

"Grasp the pole, hon," Asher says, a smaller camera in his hands. He drops to one knee and points it at me. "Let me see some more of that smolder you're so good at. What do you want, Sylvie? Think about that."

Oh boy. What I want right now is standing in the shadows. Anton said we should just be friends, but I think he's wrong. I grasp the pole in the carousel horse and tip my head so that I can get a better look at him.

"Chin up," Asher murmurs, and I respond on command. "Yes, like that. More pout. More heat."

I put a foot in the horse's stirrup and give Asher what he's asking for.

"Hop up there. Side-saddle."

It's easy enough to lift my *derrière* onto the horse. I tilt my head against the pole and give Asher my best smolder. I didn't know I had a smolder, but here we are.

Across the way, Anton shifts position. Like he's having trouble standing still.

Want something? I channel in his direction. *Am I making you uncomfortable? Well, get used to it. Because I don't think this feeling is going to go away.*

The next twenty minutes passes in a haze, as I move for Asher and feel the heat of Anton's eyes on me. I let the exquisite leather jacket slide partway down one shoulder, and Asher murmurs his praise. I arch my back a fractional degree, lifting my bust toward Anton, a scowl on my face.

This could have all been yours. There's no point in denying it.

Anton licks his lips. And then? I see him adjust the way his jeans are fitting in the crotch area.

Holy hell, the power I have right now. I move like a puppet

wherever Asher tells me to, although the man I'm really focused on is ten or more yards behind him. Every little thing I do makes Anton's stare burn more brightly.

It's intoxicating.

"Okay, wow. That's amazing. You can hop down," the photographer finally says.

My whole body feels warmed from within, and I'm strangely breathless.

"That will be a tough act to follow," Samantha mutters from somewhere behind the bright lights.

"No shit," Charli agrees.

I sort of ooze off the set on spongy knees, past a wide-eyed Bess, and head for the changing area, which is nothing more than several moveable screens that are hiding an alcove.

Keyanna greets me with a warm, damp towel. "For your face. That was smokin', girl. Just damn."

I press the towel to my face, wiping away an impressive amount of makeup, but the damp heat makes me feel even crazier than I already am. I duck behind those room dividers and replace the jacket on a clothes hanger.

Then I hear footsteps approaching.

When I glance up, Anton is standing there, his gaze on fire. "I have to know, Sylvie."

"What?" I whisper, even though the music that's still playing makes it hard to have a conversation.

"I have a question for you that I have no right to ask."

"Then maybe you shouldn't?" My words are sharp, but my heart is pounding with expectation. Because I want him, but I also *miss* him. We're friends, but we could be so much more.

"You told Campeau you were seeing someone."

"Already?" I squeak. "Does he blurt out everything I say?"

He takes a step closer. My vision is full of Anton Bayer. It's a struggle not to reach out and put my hands on his body. I think I can feel the heat radiating off of him. "Was it me that you were talking about?"

"I didn't give him a name."

"I know that," he says, moving closer. "But he thought you

190

were texting someone at the time. And you said you'd started something with the guy you were texting. Was it me?"

This is potentially embarrassing, because I *had* been texting with Anton, while also wishing he were more than just a friend I slept with once.

"Yes," I admit. "You said you couldn't be my dirty little secret. So I thought I should just tell Bryce that I was moving on. And then—if I hadn't already screwed things up with you too badly—you might realize that he and I are really not a thing."

"Not a thing," he repeats, stepping closer, until I back right into the brick wall.

"Not even a tiny little thing," I agree, and we're so close that I can sense the rapid beating of his heart.

His lips twitch, and he runs a finger down my nose, which shouldn't be sexy. But since it's Anton Bayer we're talking about, it's basically foreplay. "Never call it a *tiny little thing*. A man will get offended."

"That's not what I meant—"

He kisses me.

TWENTY-EIGHT

The Back Entrance

ANTON

I KISS Sylvie because I need a moment to think. And it works just about as well as you'd expect, since her gorgeous mouth already has my body on speed dial. So this is no ordinary kiss. It's wet and dirty and a little angry.

I don't know why I thought I could stay away from Sylvie. Good luck with that, seeing as I've got her tongue in my mouth, and her hands pinned against the brick wall.

In between kisses, I pull back and study her flushed face and her heavy-lidded brown eyes. "You make me crazy. You know that?"

We kiss some more, because we can't seem to stop.

"I really like you," she pants. "I know you're Mr. Casual and everything. I'm not expecting to pick out wedding china. But we—"

More kissing.

"We're good together. Don't even try to pretend that it's not true."

Like that would even work. Instead, I lift her up in my arms until she wraps her legs around me and whimpers. Quitting Sylvie has proven much more impossible than quitting late nights and hard alcohol. "This what you want?"

"Yes. More."

"I got more for you." I give her a dirty grin. But it backfires, because my aching cock is damn close from its favorite place in Brooklyn. And I don't think we even come up for air for several more minutes.

When I hear voices close by, I break our kiss and lower her quickly to the floor. "Meet me outside."

Before she can even respond, I duck out of the far side of the makeshift changing room. A split second later I hear Sylvie stammer a greeting to her teammates, as I hustle toward the exit.

When I find my coat and step outside, the cold Brooklyn air hits me. The photo studio is located in the Brooklyn Navy Yard, so we're an easily walkable distance from home.

Sylvie emerges onto the sidewalk not two minutes later, and we set off silently together at a fast clip down the street.

"My place?" I ask as the building comes into view.

"Back entrance?" she prompts.

"You dirty girl."

"I meant the *building*." Her glance cuts in my direction, and I grin. "Oh. You were joking. Fine. Tease the virgin. I see how it is."

I jog the last few steps and unlock the back entrance which is — as she suggested — closer. "Just trying to keep things light. Besides —" Inside, I tap the elevator button several times in hasty succession.

"What?"

A door slides open, and I nudge Sylvie into the car with a haste that's not very polite. "Besides," I repeat as the door slides closed, leaving us alone. "I don't see any virgins here."

Then I kiss her again until the elevator dings for my floor. We stumble out and hurry down the hallway toward my place, where I fumble the keys until we're finally inside.

We barely make it into the apartment before I'm all over her again, her back against the door, my fingers threaded into her hair. Another few seconds of this, and I'm going to lose my capacity for speech. "This is still complicated," I remind her.

"I know."

We come together in another brutal kiss, whether this is a bad idea or not. "Sylvie, you drive me crazy. Every time I get into bed, I wish you were underneath me."

"So shut up and do that already," she pants. "Consequences later."

"You want to go upstairs?"

"Unless you're going to do me against the door." Her brown eyes flash with impatience.

And my poor heart quivers as I stand here on the precipice, trying to figure out how badly I'm going to regret this.

It's chemistry, she said. I wouldn't question that logic from any other woman, but I'm all tangled up when it comes to her. Only part of my confusion can be blamed on her relationship with my teammate.

It's also me, I realize. I'm the one who's afraid of this. Nobody has made my heart beat so fast in years. I'm probably going to fuck up our friendship before this is through.

And now I've got us locked into a staring contest. Neither of us blinks as my achy heart does battle with her fiery will.

It's probably a bad sign that I cave first. I let my eyes fall closed and take her mouth in a kiss that's sweeter than before. If we're doing this stupid thing, then I'd better slow down and enjoy it.

I tilt my head and kiss her again. "Come upstairs, baby." I thread my fingers through hers and lead her to the stairs, then charge up there ahead of her, so I can grab the book I'm reading off the pillow and toss it to the floor.

Otherwise, it's tidy up here. The loft is small—just a bed and a small table for whatever book I'm reading. And there's a round old window, too, spilling daylight on my white comforter.

This is my private hideaway, and it's rare for me to bring anyone up here. This season I haven't had a female guest at all. Not once. On game day, I usually rest here alone, gathering my thoughts, getting into the zone.

But now I shrug off my shirt without a second thought. I open the drawer beside the bed to confirm the existence of my condom stash, since I haven't needed one in a while. "Come here, baby." I lie back on the bed, tuck my hands behind my head, and wait.

The barest flicker of uncertainty crosses her face as she steps out of her shoes. But then I see her shove that hesitation aside as she puts one knee on the bed.

I crook my finger at her and roll onto my side, so that we're face to face as she settles onto the mattress. I smooth her hair back from her forehead. "I dreamed about you. That's how I felt about our night together—like it was a dream that I had to wake up from."

She gives me a flash of a smile, but Sylvie has lost patience for talking. She leans in for another kiss.

I am happy to supply one, before she pulls away to tug her shirt over her head and sheds it to the floor. When she reaches back and unhooks her bra, she isn't shy at all. And she's telling me that with every action.

She's *daring* me to get out of my head and move things along. She's smart and brave and she totally has my number. That ought to be terrifying, I guess. But right now it's just hot.

Sylvie flings her bra off the bed, and I lose a few more points off my IQ. "Keep going," I say, reaching down to push her pants down her sleekly muscled legs. "If my dreams are coming to life, that means you're naked in my bed."

As soon as she kicks the pants away, I run a hand down her body, between her breasts, down her tummy and right into her panties.

Her body jerks with surprise as I rudely spread her legs and stroke her once, quickly.

"Anton," she gasps, and then relaxes on the bed just as quickly. She spreads her legs obediently, waiting for more.

Good lord. Her fearlessness is such a turn on. I tease her pussy again, circling her slowly with my thumb, and she groans as I come away with slick fingertips. I lean down and take her nipple in my mouth, teasing her tip with a rough tongue.

She arches into my hand and my mouth and moans. Her hands fumble across my body, seeking more.

"That's a good girl," I say, releasing her breast. I take her hand and place it right over my cock. "You want this?" It's a cheesy thing to say, but I'm trying to hold up my bravado, here. Nobody undoes me like Sylvie.

In answer, she sits up, face flushed, and tugs down my track pants and briefs. I let her have the whole lot of it at once. I chuckle when her eyes get big as my erection flops up, larger than life and hard as nails, smacking me in the stomach.

"Don't get shy now," I murmur.

Sylvie doesn't even bother to clear me of my clothing. My ankles are still tangled in fabric when she reaches down to grip the base of my cock.

And then she bends right down and takes my tip between my lips.

I let out a moan of pure shock and awe as her hot tongue swirls on the sensitive underside of my cock head. "Fuuuuck, baby."

Serious dark eyes look up at me. There's no smugness in her expression at all. Just heat.

I could say every cocky thing in the book to this girl, but I'll only be fooling myself. She's owning me with that hot glance and her fearless hands as they stroke me.

My toes curl as she experiments with taking more. I wind her long hair around my hand and groan lustily. Sylvie wants to prove herself, I think. She's letting me know that she's all in.

It's working, too. I can't hold still as she pleasures me with her tongue. I'm breathing hard after just a few minutes of her sweet attention.

Every time she glances up at me with that hot expression in her eyes, I get even more turned on. But this isn't how I want it to end, so before she gets me too far gone, I give her hair a tug. "Come up here, honey. Let me have that mouth on mine."

She melts onto my chest, and I let out another groan of desire. Our kisses are bottomless. I drink from her lips and run my greedy hands all over her skin. Her panties are the final barrier between us, and I push them down in a hurry, kicking every scrap of clothing off the bed in the process.

"That's it," I whisper as she settles onto my body again, the base of my cock cradled beneath her sweet heat. "You're going to get it so good."

"Please," she whimpers, rocking against me as we sink into another kiss. "Hurry."

"Soon," I promise, reaching down to tease her. She clenches strong thighs together around my hand. Her physique is a turn-on and so is her eagerness.

And if it's true that she's inexperienced, then I'm the guy who gets to show her how good the build-up can be. I tease a single blunt fingertip across her entrance. I take her mouth in a sequence of deep kisses, stroking her with my free hand.

"How do you want me?" I whisper against her lips. "How about right here?"

"Yes," she whispers, the sunlight shimmering in her hair.

I reach for the condom, but I don't open it yet. I just pause to kiss her one more time. "You're so hot when you want something. So beautiful when you're turned on for me. Have you been thinking about this?" I cup her breast and give it a dirty squeeze.

"I can't stop thinking about it," she says, tipping her forehead against mine. "I don't even want to."

Damn. This thing between us isn't going to just burn out. I was a fool for thinking I could walk away. I tear open the condom, and Sylvie backs up a few crucial inches, watching me suit up.

"All right," I say, sitting up a little, leaning back against the headboard. "Don't get shy on me now." I give her a teasing smile.

She moves to straddle me, and I wrap a hand around myself to make this easier.

As I watch, Sylvie takes a deep inhalation. Then she sinks carefully down onto my cock, all that slick heat surrounding me with agonizing slowness.

I let out a curse and drop my head back, because I don't know what to do with everything I'm feeling right now. She blinks down at me with flushed cheeks, and then she remembers to breathe.

"You okay?" I whisper, lifting my head until we're nose to nose again. It's ridiculous, but I suddenly feel as though I've never been this close to anyone in my life.

"Better than okay," she whispers back. "And so full of you."

Ungh. My hips give an eager twitch. I want to move so badly, but I promised myself I'd go slow. "This is more fun than running on the East River," I gasp. "Just saying."

She puts both hands on my face and kisses me quickly. "But you'll still go running with me, right?"

"Yeah. I'd promise you anything right now, though."

"Then promise me we'll stay friends," she says, rocking forward, taking me even deeper than before. "No matter what."

It's so good I can't speak.

"Promise," she whispers, kissing me again.

"I promise," I murmur. "Friends. Friends who sometimes do this."

Then I push my tongue into her mouth and groan.

TWENTY-NINE

I Have a Reputation

SYLVIE

THERE'S a feeling you get in the middle of a good workout, when your body is warm and supple, and you feel invincible. Sex with Anton is just like that, but better.

I'm not even shy, because I've forgotten that such a thing exists. There's only heat and friction and the magic of our two bodies coming together.

But that doesn't mean I don't have more to learn. I'm closing in on bliss when Anton lifts me off his cock and flips me onto my back. When he climbs on top of me, it's a revelation. I groan into his mouth as he reminds me how intense it feels to have his weight spread out on my body.

Just when I've decided that nirvana has arrived, he mixes things up again, turning me over, placing my hands on the headboard and bucking against me until I let out a delighted sob on every stroke.

Only then does he kiss the back of my neck and let fly a string of dirty, lovely nonsense from those honeyed lips. "Perfect. Baby. Yes," he pants. *"Now*, sweetheart. Take it."

We reach our peak with twin shouts of pleasure before he collapses onto me in a sweaty, glorious heap.

Afterward, we lie there in a blissed-out stupor as the sun moves past his windows. I'm too spent to speak until after we nap a little. When I wake, he's finger-combing my hair and sitting on the edge of the bed dressed in workout clothes.

"Hey, beautiful," he says. "I have to leave soon. And I bet you have practice tonight."

"Hell." I sit up suddenly. "It's game day, isn't it? You're playing San Jose. Are you late?"

He shakes his head with an amused smile. Then he sits closer and cuddles me against his chest. "I'll be on time. So you've still got an hour or more to get to practice."

"Okay. I didn't mean to fall asleep."

"I did." He kisses the side of my face tenderly. "But I didn't want to leave without saying goodbye. Trying not to make all the same mistakes again."

"So you won't lose my number this time?"

He chuckles, stroking my hair. "I won't even try to stay away from you, Sylvie. I don't think I could do it. You make me too happy."

I eat up every little caress and each whispered word. This is all new for me. But I still have questions. "Where do we go from here, then? Apart from not losing each other's numbers."

"Well, I'm not a hundred percent sure," he admits. "I'd like to spend time with you."

"But we'll keep it casual," I hear myself clarify. The truth is that I don't really know what that means. I can't imagine a day when I look at Anton and think, *Eh, I feel so casually about you.*

"Yeah," he says, rubbing my shoulder with one of those talented hands. "There's also the matter of a certain teammate of mine."

"You could just tell him," I say immediately. "I mean if we end up spending enough time together that the sneakiness gets awkward."

"Maybe," he hedges. "I don't want to make you uncomfortable, either."

"He's your friend," I point out. "He likes you. It's not going to upset him."

Anton makes a face like he disagrees. "I have a reputation — not always deserved. And he's overprotective of you..."

"Which is not always deserved," I grumble.

"Exactly. But that means Campeau is never going to think I'm good enough for you."

"Good enough for what, though?" I press. "For jogging on the river, and spicy chicken and —"

"Sex," he says silkily. "He won't like our little arrangement, because he'll think I'm using you."

I make a rude noise. "That's so sexist. Who's to say I'm not using you for sex?"

"You can use me anytime." He nudges me back onto the mattress and spreads himself on top of me. "Now I have to go. It's sad but true."

"Okay," I whisper up at those brilliant eyes. "Just think about it. Maybe find a moment when you can tell him that the mystery man is you."

"If that moment presents itself, I'll do it," he says.

Then I get one more perfect kiss before he goes.

THE NEXT FEW weeks are full of joy, for so many reasons. My coach asks me to start another game against Providence and then also a game against Albany. We win the first and tie the second. My save average remains enviable, even if my game minutes are still modest.

My personal life is on even more of a winning spree. Anton and I spend a lot of time together. We still go running, in addition to our newest activities. And our classes at the pool are even more fun than usual, because the kids are working hard as the date of their test approaches.

"Did you see that race between Trina and your tall guy?" I ask in the cab on the way home. "What's his name...?"

"Manny," I supply. "Trina kicked his ass!"

"On the first race," she corrects me. "But not on the second one. It was a photo finish."

"Do you think they're all going to pass?" he asks me, his golden hair darkened by pool water, because he doesn't like to dry it. "I'm worried about Cedric."

My heart gives a little squeeze at the thought of my happy-go-lucky hockey player worrying about one of these teenagers. "Don't forget what adrenaline is capable of," I point out. "If Cedric wants to pass, I'll bet he'll find a way."

Anton hitches a little closer to me and puts an arm around me. "I hope so. He tries really hard."

"You are a softie, you know that?" I put my head on his shoulder, and he kisses it.

"Don't tell anybody. I have a reputation to uphold."

"You and your reputation."

He chuckles. "You're coming back to my place, right? For lunch?"

"I haven't decided. What are we having for lunch?" I tease.

"Mmm." He makes a sexy noise and kisses my neck. "We're having all of my favorite dishes. I'm going to savor each one of them. Slowly."

Okay, that's the cheesiest line I've ever heard. But it doesn't matter at all. I'm already glancing out the window, hoping we're almost back to our own neighborhood. This wouldn't be the first time we race inside his apartment and chuck all our clothes on the floor in a mad dash to his bed.

He'd jokingly referred to it as our "pornado." And that's not a bad description for our hasty trip into ambitious, athletic, all-consuming sex.

There's a block left before we arrive, so I lift my chin and kiss him squarely on the mouth. He tastes like chlorine and sex, and I am here for this.

Anton leans in for more until I'm breathless. Then he pushes a twenty through the slot to the driver and bids me to get out of the cab at the rear door of his building.

We're still sneaking around, as it happens. I wish he'd just call up Bryce and say, "Man, I have to tell you something." But he hasn't.

In his defense, Bryce's injury has kept him away from practice, and he's missed several games. "I haven't exactly been swimming in opportunities to talk to him," Anton has pointed out.

It's true. Although I worry that Anton just doesn't want to do it. Maybe he thinks that our fling will run its course, and that telling Bryce about it would only create a problem where none was necessary.

Anton opens the back door for me, and we head for the elevators. None of his teammates appear during our short stay at the elevator bank, so we sneak in undetected.

In the elevator, Anton pulls me into a hug, and holds me close. And then he leads me into his place, pushes me up against the wall, and kisses me silly again. "Should I order now?" he asks in a strained voice. "Are you hungry?"

"It can wait," I breathe.

That's the answer I'm always going to give him. Because everything pales in importance to more of his attention and more of his love.

I'm such a goner already. Someone pass me the manual for how to have a casual fling, because I have not figured it out yet.

I doubt I ever will.

THIRTY

Your Shot, Baby Bayer

ANTON

CHRISTMAS COMES AND GOES. We only get a couple of days off, but Sylvie gets more, so she meets her dad in Montreal for a weekend to visit some relatives.

I stay in the city, a little lonely and a little bored. I have Eric and my teammates, and a visit from my Mom. But things just aren't the same when Sylvie is out of town.

And, wow, I don't know what's happened to me. Because I'm the one who insists I'm not boyfriend material. I'm Mr. Casual. But I miss Sylvie like a lost limb, and she's only out of town for seventy-two hours.

When she comes back, I'm all over her like a Doberman on a T-bone. I take her out to a terrific sushi lunch, and then we spend many perfect hours in my bed. And in my shower.

As always, she has to go to an evening practice. But when she asks if I want to come over later, I say that I can't. I'm having trouble making sense of how I feel about her. And I don't want to misrepresent my intentions.

On the Wednesday night between Christmas and New Year's, there's a rare evening where my team is neither playing nor traveling. So naturally quite a few of us are at the Tavern. It's Crikey's birthday. By ten o'clock, we've toasted him thoroughly, and I've had to stretch a light beer further than it was ever meant to. The Bombshells are playing their last December game before a New Year's break. I would have gone to watch, but Sylvie wasn't playing tonight. I checked with her before I came over here. If she'd gotten a chance to start a home game, nothing could keep me away.

Since I can't drink, I'm playing pool, which is easier when you're sober. Who knew? But as the evening wears on, I start watching the door.

The Bombshells game is already over. They lost, which I know because Sylvie texted me a frowny face about an hour ago. *2-4* she wrote.

Who had a bad night? I'd asked.

Everybody. And I had to watch.

Sorry, babe. Come to the tavern and I'll buy you a drink.

She hadn't replied. But eventually the door opens and I spy one of her teammates. My heart gives a kick as I wait to see her face.

And then she's right there, walking in with Charli. She doesn't spot me right away. She's laughing at something her teammate has said, her color high, her hair wavy from the shower.

All I can do is stand here like a fool and drink her in. I'd rather drop this pool cue and pull her into my arms. The urge is strong. I can't, though. Because I'm the dumbass who hasn't told Campeau that Sylvie and I are spending time together.

This is not entirely my fault. Until an hour ago, I hadn't seen my teammate's face in two weeks. Sure, I texted and called to check up on him after his injury. But, in typical Campeau style, he hasn't shared much. Either that, or he's been in a state of denial over how long they were going to bench him.

It sucks. It really does. I feel for the guy. I hadn't wanted to visit his bruised, aching self on my way out of town on the jet to say, "Hey, I hope you feel better soon. And by the way I'm shagging Sylvie every chance we get. But don't worry. She's down."

Yeah. No.

The women crowd around their favorite round booth, and Sylvie has to step aside for a second to wait for her turn to sit down. That's when she spots me watching her like a hungry dog from the pool table.

She flashes me a quick smile before she disappears.

"Your shot, Baby Bayer," Drake says.

"Fine." I've about had it with pool, so I take care to make this a good one. I line up a combination and sink my two remaining balls. Then I hand the stick to Crikey. "Take out the eight ball and you can have my next game."

"Dude," Drake says, still staring at the table where my two balls have just disappeared. "Where were you during the battle of the sexes?"

"Drake wants a rematch." Crikey chuckles. "He's not over losing that thing. I swear, he thinks about that exhibition stunt more than he thinks about our actual games."

I clamp a hand on Drake's shoulder. "Next year, big man. You'll have your revenge."

Then I leave them to it and look around for Campeau. Has he left already? I'm not proud to admit it, but when I can't seem to spot him, I'm relieved. I'm not in a hurry to tell him that I'm sleeping with the woman he feels he's taken some kind of a blood oath to protect.

But wait. He's still here. He's at the far end of the bar, deep in conversation with Petra, the grumpy bartender. Campeau is the only one who can stand her.

So I guess this is it. Time for my big confession.

I thread my way through the crowded space, passing the Bombshells at their table. It's so full tonight that they're squished in like sardines. My gaze collides with Sylvie's for a split second. I send her a look of longing.

She puts her chin in her hand and seems to make a point with her eyes. And that point is something like: *I could climb over this table and kiss you right now. Except you're the one who continues to let this be awkward.*

Or maybe I'm projecting. But Sylvie's eyes are really fucking expressive.

I *am* the one who's making this awkward, so I head over to Campeau and sit down on the last empty barstool—the one nobody wants because it's practically out the front door. "Hey man," I say as soon as Petra moves on to pull a pint for someone. "Long time no see."

"Yeah well. I see you every time I turn on the fucking TV."

Uh-oh. Campeau is drunk. That's unusual. "You okay? Anything the matter tonight?"

"What, besides everything?" he snarls. "I'm out two more games. Then I can attend practice, so long as it's no contact."

"Oh shit." My man is in a bad way. "Bryce, listen to me. You're coming back. Unless there's something you're keeping from me, this injury is an inconvenience. But it's not a career ender."

He snorts. "It's a disaster. And I turned down my contract extension like a bone skull."

"Bonehead," I correct before I think better of it.

He throws up his hands. "Say whatever you want. I know you were waiting for this to happen."

"What?" I grab the soda that Petra left for me and take a gulp. "Why the fuck would you say that?"

"You think I'm stupid to turn it down before. You think I'm crazy to stay single and live in a cheap apartment."

"I never said that." But I totally thought it. Still. "Do I look like a guy who has everything all figured out, though? Who'd listen to me, anyway?"

The door flips open beside me, blasting cold air all over us. "Hey guys!" Bess says, oblivious to the uncomfortable conversation we're having. "How is everyone?"

Campeau lifts a stiff hand in greeting. Although, since he looks a little stiff even on his best days, Bess probably doesn't notice that he's off tonight.

And anyway, Bess is waving at Castro across the room now. "Come see these photos I got back today! You too, Bombshells. The Brooklyn Outfitters campaign looks smokin' hot!"

Tank, her husband, gets up from the table he's sharing with O'Doul. "Show me these photos, babe. I don't think any of these chuckleheads can top my modeling career."

"I am partial to a certain photo of you in tight green underwear," she says, pulling a portfolio out of her backpack. "But we're going for a different look here."

Charli skates over to Bess and Tank. "I want to see! That photographer made Sylvie look like a goddamn supermodel."

At that, Campeau perks up, too. He pushes back his stool. And a couple of minutes later the whole bar is surrounding Bess as she opens the portfolio.

I hang back, though. It's crowded, and I don't really need to see photos of myself posing on the set wearing two-hundred-dollar sweatpants and a tight T-shirt, even if I had a blast doing it.

And I *really* don't want to see those pics of Sylvie, unless it's just the two of us looking at them together. I'm never going to be able to think about that day without remembering how turned on I was when she looked back at me. And how fearlessly she just went with it—mirroring my supercharged libido right back to me like a weapon.

I don't think I can stand in mixed company and remember that afternoon without everyone reading that memory right off my face.

"Here's Samantha!" Bess says, and I hear applause from the Bombshells who've gathered around to see. "And Charli. And who knew Sylvie walked a catwalk in her previous life."

"Whoa!" say several of the onlookers at once.

"Hot!" calls out one of my teammates.

"Let's see... Ladies and gentlemen, Anton Bayer."

There's some good-natured hooting from my teammates, several of them look in my direction to rib me. "Work it, baby!" Crikey calls.

But then I spot Campeau's mouth, which is twisted into a snarl. He walks unsteadily back to the bar, glaring at me.

Whoa. Does he *know* that...

"You took my sponsorship," he spits.

Wait, what?

"Wait, what?" I say. "Bess asked me to fill in. She was in a jam. I didn't think it was that important."

He shakes his head. "You don't think anything is important. That's the problem with you."

"Bryce, *Jesus*." I put my glass down, because it's obvious that we're done here. He's drunk, and in the shittiest mood I've ever seen him.

Way to push my buttons, though. He couldn't have landed that punch any better if he'd tried.

I weave my way through the bar once again. Sylvie is surrounded by her teammates, so I can't easily get near her to say hello. They'd make way if I were her boyfriend.

But I'm not. And that's my own decision, I guess. Doesn't feel like a good one now.

I find my jacket on a hook near the pool table. "Leaving already?" Crikey asks, following me back toward the front. As if I hadn't been here three hours already.

"Yup. Trip tomorrow. You know I like my beauty sleep."

"Can't believe you, man!" the birthday boy crows. "Our Baby Bayer's got his shit together this year. Takin' hockey by storm! Got your first sponsor. You're livin' the dream!"

Campeau glowers at me from his barstool, and I am officially done with this night. If this is what success looks like, it isn't half as great as I'd hoped. "Happy birthday, man. See you tomorrow."

I survive another bone-jarring back slap and head for the door.

Eric meets me there. "Hey, got a second? I'll walk you home."

"Sure, if you want." I'm honestly not in the mood for more company, but Eric is not somebody I ever blow off. I'm lucky to know him, seeing as my asshole father burned bridges with his dad a long time ago.

We head outside together and turn right, toward my apartment. Which is actually his apartment. "You okay?" he asks.

"Yeah. Just grumpy. Campeau's pissed at me."

"I saw that. He's only pissed at himself, though, and taking it out on you."

"Like that's fair?"

Eric shakes his head. "Of course not. Campeau will probably snap out of it."

"Probably," I grumble, because the truth is that I've never seen him act like such a turd. "He's been through a lot and handled it like a champ, right? And now this one injury turns him into a whiny little bitch?"

"You know, buddy." Eric chuckles. "I got to hand it to you. Last spring was rough. And you didn't take that shit out on anyone. Good on you for that."

"Seein' as I was the only one to blame, I wouldn't, though." We walk in silence for another moment. "Tell me this—how much do I owe team unity? Like, how much crap do I take from my team-mates so we can achieve greatness together?"

"Is this about Sylvie?"

"What?" I ask, and I'm probably about fifty percent convincing in my surprise. "Why do you ask?"

"Because I'm not an idiot. Anyone with eyes can see you two circling each other."

"Well, there's been a lot of... *circling*," I admit. "If that's what we're calling it."

"You sly dog. And he doesn't know?"

"Nope."

"They're not a couple, are they?"

"*Hell* no. Not now, not ever. But they have some kind of child-hood pact to look after each other. Sometimes it feels like I'm trying to join a cult. Like I don't know the secret handshake."

"How serious is it?" he asks.

"It's not," I fire back. "I'm not a serious guy, remember?"

"Everyone is a serious guy when the right person comes along."

"Not true," I argue. Although I have to admit that Sylvie is the kind of woman who makes me wish I was the right kind of man.

The real reason I haven't found a way to make my case to Campeau is brutally simple. I see the man's point about me.

I really do.

THIRTY-ONE

Make a Resolution

SYLVIE

I WAKE UP SLOWLY. And—as always—I'm alone in my bed, wishing Anton were here. I want to roll over and find him in the bed with me.

He's never there, though. The way our schedules work, we tend to spend time together in the middle of the day. He travels a lot. And when he's here in Brooklyn, our games are on alternating nights by design. That means one of us is usually up later than the other one.

If we were a real couple, though, one of us could climb into bed after the other on those late nights. We could wake up together in the morning and make sleepy love.

I want that. I want to be the first one to see Anton's smile at the start of his day. And I wonder why he doesn't want that, too. Because it's nice here in bed, thinking sleepy thoughts. My body is heavy and serene. My thoughts drift inevitably to memories of our time together. The heat of his skin, and the weight of him over me. In the mornings, he's all I can think about.

So imagine my surprise this morning when I stumble out of my bedroom a little later to make coffee, only to find Bryce asleep on my sofa.

Whoops! I'd forgotten all about bringing him home last night when he was drunk and sad and unable to locate his keys.

As I tiptoe past him toward the coffeemaker, he lets out a groan.

"Morning, sunshine," I say, in a chipper voice.

"*Bonjour*," he greets me blearily. "Oh, my head."

A year ago, I always woke up wishing Bryce were nearby. Now here he is, and he's not the person I'm looking for. Funny how that works.

"We need egg sandwiches," he says, pulling himself upright. "Let me order some breakfast for us."

"That sounds nice," I admit. I'd rather eat breakfast in bed with his teammate, but I'm not going to look askance at a bacon, egg, and cheese with my old friend.

I sit down on the edge of the sofa next to Bryce's feet. Fiona left town after last night's game for a quick holiday visit with friends in Philadelphia. So it's just the two of us, which makes this the very scene that I used to picture — Bryce and me at home together in the morning.

It feels one hundred percent wrong now. Go figure.

"Your face looks better," I point out, examining the fading bruises near his eye.

He shrugs. "I was never going to enter any beauty contest. And it's not my face that keeps me from playing."

"I know you want to get back out there," I say gently. "And you will. But Bryce — don't take this the wrong way — I think you could really use some downtime."

He flinches.

"I didn't hear whatever made you so upset last night, and I don't know what you're going through. But you seem really strung out. If you're not allowed back at the rink for a few days, can you find a way to spend the time on some self-care?"

His dark blue eyes take on an expression of horrified disbelief. "Like…you want me to get a massage and a manicure?"

"Easy, now. It doesn't have to be a day at the spa. You have to learn to walk before you can run. But what about a day at the movies? Or a museum? Just change your scenery. Think about something besides hockey for a change."

His expression is still dubious. "I do not know how to do that."

"I know. That's kind of the point. Do you want me to order breakfast for us?"

"I got it," he says, reaching for his phone on the coffee table. "Ah, lucky! Petra found my keys."

"That is lucky," I agree. "I'll start the coffee, and then I'm going to shower before the food comes."

"Yes, go," he says, waving me toward the kitchen. "I will order breakfast. I already have ideas about—what did you call it? Care for yourself?"

"Self-care," I say, biting back my smile as I stand up. "Learn that word, Bryce. You need it."

THIRTY MINUTES LATER, we're seated side by side on the sofa enjoying coffee and breakfast together. Bryce has pulled himself together, gotten dressed, and folded all the blankets before returning them to the closet. Say what you will about the man, but he cleans up his messes.

"Tomorrow night is New Year's Eve," he says now.

"I guess it is. Are you going to make a resolution?"

He shakes his head. "But yesterday your father asked me if I wanted to visit him for New Year's. I have not been to see him in a long time."

"Oh," I say brightly. "That's a nice idea." It's probably my doing, too. Yesterday, even before Bryce got drunk and sloppy and upset, I'd told my father that he was having a rough time.

"I'll call him," Dad had said. And it seems like he did.

"If you can find a last-minute flight, you should go," I urge him. "That sounds nice, doesn't it? I haven't been home in a while, either."

Bryce gives me a sideways glance. "What are you doing for New Year's? Are you going to some big New Year's Eve party with your new man?"

"Oh no," I say automatically. Because of course I'm not. Anton has a game on New Year's Eve. And even if he didn't, we don't go to parties together. Even if I wish we did.

"You look sad about it," he says.

"Oh, no way," I argue. "It's not serious with us."

"You say that, Sylvie. But some people are just serious people. I think you are, and so am I. That's just how we're built."

Oh jeez. I *really* don't want to hear his advice about my romantic life, even if I suspect he has a point. I may not be cut out for casual sex. But that doesn't mean I shouldn't try it if I want to.

"You have a break in the schedule, no?" Bryce asks. "For New Year's?"

"That's right," I say, happy to change the subject. "Ticket sales aren't great during the holidays, apparently."

"Then come with me to Ontario," he says. "Just a three-day trip."

"Wait, what?"

"Come. We will take your father to dinner. We will go to a museum. I draw the line at a spa day, though. Come with me, Sylvie. You have not been home since the summer. Why not do it?"

"Well, I have to be back in New York on January fourth." That's when the lifesaving test happens. And I have a game that night. "The flights would have to line up just right."

"What if I charter?" Bryce says, pulling out his phone. "We would come back on the third. That would be luxurious, no?"

"And spendy," I point out.

"I know it. But you are right—I never do extravagant things. Never anything just for me. And here is this opportunity. I could spoil both of us." He taps on his phone. "You think I'm incapable of doing anything spontaneous."

"Hey—I never said that."

He gives me a wise look. "Come on, Sylvie. It's what you think. Isn't that why I bought a Vermont getaway in the silent auction? Because you were trying to teach me to have more fun?"

"Oh shit," I blurt out. "Did you win that thing?" I'd forgotten all about it.

He gives me a soft smile. "I did. But those cabins are not open in the winter. I checked while you were in the shower."

I give a slow blink. Bryce wanted to go away to Vermont for the weekend? He didn't mean with *me*, did he?

He couldn't possibly mean that.

"Let's go home to Ontario," he says, unlocking his phone. "One time I saved this number for a charter company. O'Doul gave it to me. Why not go? Unless you have plans..."

We both know I don't have plans. "I absolutely have to get back on the third," I say. "It's nonnegotiable."

"Let me just see what is available."

THIRTY-TWO

That Someone Isn't Me

ANTON

WHEN THE TEXT comes from Sylvie, I can barely believe it. She's in Canada? With Campeau?

It was a spur of the moment thing. And I haven't been home since summer.

Okay, this is no big deal, I tell myself. It's not a romantic getaway. She didn't run away with him on a cruise to the Virgin Islands.

Besides, Sylvie is a grownup who can go wherever she wants. I don't get a say.

So why do I want one all of a sudden?

At the very least, I can't resist pointing out that we have some important business to attend to this week. *I sure hope you make it back in time for the big lifeguarding test on the 4th.*

I will! I have a game that night, too.

That's right. And I'm hosting a bunch of teenage lifeguards that night. Go Bombshells.

That is so cool of you. I wish I could help you plan it.

I wish she could, too. Although Georgia, Rebecca, and Heidi have already offered. So I don't even need the help.

I'm just jealous, damn it. Someone is away on a trip with Sylvie, and that someone isn't me.

Have a good time in Ontario, I say, instead of saying all the things in my heart.

I will! Heading out for a nice lunch! Talk later!

THE NEXT DAY is New Year's Eve. We have a game, which I suppose will be watched by all the single men who don't have a date for New Year's Eve.

At five o'clock I walk to the stadium, past shops festooned with balloons and glitter, and I feel exactly like one of those lonely, dateless guys.

There's no reason for me to feel particularly solitary. I have the same number of friends as I did last New Year's. My game is on point, my stats are up, and I want for nothing.

Except for one thing. I want Sylvie in my life, and in my bed. I want more of her, even though I shouldn't.

WE BEAT New Jersey five to three, and then I attend a spontaneous New Year's Eve celebration at the home O'Doul shares with his fiancée, Ari.

There's pizza, and I bring a six-pack of light beer, which Tank drinks with me out of pity, I think. "We crushed 'em tonight, Bayer. Got a New Year's song for us?"

"Didn't bring my guitar." I'm not in the mood for singing, anyway. I can't stop wondering what Sylvie is up to tonight.

Just before midnight, we watch Silas's wife sing a short set from Times Square on O'Doul's big-screen TV. And then we watch the ball drop.

Stepping away from the crowd, I find a quiet corner and pull out my phone to call Sylvie. But then, with my thumb on the screen, I hesitate. She probably doesn't want to hear from me right now. Since I haven't found the balls to do my part and have a talk with Campeau, it would just be awkward if I called at midnight.

I put my phone away. Then I make my excuses and walk out into the cold night by myself.

ON THE THIRD OF JANUARY, I'm gearing up for another home game, this time against Florida. But right before I leave my apartment, my phone rings.

Sylvie. The sight of her name on the screen is like a drug. I feel warmth flood my veins as I answer the call. "Hey girl! Happy New Year. How's Canada treating you?"

"Anton! Canada is great. And I know you're probably headed to the rink, but I have to tell you something, okay? I feel really bad about this."

My stomach bottoms out. Because I'm a hundred percent sure that she's about to say: *Campeau removed his head from his ass. We're getting married, and we're going to have little babies together.*

Why else does a guy take a girl out of town? They went to visit her *father*. He probably wanted to ask permission. That's exactly the kind of guy he is.

"I have to miss the Red Cross test," she says.

Oh.

"*Oh*." I say, stunned at this development. "Is there a problem?"

"Well, no. My coach just called, and I'm playing tomorrow night. So they want me at another goalie practice as a warmup. It's at the same time as the test."

It takes me a second to completely rearrange my brain to this new reality. But then I realize what a huge deal that is. "Holy shit!" I gasp. "That's terrific! You got a home game." *Finally.* I sit down on my couch so I can concentrate on whatever she says next.

"I'm pumped up. You have no idea. But I can't believe I have to bail on the test! After all that."

"It's okay," I say smoothly. "Really. The Red Cross guy is going to run it, right? What was his name?"

"Randy Fineberger."

"How unfortunate." We both snicker, and it feels like *us* again.

Sylvie and I always have a good time together. When it's just the two of us, everything makes more sense.

"I'll email him," she says. "And please apologize to the kids? Heck, I'll email them, too. I really didn't want to bail."

"Hey, I know. It's okay. You've been waiting for this."

"My dad is going to fly back with us so he can see the game."

"Awesome. I'll be there, too. It's the night of my hockey party for the swimmers. They'll get to see you play, and so will I." It's so fortunate, since our schedules almost never line up like this.

"Yeah, like I need any more pressure." She laughs nervously.

"You got this," I say, wishing I could reach through the phone and pull her into a hug. "It's going to be amazing. In twenty-four hours it's all happening!"

"Thank you," she says softly. "Thanks for all that you do. For the kids, I mean."

"Yeah, no problem." There's a beat of silence. And I want to fill it with so many things. *It's really good to hear your voice. I miss you more than I'm supposed to. I'm lonely without you.*

But I don't say any of those things. Not one. She's probably not alone right now, anyway. And she probably doesn't want to hear it.

"You take care of yourself. I'd better get to the rink."

"Oh, of course!" she says quickly. "Here I'm babbling about my game, when you have one right now."

"I'll get there. You take care, okay? And I'll see you tomorrow night."

"Bye, Anton," she says quickly. "I, um, thanks again. Bye."

We hang up, and I feel unsettled, but I head to the rink like a good boy. We lose to Florida in overtime, but I get an assist. I can hold my head up high.

As soon as I leave the arena, though, all I can think about is the damn test tomorrow. I skip the bar and head home, thinking about the rescue portion of the exam. I take off my suit, thinking about the treading water part. And I climb into bed, thinking about the last skill—fetching the weight off the bottom of the deep end and swimming it across the pool.

We didn't have the right kind of weight for practice, so we had to use those rings. And I never demonstrated the full skill. I let

Trina demonstrate, because I didn't want to screw it up and look like a dingus.

Most of the kids practiced the whole skill with the ring. I don't think Cedric did, though. I wonder if he'll pass the test.

It's not all that surprising that I dream about the lifeguarding exam after I fall asleep. In the dream, Sylvie is there, but I'm in charge, and I have to demonstrate every skill before the kids do it.

"But don't worry," Sylvie says. "We'll just keep it casual."

She's smiling at me as I get into the pool to swim the laps and perform the rescues. Because this is a dream, there's also a Coney Island-style hot-dog-eating contest going on at the same time, over at the side of the pool. If you're really into Freud, make of that what you will.

Eventually, it's time for the very last skill, the dreaded weight.

"Here it is," Sylvie says. Then she throws a giant cinder block into the deep end. "You have two minutes."

I'm supposed to swim down and fetch it. But I don't want to.

"Go on," my father prompts. "You pussy. Just get the damn thing. Everyone is waiting."

So I do it. I dive under water, and kick down into the blackness. I can't see anything, but I find it anyway, and I pick up the block. It's lighter than it should be.

I push off the bottom and propel myself to the surface, bearing the weight toward the edge of the pool. I need both hands to hold the weight, so I swallow a mouthful of water as I kick toward the side. I choke and cough as I kick toward relief.

But my father is waiting there for me, and every time I get close, he reaches out with a long arm and pushes me backwards, away from the safety of the edge.

I start yelling. "Dad! I need to put this down. It's heavy."

"Too late," Dad says. "You blew it. He's already dead."

I look down at the weight in my arms. And I find I'm holding my brother Rudy's lifeless body. His lips are blue and his skin is pale.

Waking up with a gasp, I sit up in bed so fast that I almost sprain something. I'm sweating, and my heart is pounding.

Holy shit. "Thanks, brain," I wheeze. "Thanks for that healthy serving of what-the-fuck."

I flop back onto the pillows and groan.

It's the only time in the last few weeks when I've been glad Sylvie wasn't here with me.

THIRTY-THREE

Two Minutes

ANTON

I WAS right to assume that the Red Cross guy would run the test. Randy Fineberger is here with his clipboard. And even though I've worn my swimsuit, nobody expects me to get wet today.

Maybe it's the humidity in here, but I start to sweat as Fineberger starts the clock. If these kids don't pass, I'm going to feel like an asshole.

So far the test is going fine. Everyone swims the lengths they're asked to. And then every kid performs a rescue on another kid, using first the hook and then the flotation device.

I'm feeling optimistic as they push on into the next task—the two-minute water-treading. Without arms, of course.

Last week Sylvie explained that you can roll onto your back for this, and that's what most of the kids do. Although Cedric stays vertical, kicking his legs. And he's getting tired.

"Find a way to slow your breathing," I coach from the pool deck, feeling like a poser. I'm so anxious for these kids that I'd probably sink like a stone if I were in there with them.

Cedric sort of rolls onto his back, like a cartoon manatee. I see him take a slow, measured breath and bear down into the eternity that is one hundred twenty seconds.

I don't know what's happened to me. I signed up for this job to see Sylvie in a bathing suit. I don't like pools, and I didn't care all that much if these kids passed this test.

And here I am losing my ever-loving mind, sweating over the last twenty seconds of the task. Damn, I really wish Sylvie was here. She's the one who got me into this. She should see how it plays out.

There's only a few seconds left when Benjamin accidentally sucks back a mouthful of water, and then makes a choking sound, followed by a harsh cough. *Ugh*. I can feel my own lungs burning in sympathy.

And then—hell—I see his fingers reach out for the wall in a natural impulse to steady himself.

"No hands!" I bark like a corrections officer.

Benjamin gives me a wild look but does not touch the wall.

"Time," Fineberger says.

I let out a whoop and pump my fist. "Good job, guys. You're doing it."

"There's just one skill left," Fineberger says, leaning over to open a plastic crate. "We'll do this two at a time. You'll start in the shallow end, swim down to the deep end, and pick up the weight off the bottom."

Okay, at least it's not a cinder block. It is a dumbbell that's coated in rubber foam, probably so that it would bounce off the bottom of the pool instead of breaking it.

But, Lord, how do you *swim* with a dumbbell?

"Would you mind putting these in?" Fineberger asks me. "They should be spaced out at the deepest part of the pool, so the kids don't get in each other's way."

"No problem," I say, lifting the first weight and carrying it to the pool's edge. Twenty pounds is nothing in the weight room. But it feels like Wile E. Coyote's anvil as I toss it into the deep end and watch it slowly sink. Then I toss the other one.

"I didn't practice this," Cedric says in a low voice after I'm done. "I only used the ring that first time."

"We didn't have this kind of weight to use," I say, kicking

myself now. I could have brought something for them to practice. I should have, damn it.

"Really don't know if I can do this," he mutters.

And I say nothing. Because that seems like a perfectly reasonable position to me.

"Is there anyone who wants to lead the charge?" I ask the kids. "You could be first to complete all the skills." Sometimes a little peer pressure is all that's needed.

"I'll do it." Trina raises her hand. She's one of Sylvie's best swimmers.

"Me too," a kid named Manny volunteers, possibly because he can't stand the thought of being shown up by a girl.

I clap my hands with much more confidence than I feel. "Okay, guys. Once you enter the water, you've got two minutes to complete this task. Show us how it's done."

The proctor holds his stopwatch. "And... *go*." He pushes the button as Trina and Manny hop into the shallow end and start swimming.

Manny is the faster swimmer, but he burns some time looking around with his head under the water, finding the weight.

Trina just takes a big breath and kicks under, disappearing beneath the surface.

I feel an honest-to-God cold, sweaty chill when she doesn't instantly reappear. Just the thought of the water forcing itself into my nostrils while I try to tug a weight up to the surface makes my heart pound.

Trina pops up, though, after several long beats. She's smiling. And right away she starts to kick toward the shallow end, weight towed under one arm. And Manny is about fifteen seconds behind her.

"Excellent," Fineberger says. "Walk the weight back down to the deep end please. Mr. Bayer will toss it back in."

"This thing is so much lighter under water!" Trina exclaims as she hauls the weight out of the pool.

"You hear that?" I ask Cedric. "It's easier than it looks."

He gives me a dubious glance, and I know for a fact that I'm the world's biggest hypocrite. Size XXXL.

The next pair of kids jumps in, and then the next. Two by two they struggle their weights across the pool. One girl drops hers and has to snatch it off the bottom again, but the proctor waves her through.

Before long, it's only Cedric who's left. "You're up, man," the proctor says. "Ready? And…go."

Cedric slides into the pool and swims down to the deep end. *Come on*, I beg the universe. *Let him pass*.

He ducks his head beneath the surface to spot the weight. Then he comes up again to breathe. His eyes find mine, even as the seconds tick down.

"You got this," I say in my jocular, athlete voice.

Cedric ducks under again and kicks until only his feet are visible, churning beneath the water.

I'm holding my breath too, in sympathy.

He surfaces again, gasping. "It's too far down there. I can't."

"You can!" Trina cries.

"Come on! Let's go!" The other kids shout their encouragements, and I'm feeling pretty good about humanity.

Cedric swims to the ladder and gets out. "I tried. I'm sorry."

Fineberger frowns down at his clipboard. "But you won't pass."

Cedric shrugs, his chin high. He's daring anyone to argue, and they don't. The kids look everywhere but at Cedric.

"All right." Fineberger sighs. "Let me sign certificates for those who passed. You can meet me in the lobby in ten minutes to pick them up."

The kids, with a last look at Cedric and me, shuffle off to the locker rooms, leaving the two of us alone.

"I'm sorry," he says. "Can I still come to the hockey game tonight?"

"Of course you can. But let's talk for a minute. Are you sure you don't want to try again? I would ask Fineberger to come back in here."

"I'm sure, man. When I was a kid I went swimming at Coney Island on this day when there were waves? And I got, like, sucked under. I always hated the water after that. Still do." He shivers. "I didn't like everybody watching me. And it doesn't matter. I'd make a shitty lifeguard."

"Nah, I don't actually believe that," I argue. "I get the feeling that lifeguarding is more about paying attention than being a swimming stud. You could be the best swimmer in the world and still fail."

"Whatever, man. It wasn't meant to be. I'm not gonna be a big stud like you, I guess."

"Shit, Cedric. Sit down. I need to tell you a story." He gives me a dubious look but sits down on the pool's edge. I do the same. "Do you know why I came to teach this class?"

"Because you're a professional athlete, and you're supposed to, like, inspire us."

"That's not why. The real reason is that I have a giant crush on Sylvie, and I wanted to spend time with her."

Cedric puts his face in his hands and laughs. "You're shitting me, boss."

"Nope. The truth is that I hate the water, too. When I was five years old my father took us on this fancy trip to a resort in the Virgin Islands, with water so blue that it's like a movie. Besides my parents and me, there was my dad's boss, and his family. I didn't know these people, and I didn't like the kids. But I had to do everything they wanted, or my dad got angry. He wanted to make a good impression."

"Gross."

"I know, right? There we are in fucking *paradise*, but it isn't enough for my dad. We have to impress these people and their snotty kids. So my dad signs us up for this boat trip where we're going to snorkel and see fish underwater. But guess who doesn't want to breathe through a snorkel and look underwater?"

"You?" Cedric guesses.

"That's right. I'm this little kid a million miles from home, standing on a boat, afraid the fish are going to eat me. But I get in the water anyway, because I do not want my dad yelling at me. And I put my face in the water a few times to make him happy."

"Then what, boss? If you tell me a fish tried to eat you, it will not make it easier for me to love the water."

I bark out a laugh. "No. The fish weren't the villains. My dad got pissed that I wouldn't dive under like the other boys. So he pushed me."

"Off the boat?"

"No, he pushed me under. He held me down. And when I came up screaming and coughing, he told me I was a pussy, he slapped my face, and then he held me under again."

Cedric's eyes are huge as dinner plates. "That's some next-level shit."

"Yeah, he's not a good man." I look down at the calm pool water. "But the point of this story is that swimming down to grab that weight appeals to me about as much as it does to you. And I didn't want you to walk out of here thinking you were the only guy with an uneasy relationship with the water."

He's staring at me like he's not sure I'm being serious. "But you taught us all those other things—treading water and everything."

"Sure. There's a fair amount of fake-it-till-you-make-it in every man's life. You can bullshit your way through a lot when you need to. But there always comes a day when you have to fess up and own that you don't know what the hell you're doing. I guess that's today."

The proctor opens the pool door and sticks his head through. "I just realized my weights are still down there. Would you mind grabbing them for me?"

Cedric laughs. "You might have to ask someone else."

"No," I say, getting to my feet. I yank off my T-shirt. "I'll do it."

"Really, boss?"

"Yup. You going to help me?"

He hesitates. "Do I have to?"

"Nope. But..." I turn to Fineberger in the doorway. "If he gets a weight off the bottom, will he pass?"

The guy frowns. "If you hurry. Sure."

"Come on, Cedric. Just try one more time. There's nobody here to see what happens if it doesn't work out."

He groans. "Are you gonna get them both if I don't?"

I slip into the water. "Can't say for sure," I admit. It's the most honest I've been in a long time. "Could really go either way."

"Hell," he says under his breath. Then he walks over to the ladder and lowers himself back into the water. "That story you told me better not be something you saw in a movie once. Or I'm gonna be pissed."

I laugh. "It's not. I swear."

"Two minutes," Fineberger says. "And…go."

I swim out into the middle of the deep end. I put my face under the water and look down. The weights are right under us. So close, but so far.

Cedric is watching me when I raise my head. "Count of three?"

"Yeah."

He shakes his head. "This is so dumb. One. Two. Three."

I take a deep breath, and I don't wait to see if he's going under. I just go. And it's harder than I thought it would be to dive so deeply underwater. The last foot or two feel the worst, with my lungs bursting and my nose burning.

With a fierce kick, I close in on the weight, grabbing for it just as I see a Cedric-sized thing flailing to grab the other one.

Once my hand closes around it, I know this is going to work. I tug, putting my feet down at the same time. That gives me leverage to push off the bottom, and I go shooting toward the surface.

The damn weight practically floats through the water with me. Who knew?

When I break the surface, I'm alone up there for several rapid beats of my heart. But then Cedric pops up with a whoop.

"Swim down here, guys," Fineberger says, because he's some kind of aquatic drill sergeant.

"Piece of cake!" I yell, and Cedric laughs.

Then he inhales water and starts to choke, damn it.

But never mind. He coughs his way to the shallow end and puts that stupid weight onto the side of the pool.

"Good work," Fineberger says. "I'll go sign another certificate." He puts the weights into his crate and wheels it out on a luggage cart.

"You don't get a certificate, boss?" Cedric asks.

"Nah. But I haven't earned it yet. Still got some skills I need to man up and handle today."

"You gonna tell Sylvie how you feel? The class is over, boss. Better learn some new tricks if you want to see her in a bathing suit."

"Get out of my head, Cedric."

He cracks up.

THIRTY-FOUR

Dude Should Get Hazard Pay

ANTON

"WHY IS SHE ALWAYS SKATING BACKWARDS?" Cedric asks. "She gonna crash into something if she don't look where she's going."

Who knew it would be this much fun to take a bunch of teenagers to their first hockey game?

"That's Charli. It's her one job," Drake explains. "She's a defenseman. I mean—a defense*person*. That's Anton's position, too. The D-man is supposed to get in the other guy's face and make trouble for the forwards."

"I could do that job. I'm a lotta trouble." Cedric cackles. "Hey—how come the refs don't have pads? They only got, like, that shitty little helmet. That better be a high-paying job. That dude should get hazard pay for skating around all these angry women."

"They're not angry," Trina says. "The word you're looking for is *fierce*."

Cedric pulls a face. "Same difference when you got blades on your feet."

"The kid makes a few good points," Drake says, his hand dipping into my popcorn. "Bayer—did you notice? This is really good popcorn."

"Yeah. Sure it is." I'm not very focused on the popcorn, though. I'm watching Sylvie. She hasn't let anything in at all yet.

"You think the popcorn is better at the women's games?" Drake asks, dipping in for more.

I hand him the whole box. "How would you know? You're never in the stands at your own games. You hearing this bullcrap, Campeau?" I call down to our teammate, who's seated two rows beneath us.

He doesn't even hear me. He's spent the whole game so far bent forward in his chair, eyes glued to Sylvie even when the puck is at the other end of the rink. Beside him, Sylvie's dad is watching with the same intensity.

Sylvie looks good tonight, too. Her skating is smooth and her stance is confident as she directs her players in the defensive zone.

"What is Sylvie yelling about, anyway?" Manny asks. "Is she the captain?"

"No, but the goalie has a lot of jobs besides stopping the puck. She issues defensive-zone guidance. She's everybody's eyes and ears, letting players know when the opponent is closing in, or when they have time to make a play."

"Cool. Doesn't look easy."

It doesn't. This game is hard fought. Boston is scrappy and unafraid to draw penalties. The score is zero-zero near the end of the first period. It's still anyone's game.

Boston hasn't mounted many challenging offensives, but they're frustrating our team. I can see it on Fiona's face. She wishes Boston would stop tripping her every ten seconds and play the damn game.

Boston pulls another dick move, and now Charli looks ready to blow.

"Hey, are we gettin' a fight now?" Manny asks. "I heard this was a bloody game. I want to see somebody drop the gloves." He rubs his hands together.

"The women don't fight as much," Trina says. "They play a smarter, more cerebral game."

"You saying boys are dumb? That's sexist," Manny says with a chuckle. "I'm offended."

"Well, sorry," she huffs. "The women's rules change the game.

There's no body-checking, so you have to use different techniques to shake the puck loose."

Who knew our Trina was a hockey expert?

"I'm only funnin' you." Manny nudges Trina. I think he has a thing for her.

Down on the ice, our opponent continues to make trouble. Charli trips a player and gets called for it, giving Boston a power play.

The Bombshells set up for a faceoff, looking aggravated.

The only one who doesn't look rattled tonight is Sylvie. Her stance is fluid and her motion is as smooth as that first day when she'd caught my eye. Whenever Boston manages to pull together an attack, Sylvie has no problem dismissing it.

She's doing it. She's in the game. And I can't believe I get to be here to watch.

IT'S A LONG, tense battle. At the first intermission, I pass out food that I arranged for ahead of time. And during the second intermission, I lead the whole gang on a tour of the men's facilities and the smaller practice rink. We tour the video room, the weight room, and the players' lounge.

Along with my students, I've got Leo Trevi and his buddy from college, Bridger McCaulley. He's Scarlet's husband, and he's probably having a pretty boring game tonight, because Scarlet is sitting on the bench.

This pleases me to no end, even though Bridger seems like a cool guy. "Nice digs," he says as I lead my crew through the locker-room door. The room is empty, as it should be at this hour of the night.

"Dude, classy," Manny agrees, looking around. "You ever use that ice bath?"

"Only when the trainer makes me," I admit. "You don't know cold until someone pours a bucket of ice all over your naked body."

"For your paycheck, I'd do it," Manny says.

"There is that," I admit.

"Hey! Got a lot of fancy stuff in your bathroom," Cedric says from around the corner, where he's snooping near the showers. "This cream says it polishes and brightens. And it smells like mangoes."

"I play better when I smell like mangoes," I tell him. "Come on. Let's get back for the third period. Anyone want ice cream?"

That gets them moving. We sit back down in our seats during the fourth minute of the third period. The score is still zip-zip.

Just when I start to think I've accidentally brought these kids to a soccer game, Brooklyn scores on Boston.

"Yeah!" I holler, standing up to cheer. "Let's go, Fiona!"

"Don't you owe her ten bucks for every goal she scores?" Trevi reminds me.

"Totally worth it," I argue. I want this win for Sylvie. She's got a shutout, which is going to be great for her stats if she can hang on another fifteen minutes.

No matter what, though, I'm going to find Sylvie after the game. And I'm going to tell her how much I miss her. And then I guess I'm going to find Campeau and finally let him know that I need Sylvie in my life.

For real. I don't think this is casual anymore.

While I'm making these plans, Samantha scores for Brooklyn.

"Two goals!" Cedric yells. "This is great. They can't catch us now."

"God, don't jinx it!" Trina shrieks.

The whole section laughs. But then Boston gets a damn break-away. Now we're all leaning forward in our seats.

"Lookout, Sylvie!" Trina screams. "Incoming!"

Oh shit. The Boston player bears down on Sylvie. Our defense can't get there in time, so it's one on one.

Sylvie's in the zone, though. I can tell. *Come on, honey*, I privately beg. *You got this*.

The shooter tries to deke the shot with her shoulders, but Sylvie is watching so closely that they both move in the same direction at the same time, like a pair of well-trained dancers.

The puck smacks into Sylvie's glove a split second later.

"YESSSSSSS!" I scream, rising to my feet with the rest of our section. "Go Brooklyn!"

"Yes, baby, YES!" Campeau puts his fingers in his mouth and lets fly a deafening whistle of approval. It's basically the most emotion I've ever seen him exhibit off the ice.

Brooklyn's shutout is still intact with eleven minutes left in the game. But Boston is pissed off about it and getting chippy. They're playing like a bunch of trolls now, with more elbows than a box of macaroni.

Whoever called women "the fairer sex" never watched this team trying to make up for their scoring deficit with pure physical violence.

But they're running out of time. The speed of play amps up as the clock runs down. Even when you feel completely depleted, there's always a little more gas in the tank, and both teams are drawing on that right now.

Sylvie, the warrior queen, stays loose and composed in the net, watching the action and coaching her teammates. She's just fun to watch, and even though several of my teammates are sitting here enjoying her performance, I feel like a man with a secret.

She's exciting to me on so many levels. In my whole life I've never gotten turned on by somebody's hockey skills. But I guess there's a first time for everything.

I'm actually daydreaming a little when Boston gets another chance at a breakaway. This time Charli is on her, though. She angles her stick to prevent a shot. The Boston player uses her fist to try to shake her off. It's illegal, but she doesn't get called.

And then everything starts to happen really fast. Charli goes for the poke check but somehow she gets tangled up in her opponent just as the shooter makes her shot.

Both skaters go down, but they've got so much momentum in their bodies that they skid toward the net, where Sylvie is diving for the puck.

Charli rolls out of the way to avoid colliding with her teammate.

But the Boston player doesn't bother. Nor does she move her

stick out of the way. She just slides like a missile into Sylvie's outstretched upper body.

I'm on my feet again before I realize it. Sylvie's helmet has popped off, and now she's clutching her... Jaw? Neck? Cheek?

"FUCK!" Campeau shouts.

That's when Sylvie sort of curls forward, as if collapsing onto the ice. She doesn't move.

"Holy shit," Cedric whispers.

I see something red where there shouldn't be anything red.

"Omigod that's *blood*!" Trina shrieks.

Campeau climbs over a row of seats, heading for the aisle, his eyes wild.

Drake makes a grab for him. "Hey, hey. Slow down. The doc is down there."

Sure enough, Doc Herberts is already running across the ice, the trainer right behind him.

"Hands off me." Campeau shakes off Drake. "*Les ostie de fuckés!*" He follows that up with more French cursing.

I watch him run for the exit, with Sylvie's father on his heels. I want to follow, too, but I know I can't. I am entertaining seventeen guests, and Doc doesn't want me in his way.

"Is...is she gonna be okay?" Manny asks in a hushed voice.

"Yes," I say immediately. But the popcorn curdles in my belly.

Sylvie is helped off the ice a moment later. She's on her feet, but I can't see her face at all, for the swarm of people around her. It's a lot of people—her coach, the doctor, and at least one trainer. Her teammates are clustering close by.

Jesus Christ. What the hell is wrong?

I feel the strangest sensation in my body right now. Like my hands and feet are suddenly cold and numb.

"Mr. Bayer." Cedric clears his throat. "Man, you look pale. Breathe, dude."

Oh, right. Oxygen. I take a long, gasping breath and feel a little less dizzy.

"The game is over, right?" Trina asks. "There's blood on the ice."

My stomach lurches. There's a trail of blood from the crease toward the chute. And now that cold feeling is back.

"This is the pros," Drake says. "They'll almost certainly finish the game."

Sure enough, Scarlet skates out a moment later, looking a little stiff as she stands in front of the net.

"This is grisly," Scarlet's husband says from behind me. "Shitty reason to get some more playing time."

The players set up for a faceoff, but I'm no longer paying attention. My mind is on Sylvie in the locker room. I'm counting down the seconds until I can get out of here and go to her.

"She's going to be okay, right?" Trina whispers.

"*Yes*." But I've never been so worried about anyone in my life.

THIRTY-FIVE

There Goes My Modeling Career

SYLVIE

"HOW BAD IS IT?" I ask my father.

I'm lying in an ER bed, with a mask covering my eyes. The mask is shielding me from the bright lights that the plastic surgeon needed to see the gash on the side of my neck and jaw. There are something like fifty tiny stitches there now.

"It's nothing we can't handle," my father says gently.

"There goes my modeling career, right after it's begun."

"The wound is not on your face. Not really."

"I was joking."

"I know. But you're still beautiful. Just saying."

My skin is still numb, which is a really weird sensation. And I'm told that it will hurt when the numbness wears off.

I don't remember skating off the rink. I passed out in the dressing room, probably more from shock than blood loss. Although I'm told the blood loss was quite dramatic-looking, if not life-threatening.

And my poor dad had to witness the whole thing. "I sure am sorry to make you worry."

"Been worrying about you since the hour you were born. This is just another day at the office."

"It's not fair, though. After the year you've had."

He squeezes my hand. "I already know how fragile life is, pumpkin. I regret nothing. When you got the call to come to Brooklyn, I was so happy for you. I'm glad you went for it. Even if I'm going to be seeing that reckless skater aiming for you in my dreams."

"I came to New York for an adventure."

"You found it." His chuckle is dry.

"Did I, though?" A wave of despair passes through me. The reality of what's just happened to me is finally starting to sink in. "If they put me on an extended concussion protocol, they'll need another goalie."

"That could happen," he agrees gently.

"If they love that other goalie, then I'm out, Dad. There's no budget for a third goalie. I'll be back in Ontario wondering what happened."

"Oh, honey. I hope that doesn't happen. But it's too soon to worry about that."

It isn't, though. "There are no guarantees in hockey," I mumble. It's something he tells his players all the time.

"True." He lets out a sigh. "Let's just wait and see."

That's what a father says when he doesn't want you to panic. But pro sports waits for no man. Or woman. Injuries disrupt careers all the time.

I can't believe that skater was so careless as to slash me like that.

I can't believe I have a gash so impressive that I bled all over the rink. And I may have a concussion.

And I *really* can't believe that I might have just played my last game for Brooklyn. It was a shutout, and I didn't even get to finish it.

That last thing stings the worst. And that's saying something, coming from a girl with a lot of new stitches in her body.

And then there's the idea so terrible that I almost can't think about it. If I get cut from the team, I'll have to go home. I won't have a work visa anymore.

Anton will be here in Brooklyn. And I'll be in Ontario, alone.

My eyes burn behind the mask. "When can we get out of here, Daddy?"

"Soon, pumpkin. Bryce is blowing up my phone with questions. What am I allowed to tell him?"

"Whatever. I don't care," I grumble. My phone is probably blowing up, too. My teammates will be worried.

And Anton, too. Even if he won't say so, I believe in my heart that man cares about me.

"Hey now," my dad whispers. "What's the matter? You don't know how long you'll be on the bench. And it's not like you to panic."

"I'm not ready to be done," I croak.

"With hockey?"

"With Brooklyn. There's a guy."

My dad laughs. "Ah. So how come I don't know about this yet?"

"I…" *Love him.* "I really like him. But I don't know if it's mutual."

"We're not talking about Bryce, are we? I didn't get that vibe this week."

"Nope. He and I are just friends. But I have a type, I suppose. Hockey players with commitment issues."

"Oh honey. I'm sorry. There are a lot of those, though. So which one is this?"

"It's one of Bryce's teammates."

"Is that awkward?"

"He thinks so. Or maybe it's just an excuse. I guess I'm going to find out soon enough."

And I must be correct, because the door swings open, and another doctor enters the room. "Hello, Miss Hansen. Let's take a look at that head of yours. I'll need you to answer a few questions."

"Okay," I say, my voice unsteady. "I'm ready."

Maman, if you've got any pull at all in heaven, please don't let me have a concussion.

S'il vous plaît.

THIRTY-SIX

This is the Guy?

ANTON

WE'RE at the Tavern on Hicks. And by "we," I mean a whole lot of people. It's like a vigil for Sylvie. Her teammates are here, huddled in that circular booth they always take, talking in hushed voices. They officially won their game, even though the Bombshells looked shaken during those last ten minutes. Scarlet allowed a goal, unfortunately, so it's not a shutout anymore.

Sylvie is going to hate that so much.

If she's conscious.

Please let her be conscious.

I'm basically drowning here on my barstool, worrying about her. We all are.

Eric is sitting beside me in quiet solidarity. I ordered us each a twelve-year-old Macallan. He didn't even blink when I asked for something that wasn't a light beer.

The scotch isn't helping, though. I need to see Sylvie. I need to know that she's okay. My texts to her have gone unanswered.

Bryce is a couple seats down the bar. He's hunched over his phone, too. "She answer your text?" I ask, even though I know I sound way too invested right now.

"No, but now I try her father." He looks up. "Petra, could I have another beer?"

"Later," she grumbles. "I'm busy worrying about other people who matter more than you do."

Wait, what? I glance up at the bartender who is, admittedly, always a little frosty. But she's never actually rude.

Bryce seems not to have noticed, and Pete also looks unfazed. He does, however, grab Campeau's glass and refill it without a word.

"More scotch?" he asks me. "Seems like a difficult night here."

"No thanks." I sigh. There's no point in getting drunk. It won't help. "But please send a round to the Bombshells on me."

"Good man."

"They're on their way," Campeau says suddenly.

"Yeah?" my voice breaks on the word. "She's okay?"

"Fifty stitches and an inconclusive concussion result."

"But they're on their way *here*?" I clarify. If it's true, it can only be good news. Nobody goes to a bar when they're in mortal peril.

I feel the first small hint of relief. And when I glance at Eric, he's grinning at me.

"What?"

"Hang in there. You're going to be okay."

"It's not me who's in trouble."

He laughs. "So you say. This could be fun to watch."

"What are you talking about?"

"You were so wise and bossy when I was falling in love."

"What? I was not."

"You were *full* of advice. We were sitting in this same bar, for chrissakes. *Balls to the wall, man!* Sound familiar?"

"You shut up."

He snickers.

Then the door opens, and I forget all about Eric. Because Sylvie's dad is leading her into the bar. The women's table lets out a cheer, and I'm on my feet and crossing the floor toward Sylvie.

The problem is that two men are homing in on her at the same time. Bryce from the left and me from the right.

But I'm faster this year. My game is on point. All those light beers must count for something, because I get there first. The relief I feel as I gently fold Sylvie into my embrace is just indescribable. Like I can breathe again for the first time in three and a half hours.

"Are you okay?" I ask in a shaky voice, as she rests her forehead against my mouth. I give her a quick kiss on the head. "I was so worried. Does it hurt?"

"I'll be fine," she whispers. "I promise."

"What are you doing?" Bryce howls. "Be careful! She has a concussion!"

I loosen my arms immediately. I don't think I'm hurting her, but I need to be sure.

Sylvie isn't okay with that, though. She grabs me and kisses me right on the mouth.

Hell yes. I give her a slow, soft kiss.

"So I take it this is the guy?" Sylvie's father asks.

"No!" Campeau thunders. "Fuck no. Anyone but *him*. He is *not* the guy."

"Why not me?" I ask, staring into Sylvie's sweet eyes. "I'm not perfect. But I really care about you."

"You're a player! You're a *mess*," Campeau says.

"Watch it, Bryce," Eric murmurs.

"No," he growls. "You're a *snake*, Anton. You sat there and listened to me talk, nodding your head like you care. And the whole time you're sneaking around and—"

Sylvie flinches, and I guess we're both pretty glad he doesn't finish that sentence.

"Now, calm down," Mr. Hansen tries.

Campeau isn't having it. "*This* is the kind of teammate you are? Fuck you."

"Bryce," several people say at once.

But he's in a full-on rage. I watch with growing horror as his face reddens even further. This is exactly the moment I'd been trying to avoid. "Lies? Sneaking around? Is that what Sylvie deserves? That's what it means to be a good teammate?"

I feel a million people staring at me. And the truth is that I did all those things. I did sneak around. "I don't feel good about that," I say quietly.

"Wonder why?" He snorts. "You—"

"Shut up," someone else shrieks. "Just *stop*."

The whole bar turns to see who's yelling now. It's Petra the bartender. She has laser eyes for Campeau. "You idiot!" she hisses. "Sylvie is fine. Anyone with eyes can see that she's fine. And they're happy together. Just get over yourself already. You're making a scene for no reason at all!"

My gaze collides with Sylvie's, and we mirror confusion back at each other.

"Who would confide in you?" Petra continues. "You're so judgmental! Guess what? You don't get to decide what other people care about! You can waste your whole life trying to get your stats up! Go ahead. But don't tell *them* how to live."

Having said her piece, she turns around and stomps back over to the server's station, where she begins to angrily toss rolls of silverware into a pile.

Campeau's face is red. He's wearing the same intense expression he wears during a difficult game. Every head swivels to watch as he storms toward her. "Petra," he barks.

"What!" she snaps.

"I am sorry."

"Then go somewhere else and be sorry!"

We can hear every word because the bar is dead silent. Everyone is watching this drama unfold. Even Pete the bartender is standing perfectly still, a look of trepidation on his face.

"You are right," Campeau barks. "*Désolé.*"

She still doesn't turn around. Her hands are braced on the server station like she's afraid a strong wind will tear her away from terra firma.

Campeau grasps Petra by the elbows, turns her firmly around, and leans in. Then he gives her a passionate kiss.

She yanks herself back and lifts a hand. It hovers above his face. The whole bar braces for her slap.

But it doesn't come. Instead, she grabs him by the jacket and kisses him again.

"What is happening?" Charli says from somewhere nearby. "I'm so confused right now. And kind of turned on."

"I don't know. But it's fascinating," Sylvie says. She leans against my body and starts to laugh.

Her father is laughing, too. Like, doubled over and struggling to breathe. "The quiet ones," he gasps. "You never know what's going on in there."

Indeed, Petra and Campeau are now staring into each other's eyes, whispering to each other, and ignoring everything around them.

"Sylvie." I settle my arms around her and close my eyes. "Baby, I'm glad to hear you laughing. I was so worried about you."

"Sorry about that," she whispers, and hugs me even more tightly.

"We could sit down, okay? How's your head?"

"My concussion exam was inconclusive." She takes a seat on the stool that I offer her. "I answered all the questions correctly. But if you black out—even for a moment—you end up on the concussion protocol. Which I did."

"Oh, baby. I'm sorry." That means she'll miss games. "That just *sucks*. But I'm just so glad you're going to be okay. I need you."

She looks up, no longer laughing. "I need you, too. But my position is pretty precarious. They'll have to roster another goalie."

"God, I'm sorry." I take both of her hands and squeeze, knowing full well how much it hurts to watch your team go on without you. "Does it make me a hypocrite to say that it doesn't matter as long as you're okay?"

"A little?" She gives me a shy smile. "But I like hearing it."

"I'm sorry it took me too long to tell you. But guess what? The way I feel about you isn't casual at all."

Her expression softens. "That's good, because I skated past casual a while ago myself."

"God, I've missed you. So much." Very, *very* carefully, I kiss her.

Someone clears her throat nearby. "Excuse me, lovebirds, but we are all waiting to see Sylvie." It's Fiona standing there, her arms crossed, and Sylvie's coach is also waiting nearby.

"Oops," I say, letting her go. "I'm monopolizing your teammate."

"You are," Fiona says. "Take a hike, stud. Get her a soda, maybe. You can have her back in a minute."

"All right." Sylvie gives me a big smile as I move down the bar and ask Pete for Sylvie's drink.

"Just a Coke?" Drake asks. "A girl deserves a cocktail after that shitty day."

"A *woman*," Charli argues.

Drake waves a hand in her direction. "I'm not afraid of you anymore. Want a margarita? I'm buying."

Charli looks conflicted. "Um, sure. Thanks."

"Drink, Baby Bayer?" my teammate asks.

"No thanks, man." I bring Sylvie a drink and then introduce myself to her dad. "Mr. Hansen, sir. It's a pleasure to meet you."

He gives me the kind of careful perusal that they probably teach every father of a daughter, and I feel a prickle of uneasiness that might never go away. I've never been the kind of guy that women brought home to daddy.

Mr. Hansen clears his throat. He gives me a very stern look. And then he says, "My daughter thinks you don't love her."

Well, *damn*. If this is what it's like to be respectable, it's even harder than I thought. "That's my fault, sir. I'll make sure she knows. I'll clear that up tonight."

He grins. "See that you do. And you'll need these." He pulls some folded up papers out of his jacket pocket. "The hospital has some instructions for wound and concussion care. It's either you or me who's looking after her tonight."

"I'll do it," I say, taking the papers from his hand.

"Very well. That sofa in her apartment does not look that comfortable."

"Uh, right. Sir." My dad-game needs work. "Can I buy you a drink? You must have been sitting at that hospital a long time."

"Why, yes you can." He offers me his hand to shake. And I take it.

THIRTY-SEVEN

Very Motivational

SYLVIE

I CAN'T BELIEVE that it's Anton who's tucking me into bed. I guess that's a silver lining to this disaster of a night.

He pulls up the covers, then he sets a glass of water down for me on the bedside table, before walking around to the other side of the bed, and climbing in. "Are you comfortable? Should I sleep on the sofa and give you more space?"

"Oh, hell no. You're staying right here." I roll onto my right side—it's my left that has the big bandage—and reach for him. That's why I chose this side of the bed.

He catches me and pulls me against his chest. "I was really worried about you," he whispers. "You know how some injuries just look *bad*? It looked *bad*."

"My dad said the same thing," I murmur.

"Sylvie?"

"Hmm?"

"I love you."

I lift my head off the pillow, even though my upper body is starting to ache. "Anton, you're not just saying that because I bled all over the ice, are you?"

He chuckles. "Definitely saying it because I love you. I'm crazy about you. I hope someday you feel the same, but I'm willing to be patient and find out."

"Well, I think you should know…" I run a hand down his chest and sigh. "I've got it bad for you. Tonight I was lying in the ER hoping that my time in Brooklyn wouldn't end before you and I had a chance."

"Let's make that chance," he says, his feet tangling with mine. "I'm sorry it took me so long to figure out what you mean to me."

"Well, Bryce was in the way there for a while," I admit. "He was my stumbling block."

"Yeah, but I said he was my stumbling block, too. And he wasn't. Not really. It was just me and my own fool head."

"I like your fool head. A lot," I say as a yawn overtakes me.

"Oh, baby. Let's sleep," he says, rubbing my back. "You need the rest to heal."

I lean against him and take a sleepy sniff of his clean, masculine scent. "We never just sleep."

"Tonight we do," he says firmly.

And he must be right. Because I drift off very quickly.

IN THE MIDDLE of the night, though, I try to roll over onto my other side, and the jab of pain I receive from my wound wakes me up immediately.

My eyes fly open in the dark. My first reaction is, *oh shit*. But after a moment, the pain recedes to a manageable level. It stings, but I'll live.

And it's nice to find that Anton is sleeping beside me, his face peaceful, his blond eyelashes sweeping down to touch his cheekbones. He's so gorgeous that it almost hurts me to look at him.

I persist, though, and when those lashes flutter open, I realize I've been staring at him like Edward in *Twilight*. "Sorry," I whisper in the dark.

He closes his eyes, but then opens them again a moment later. Then he pushes himself into a sitting position against the headboard, like some kind of sexy phoenix rising from the ashes of the bedclothes. Moonlight bounces off his carved chest, and outlines the peaks and valleys of his golden hair that's sticking up in every direction.

"You okay?" he asks sleepily.

"I'm fine. The stitches sting a little bit. But it's really not a big deal. Can we just forget about that stupid middle-of-the-night concussion protocol? They'll quiz me in the morning, no matter what you do."

He shakes his head, and anyone else would argue with me. But not Anton. "You sound fine to me. And the truth is that I'm not that good at following directions. But if you're awake, I'd like to be, too. Wherever you are, that's where I'd like to be." He takes my hand in his and caresses it sweetly. "I'm really damn sorry that it took a blade in your face to get me to say that. But it's true."

Well, now I'm really awake. I sit up and lean against the headboard, too. The clock says two thirty, and we should both be sleeping right now. But I love this silent moment too much to try. "You know what hurts?"

"What?" he asks, sounding worried.

"The fact that I didn't get to finish my game."

"Oh, honey." Carefully, he eases an arm around me, and I tuck my chin against his muscular chest. "I bet that does hurt. I sure enjoyed watching that game—right up until the moment everything went bad. I bet your dad did, too."

"Yeah. He said the same thing a dozen times. I'll try not to whine about it too much, but it stings worse than the stitches."

"I know it. You earned that victory. What a game." He smiles for me in the dark, and that means everything.

In fact, it's making me into an emotional fool. "I also wish my mother could have seen me play."

"You must think about her all the time."

"I do. I wish I could introduce you to her. She would like you. To be fair, though, she liked everyone."

He laughs good-naturedly.

"But she would have met you, and in like ten minutes she would have been able to see all the good in you. I know I'm partial, but she was special. At her funeral, they had to set up an overflow room in the church basement with a video of the service. And even that overflow room overflowed."

He strokes my hair with loving fingers. "I sure am sorry I never got the chance to meet her. Do you have a picture?"

For a moment I almost say, *I'll show you in the morning*. But we're both awake, and one of the things I love about Anton is the way he lives in the moment. It doesn't matter if it's two thirty. His eyes are bright and warm.

"One second." I slide out of his embrace and cross my bedroom —it's only two steps—to take the shoebox of keepsakes out of the top drawer of my dresser. The only times I've opened it in Brooklyn have been to drop hairpins in there. I don't look at the photos, because thinking about my mother still hurts.

But now I hop back in bed, and then grab my phone to use as a flashlight. I lift the lid and find a ticket to my first college hockey game. Mom was seated in the front row. And here's the jeweled hairpin she left me on the windowsill just after she died. The others are in here, too.

Come to think of it, she hasn't sent me one of those in a while. Maybe she thinks I've gone off course. Or maybe not. It's possible she decided to let me handle things from here on out. I don't know if that's a good thing, or sad.

Best not to think about it right now.

I move the ticket aside. And—*bam*—right there on the top is a photo of my mother and me when I was seven years old, all dressed up to see the Nutcracker at Les Grands Ballets Canadiens in Montreal.

Tears burn my eyes immediately at the sight of her smile.

Anton makes a soft sound and takes the photo so he can see it more clearly. "You two. What a pair. So lovely."

I swipe tears away from my eyes. "Sorry."

"No, baby. *I'm* sorry. Should we do this another time?" He wraps an arm around me.

But there won't be an easier moment for it. Grief takes its bite out of you on its own time. "No, it's okay. There's a funny picture of me in high school, too. You don't want to miss it." I hand him several photos, including one where I have a really odd asymmetrical haircut.

He lets out a quiet chuckle. "Well, it's good to know that you're capable of bad decisions like the rest of us. But it would take more than a weird haircut to dull your shine."

Did I mention how much I like this man?

"Here she is frosting my birthday cake." I hand him another photo. "And here she is making my Halloween costume. She said I'd regret this costume idea. And it was one of her easier premonitions." I pass him the photo of Maman stitching me into a bulky green dinosaur costume.

"Who would have guessed that would be uncomfortable?" He kisses me on the temple. "What were her other predictions?"

Just as he asks the question, I flip to the next photograph. And it's Maman, me, and Bryce all in a row in our Sunday best.

"Ah," he says quietly. "I see."

"Nobody's predictions are right all the time," I say quickly.

"Well, good," he whispers. "Because I love you, Sylvie. You're it for me. And I wouldn't let a little thing like fate stand in the way."

My heart beats faster. "You say the nicest things."

"Nah, I'm really not that nice." He kisses the side of my face, and then my neck.

"You liar."

He chuckles, and then eases himself down under the covers. "Get some rest, sweetheart. You have to get better so I can ravish you again."

That's very motivational, and I decide that he has a point. But as Anton closes his eyes, dozing against the pillows, I look at each photo one more time as I gather them in a pile.

Before I put them back in the box, I pluck the letter out of the bottom and turn the envelope over in my hands. Maman had written it on her fine French stationery, before tucking it into a heavy envelope with a rounded flap.

And I can't resist—I open it, just to see her script on the page. It still floors me that she took the time to write this letter some time during the last couple years of her life. How did she *know?* It will forever be a mystery to me.

I examine the pages, skimming the letter again. I'd only read it once before. But my memory of what's there is fairly good. And I remind myself that I need to copy down her recipe for madeleines —on page three—someday soon, and make a batch myself.

I'd thought there were ten pages to this letter, but now I realize there were eight. I guess my memory isn't perfect. And it's on page eight that Maman had predicted my marriage. There's no point in rereading that part now. But as I fold the pages in half to put them away, my eye snags on a word that I hadn't seen before, and it makes me go completely still.

Caribbean.

Wait, what? I back up to the beginning of the paragraph and try to make sense of it.

There are times when I am not sure whether I have seen a thing in the haze of the future, or whether I have seen only what I hope to see. But there are a few things I am absolutely sure of: You will have a long and happy life, mon ange. You will know true love, as I have also known it. And you will spend your life with the lovely man with blue eyes like the Caribbean Sea.

Be patient, darling. It will happen for you. You will know great love if you allow yourself the patience to see it in front of you.

I let out a gasp, and then clap a hand over my mouth.

The sound makes Anton's eyes flutter open again—his bright blue eyes. Like the Caribbean Sea. "All good?" he asks sleepily.

"Yes," I yelp. "Just fine."

His eyes close again. I lean down and kiss his forehead to let him know that all is well, and he makes a soft sound of comfort.

But then I read the last paragraph of that letter again, my gaze darting back and forth across the words on the page.

How is this possible? I read this letter in Ontario, and I interpreted it to mean Bryce. I would have said that she'd actually named him in this paragraph. I hadn't remembered her describing the color of blue.

The fact is that I'd been impatient. I'd read what I wanted to read.

With shaky hands, I fold up the letter and tuck it back into the box. I set the box on the floor, and I set down my phone, plunging the room back into darkness.

I relax under the covers, and Anton's hand slips into mine. "Love you, baby. Sleep well, now."

"I love you, too," I whisper back.

It takes me a little while to fall asleep. My mother was a wise woman. She saw many things that I failed to see. And maybe she even predicted Anton's entrance into my life.

But I think there's something else I'm supposed to learn from those pages, first. *Patience, Sylvie.*

Let's face it, if I'd listened to that advice, I could have avoided all the heartache I had over Bryce.

You were right, Maman, I think to myself. *I must learn to be patient. If only you were here to tell me how that is done.*

THIRTY-EIGHT

Like Whiplash

ANTON

IN THE MORNING, poor Sylvie is sore. Her neck and shoulders are tight, and her stitches throb.

"It's like whiplash from a car crash," she says, rolling her neck.

"I'm sorry, baby. Let me get you a dose of Tylenol." After that, I help her to put a waterproof bandage on her wound, so she can shower.

"Sorry to be such a drag," she mumbles as I towel off her hair.

"You aren't. Stop." The truth is that I like taking care of her for once. "I do have to go to morning skate, though."

"And I have to meet another doctor, so we can argue about the concussion protocol."

"It's going to be okay," I tell her, and it's not just a platitude. "I really believe that." When she stands up, I fold her into a nice hug. "Heal fast, sweetheart, so I can let you out of sexile."

"That's a Frankenword for...sex exile?" She giggles against my shoulder.

"You know it."

I'M JUST FINISHING up a nice, grueling workout on the rink three hours later when I spot Sylvie standing over by the penalty box.

I skate over there immediately and come to a hockey stop beside her. "Hey, gorgeous. What's the news?" It must be good, because she's smiling.

As soon as I take off my sweaty helmet, she leans in to kiss me hello. One of my teammates whistles, but I don't even give him a glance.

"Guess what!" she says breathlessly. "The doctor thinks my chance of having a concussion is actually pretty low. So they're probably only keeping me off the ice for a week."

"All right!" I give her a high five, and then another kiss. For luck. "See? It's going to be fine. Thanks for coming all the way in here to tell me."

"I'm actually here to invite you to lunch," she says. "My father has made a reservation at some nice restaurant on the river."

"Sweet. Can I have twenty minutes to shower and change? And we'll walk over there together."

I steal one more kiss for the road, and then skate off to get ready. My shower is quick, but still long enough to notice that the offerings in the dispenser have changed again. Today's new shampoo smells like lime and apples.

Donning my socks in the dressing room, I'm whistling to myself until a pair of sneakers suddenly appears in my line of vision. When I glance up, Bryce Campeau is towering over me, a grim expression on his face.

Well, shit. I guess we're doing this now. I stand up and brace myself for another insult from him.

"I have something to give you," he says.

"Oh? Is it a punch in the face?" I ask, only half kidding.

"Definitely not. Here." He thrusts a card at me.

I take it, giving it a quick skim. *The bearer of this certificate is entitled to a weekend getaway at the Green Rocks Resort Community in Sweetwater, Vermont.*

"Wait, is this the thing you bought in that auction last fall?"

He gives me a terse nod. "Take it. It's my gift to you. It is my apology for being an ass last night."

I clear my throat awkwardly and offer the card back. "You don't have to do that."

"No, I insist. For you and Sylvie."

"Really?" I hesitate. "She'll love it."

I get another nod. Our Campeau never was much of a talker. Then he starts to turn away.

"Hey, Bryce? There is one thing that I'm curious about. What's up with you and the grumpy bartender? Petra."

He shoves his hands in his pockets and his mouth twitches into a quick smile.

"She your girlfriend?"

"Well, no. At least not until last night. But I have spent a lot of time at that bar talking to her and getting to know her. We are similar. Both are a little unsure where we fit in."

"Dude, that's everybody."

Bryce shrugs. "Maybe. But Petra and I understand each other. And I did not know until last night that you can fall in love with someone while sitting on the barstool and listening to her talk."

Well, that is fascinating. I hold up the card he'd given me. "Hey, you know, you could take her to Vermont. You could use this."

Campeau holds up a hand, refusing to take the card back. "No. Sylvie obviously wanted to go there. And you should take her. It is my gift to you both. You can save it as a surprise for the summer vacation."

"Thank you. I'll do that. I would take Sylvie anywhere she wanted."

"I know you would." He looks down at the floor. "You'll be good for her. I am sorry I said otherwise."

"Hey, Bryce?" We're interrupted by Bess, who's stuck her head into the dressing room. "We're ready for you upstairs. We're in Hugh's office."

He perks up. "Thank you. I will be right there."

I let out a low whistle. "Dude, is this your contract extension going through?"

"Yes, we are signing today."

"Damn," I say as a wave of envy rolls through me. "Congratulations, man."

"Thank you. I hope to earn it." He turns and walks away, looking just as serious as he always does.

I finish getting dressed, while fighting off a familiar flurry of doubts. My own contract expires in six months. If I could just be a *little* sharper, a little more driven than I've already become, then maybe I'd deserve an early renewal, too.

But hell, I've tried. And I honestly don't know what I'd do differently this season. This is the best version of me that there is. It's good enough for three goals and four assists. It's good enough for Sylvie, and all the best people in my life.

You can't please everyone. That's the only valuable thing my father ever taught me, I guess. At least he gave me that.

So I tuck that card into my pocket and put on my jacket. It's time to have a nice lunch with my best girl.

Upstairs, I spot Sylvie in the lobby. Her father is there, too.

"Sorry to keep you waiting," I say, jogging toward them.

"Oh, you're not keeping us," her father says. "I just met Rebecca and Bess, and I got a tour of the facilities. Nice place you got here."

"Isn't it? I feel lucky every time my ID works in the lock."

Her father gives me an approving glance, and I decide that I'm not going to beat myself up over not getting an early contract extension. If I keep my head down and play well, it will happen for me.

As we head for the door, Eric jogs down the stairs from the executive suite and gives us a wave. "Afternoon everyone. How's your head, Sylvie?"

"It's all right," she says.

"Glad to hear it. Bess and I got you guys a car to the restaurant. So Sylvie doesn't have to walk."

"Hey, thanks, man," I say.

"No problem. Oh, and Anton?" He steps closer and draws me aside as Sylvie and her dad make their way to the door. "You got an hour for me sometime next week?"

"Sure. What for?"

"I was just told that we're getting in a contract for you to review."

"Me?" I say, just to be sure.

Eric cracks a grin. "Yeah, you."

I feel so relieved that I have to put my hands on my head and blow out a long, careful breath. "Wow. Okay."

"You'll probably have a choice to make. Two years, or three. Something like that. We'll have to see what's in the package."

"I'll take the three-year," I say, and take a step toward the door, where Sylvie is waiting.

Eric laughs. "You need to see the numbers first."

"I probably don't," I tell him. "I'm in it for as long as they'll have me."

Eric shakes his head. "Go eat lunch. We'll talk about it next week. And rest up for tonight's game against St. Louis. It's going to be a rough one."

"They all are. Later!" I catch up to Sylvie and put my arm around her.

Her father opens the door, and we step out into the bright sunlight of the Brooklyn afternoon.

THIRTY-NINE

Hiberdating

Nashville, June

SYLVIE

I'M WEARING A WIDE-BRIMMED, floppy sunhat. I keep my head down and my phone pressed to my ear as I roll my suitcase into the hotel lobby.

"Okay, I'm in," I say, scanning the wide-open space from behind a pair of big sunglasses. "Oh, crap!"

"What's the matter?" Anton gasps in my ear. "Have you been seen?"

I duck to the right, where there's a seating area, and plop down in a chair beside a giant plant.

"No," I whisper. "But it was close." I wait, my back turned to Coach Worthington, who's crossing the lobby toward the elevator bank. I can track his reflection in the plate-glass window.

"Shit," Anton whispers in my ear. "Maybe this was a bad idea. Just more of my bad judgement."

"Are you kidding?" I whisper back. "I live for your bad judgement. Besides, I've got this. I like a challenge."

"Okay, okay. You're right. If anyone can pull this off, it's you."

"That's my boy." I glance over my shoulder to see the coach waiting for an elevator.

Tonight is game number six in the Stanley Cup championship. The Bruisers really did it—they made it all the way to the finals again. And they're currently winning three games to two. But the Nashville fans want this badly, almost as much as their home team. And anything could happen.

I'm not supposed to be here right now. The team decided to hunker down together in this hotel for games five and six. No wives, girlfriends, or other distractions. Like soldiers before battle.

"I'm sorry, baby," Anton had said. "Even Tank and Bess are staying apart."

Of course I'd understood. I'd been holed up across town at another hotel with my friends, until an hour ago, when Anton had called me three times in sixty minutes. Instead of resting before the game, he was full of nervous energy.

"Honey, do you need me to come over there?" I'd finally asked.

"Yes," he'd answered immediately. "Bring your suitcase. And some junk food. I'm going insane here by myself."

One Uber ride later, here I am, hiding from the authorities beside a potted palm. "All right," I whisper after the coach disappears. "It's go time. Where am I headed?"

"You have to pick up the key I left you. The elevator won't open on the twelfth floor without it."

"Okay." I glance discreetly around the lobby. "The front desk is wide open, though. Someone will see me."

"I thought of that, baby. So the key is with the friendly cashier in the gift shop. Her nametag says *Loretta*."

"Ooh, sneaky!"

"Once a bad boy, always a bad boy. You'll find her just past the entrance to the cafe."

"Got it." I rise and quickly make my way through the lobby, shoulders back, phone to my ear, as if I belong here. One of the Brooklyn athletic trainers is leaning against the check-in desk, but he's too deep in conversation to notice me.

When I wheel my bag into the little gift shop, it's blissfully empty. The woman behind the cash register—Loretta—looks up and smiles. "Can I help you, hon?"

"Well, I hope so. I was told you're holding a room key for me?"

"Yes, dear. But I'll need your name."

"Right! Of course. It's Sylvie."

"Ooh, yes! Your boyfriend is so cute. Those *eyes*." She gives a sigh. "So dreamy."

"Aw shucks," Anton says into my ear. "I think I made an impression. She must not meet many hockey players."

I watch as Loretta lifts a book off the counter, revealing not one but *three* key cards, each with a sticky note and a different name on it. One says SYLVIE, but there's also one for HEIDI JO and one for BESS.

Huh. I think Loretta has met quite a few hockey players.

"Here you go, dear. Welcome to Nashville. Best of luck tonight."

"Thank you so much." Before exiting the shop, I peek out toward the elevator bank, making sure the coast is clear. And then I make a dash for it. "I'm on the move."

"Awesome. Twelfth floor. Head to the left after you get off the elevator. Room 1212."

"Copy that." I press down on the button, and an elevator opens immediately. It's empty. *Yes!* "I'll be right there, unless it all goes horribly wrong in the hallway upstairs."

"You got this, baby. Go!"

Once I slide the key into the elevator slot, the car ascends smoothly upward.

Ninety seconds later, I'm hustling down an empty hallway toward the door marked 1212. It opens just as I arrive in front of it. Anton basically snatches me into the room. I yank my bag in behind me and kick the door shut.

"Finally," my boyfriend gasps, wrapping himself bodily around me. "I missed you so much." His kiss is fueled by three days of separation and—let's face it—a lot of pregame nerves.

I hug him tightly and receive several hot, furry kisses, because playoff beards are fierce. "Sit down, hunk," I say, nudging him onto the king-sized bed. "Now talk to me. How's your shoulder?"

"It's fine. Really." He rubs the spot that was sore last week. "I'm feeling good. Just *hyper*. And too deep inside my own head." He flops down, propping his head up on a hand, his bright eyes smiling. "Talk to me, gorgeous. I just need a little Sylvie time. Tell me all the news."

I spread out beside him, mirroring his posture. "Okay, Cedric and Trina *both* got summer jobs at that pool in Red Hook."

"No way! That's amazing. Can't believe he made that happen."

"Well, Trina got a lifeguard position, but Cedric is working security. He gets a pool pass as a perk, though, and he's enrolling in some swim lessons."

"Sweet! I'll send him an email." Anton threads his feet between mine. He's cuddly. We've become that kind of annoying couple who's always touching each other when we're out with friends.

"Deal with it," Anton says when people tease us. "We're here, aren't we? You can't accuse us of hiberdating." Because he still has a Frankenword for everything.

We've had a crazy, wonderful year. In spite of the pressure of all those early predictions, the Bruisers did make it to the finals again.

Meanwhile, the Bombshells finished our season in a very respectable third place. And I played four of our last ten games, with a save average that's only a percentage point behind Scarlet's. Rebecca and Bess have already made it clear that I'm invited back next season.

And in between all those hockey games, Anton and I have only grown closer. "You two are just a really good team," Fiona remarked once.

That's exactly how it feels to me, too. Like Anton and I just *work*. Our schedules are insane, so we have lots of time apart. But we're still always in sync, with phone calls and an endless text conversation that fills my days with fun and humor.

And when we're actually together? There's nothing better. Anton doesn't hold anything back. He always makes me feel like I have his full attention. For someone who claimed not to be boyfriend material, he seems to have achieved elite capabilities in record time.

I try not to wonder what the future holds. I try not to plan. As a couple, we're taking things day by day.

The days are pretty great, too. So it's not like I have anything to complain about. Besides—no matter how the Bruisers play in their last one or two games of the season, it's over in less than seventy-two hours.

Anton says he has a surprise planned for me. I think it's a getaway to Vermont. A couple of months ago, I found a certificate in his dresser drawer, good for a weekend getaway.

I can't *wait*.

"Have you seen Bess lately?" I ask him. The truth is that I'm running out of gossip to distract him with.

"Yep." He pushes a lock of my hair off my face. "She looks like she swallowed a basketball. There's a photo of her and Rebecca sitting side by side at the pool in Tampa, with matching bellies."

"It's going to be an exciting summer in Brooklyn," I point out.

"Yep." He gives me a smile, but it's full of nerves. And then he rolls me onto my back, spreads his hot body out on top of me, and kisses me like it's his last moment on Earth.

And, okay, I'm here for this. In a bossy, alpha maneuver, Anton stretches my arms overhead. I'm trapped beneath his eager body, getting kisses so hot they could power the sun.

I melt into the mattress and take it. Soon enough, we're straining against one another, daring each other to take it further. There's only one problem.

"What happened to 'no nookie before games,'" I pant between kisses. That was one of his newest rules for himself. "And if you give me beard-burn, we're gonna be so busted."

Anton breaks our kiss and then laughs. "I'm sorry. I know I'm sending out mixed signals." He lets go of my hands, and then kisses my neck softly.

"Hey, it's okay." I ruffle my hands through his overgrown hair. He and his teammates all look like mountain men. "Tell me why you're so nervous today. Is it because you think you can't win tonight?"

He looks down at me, those bright eyes warm and locked onto

my own. "No, baby. It's just the opposite. It's because I think I can."

"Yeah?" I roll to the side, so we're eye to eye. "Explain."

"I have a pretty long history of self-destructing right when my goals are in reach. I can't let that happen this time."

"But you won't," I promise him. "You've done everything right. It will either happen or it won't."

He leans in and gives me a snootch. That's what he calls a nose kiss—it's a Frankenword for *smooch* and *snoot*. "Thank you for coming here and helping me cinch up my bag of crazy."

"Any time, okay? For what it's worth, I'll love you exactly the same amount no matter what happens. You know that, right?"

He gives a slow blink. "I do know that. And it's worth a lot. It's everything."

I give him a sweet kiss. "Now let's take a nap. You'll feel better if you get an hour or two of shuteye."

"Okay, baby. Good idea." He gets up off the bed and kicks off his sweatpants. Then he pulls back the covers and gets into bed, while I set *both* of our Katt phones with alarms, just so he doesn't have to worry about oversleeping.

Then I remove my sundress, put on a cotton tank top, and lie down beside him.

He curves his body around mine and sighs.

I close my eyes and try to relax, hoping he'll settle down and rest.

But after a time, Anton's lips begin tracing the back of my neck. And then his tongue comes out to play.

"Fuck it," I say, rolling over to meet his kiss.

He pulls me in, and we come together in a slow slide of tongues and wandering hands. I hitch my knee up onto his hip, and he groans as his erection bumps against the fabric of my panties. "Baby, I think I need to break a rule."

"Are you sure," I breathe against his lips. The beard burn will totally be worth it.

"Rules are what you make of them," he says, as his hand slides into my underwear.

"What…does that mean?" I gasp.

But the pleasure of his touch is so swift and consuming that when he mutters, "I have no idea," I don't bother asking for clarification.

We kiss and touch and free each other of any remaining clothes. I forget all about hockey, and I'm sure he does, too. There are only these sheets, and this man, and the perfection of this moment. When he lifts my leg up onto his shoulder and slides home, we both groan from the rightness of it.

"Love you," he says, moving right away. Like he can't stand to wait.

"Love you," I echo as the pleasure builds. We gave up condoms right around the time we gave up sneaking around. And both the new birth control and the honesty have been equally freeing.

Today we set some kind of speed record for mutual satisfaction. It's only a few minutes later when we pull into the station together, panting and groaning and then laughing at ourselves.

"Does it count as a rule broken if it only lasts five minutes?" he asks, sinking onto the mattress beside me.

"Nope," I say authoritatively. "It's like the five-second rule when a cookie falls on the floor."

Then we both laugh like crazy people for the next few minutes. Anton's pregame stress has finally burst. When we eventually settle down together again, the next thing he says is a snore.

And I take it as a compliment.

FORTY

Much Rejoicing

ANTON

"WE CAN END THIS TONIGHT," Coach says, pacing the visitors' locker room before the final period. The game is tied — two to two. "They expected to shut us down by now. They're on edge. They thought they could break down your game and pick it apart. We're not going to let that happen."

I glance around the circle at my teammates, and I see determination on every single face.

If we lose this game, we still get one more chance. It's not over. And that's the scenario that Nashville is counting on.

But every man in this circle knows that the other outcome is possible, too. Where we finish this once and for all, and go home with the cup.

I can *feel* that possibility. Like a buzz in my veins. It's out there. All we have to do is take it.

"This is the strongest you've ever been as a team," Coach says. "This is your moment. End it during the next twenty minutes, guys. It's yours for the taking. Go get it."

A cheer rises up, and we all stand. I snap my helmet back onto sweaty hair. Every man has given a hundred percent effort, and now we'll double down and try for two hundred. There are backpats and fist-bumps as we funnel down the chute one more time.

I feel a firm squeeze on my forearm, and it's Campeau. He gives me a quick nod. *We got this.*

Things are cool between us again, as they should be. When Coach said this is the strongest we've ever been as a team, he didn't just mean physically. We're a unit. And I'm one twenty-third of that unit.

I made it to the top of the top. It's happening.

Skating out with O'Doul to start the third period, we take our positions for the faceoff. The crowd is deafening. These two teams both want it so badly.

But someone's going to win, and it might as well be us. All we need is a sliver of advantage.

The ref skates in a tight circle, positioning himself between the two centers. The arena goes quiet. Or maybe that's just in my head, as all my focus narrows to this one moment.

The puck drops, and Campeau wins the faceoff, sending the puck to me.

Later, when I look back on these most important twenty minutes of my career, that's the tipping point I'll come back to — Campeau winning that faceoff. The early possession sets the whole tone for the period. It puts Nashville on their back foot.

We don't waste the chance. Our passes are sharp. We create scoring opportunities. Campeau's first shot on goal is deflected, but Castro scoops it up and ships the puck to O'Doul.

The two of them play keep-away for a minute before Castro changes it up, firing off a shot to Trevi. Who pops it into the upper left-hand corner of the net.

The lamp lights, and now we're leading early in the third period.

There is much rejoicing on our bench, while Tank and Crikey take a defensive shift. But then I'm back on the ice two minutes later, as Coach does his best to keep our legs fresh and the other team guessing.

Maybe it's hubris, but I feel unbeatable now. That must be why, when Drake sends me a deep pass a minute later, I line up a long shot from the blue line.

Instead of passing it, or skating it in, I see the opening the goalie has created for me, and I fire on it.

The keeper moves, and we probably both think he's going to get there in time.

But he doesn't dive low enough for my puck, which drops to the ice before sliding right in, just beneath his glove.

It doesn't seem real until Campeau screams, "YEEEEEEEES!" in a display of emotion never before seen on his stoic face.

Then my teammates pile onto me like a pack of puppies, while music thunders through the arena.

Unbelievably, there's still fourteen minutes left in the third period. As I line up for another faceoff, I know that technically anything could still happen.

It doesn't, though. We play a nice clean period, avoiding the penalty box. The minutes tick down while a frustrated Nashville team fails to break us.

And when the buzzer rings, we've done it. We've won the whole damn thing.

I tip my head back and look up at the stadium, which is throbbing with emotion. So this is how it feels. Wow.

The cup is suddenly visible at the edge of the rink. Yes *that* cup.

I can't wait to touch it. And celebrate with Sylvie.

FOUR HOURS LATER, I've been showered in kisses and hugs, then showered in champagne, and then showered for real. Then I've gotten drunk on champagne with my teammates, with Sylvie, with my mom, and with the whole stinkin' world.

And then I've sobered up in time to get messages of congratulations from everyone I've ever known, including my little brothers.

But not my father, who insists on being the exception who proves the rule.

And I'm finally, finally opening the door to my hotel room again in the wee hours of the morning.

"God," Sylvie moans, shuffling in behind me. "I'm so tired that I can't feel my face. Can I have the bathroom first?"

"Go ahead, sweetheart."

She drags herself in there with a nightgown and a few toiletries. I strip down to my boxers and turn down the bed. Now we can sleep as long as we like. There won't be any practice tomorrow. Nobody will wake us up early. It's been a night for the record books.

Even so, I'm not quite ready for it to end.

Sylvie comes out of the bathroom looking sweetly sleepy. She hops into the bed and groans as she slides down into the high-thread-count sheets. "What an amazing day." She yawns.

I stroke her hair away from her face. "You know, I heard some of my teammates say, 'This is the happiest day of my life.'"

"That's fair," she says, giving me a tired smile. "It's the culmination of years of hard work. I'm sure they didn't mean to upstage the birth of their future children."

"Well, that's the thing." I chuckle. "The day I met you, I was deep in that groove—like I'd make my season pay off, or I'd die trying. Nothing else mattered. And then half an hour later I spotted you."

She slips her hand into mine. "It's been quite a year, hasn't it?"

"I got so much more than I asked for. But I was wondering if you were game to actually make this the best day of my life."

She frowns up at me. "You already scored with me, and then scored in a winning championship game. Unless you want a back rub or a drink from the mini bar, I really don't see what else I could add."

That's when I reach over and slide open the nightstand drawer, plucking a little box off the bible.

"Sylvie, I know it's been less than a year since we met. But I'm in love with you. And I plan to stay that way for the rest of my life." I open the little box and show her the ring that's inside it.

It's an emerald-cut solitaire diamond that my mother helped me choose. "A classic design for a classic beauty," my mother had said.

"*Anton*." Eyes wide, Sylvie sits up quickly. "Is…is that what I think it is?"

"Would you be my wife?" I ask, my voice nearly cracking on that last word. If I've moved too fast, or if she just flat-out says no, it's going to hurt. But as a great man once said, you miss a hundred percent of the shots you don't take.

The beat of silence that comes next is the longest of my life.

"*Yes*," she gasps. "Yes, I will. Oh, Anton! I can't *believe* you!" But she must mean it in a good way, because she throws her arms around me.

I pull back so I can slip the ring onto Sylvie's finger, and she makes a little squeak of happiness. "It's so beautiful!" She climbs into my lap, and I hold her close.

Now this really is the best day of my life.

"You were right, Maman," she whispers.

"What's that?" I ask.

"Nothing, baby. I love you."

"And I love you." I give her a slow kiss.

"I have a question." She raises her hand, the one with the ring on it. And then she flips over her hand to admire it.

"Anything, baby."

"Did this depend on winning the game?" She giggles. "Because maybe I need to thank your teammates."

"No, you goof. I was waiting until it was all over. Tonight. Or this weekend. Whenever I got the chance to focus on something other than the game. And the chance to remember that hockey isn't everything."

"It's not everything," she echoes. "But it's pretty freaking great."

I chuckle and cuddle her closer. "The day I met you I knew you were special. I just knew."

Sylvie reaches past me and shuts off the lamp. And we settle in for a long sleep before we plan the rest of our lives.

THE
END